tubi original

SIDELINED 2

INTERCEPTED

tubi original

SIDELINED 2

INTERCEPTED

Based on the motion picture written by **CRYSTAL FERREIRO**

By **RACHEL ESPY**

Based on characters created by **TAY MARLEY**
from the book, ***The QB Bad Boy and Me***

wattpad books 

wattpad books
An imprint of Wattpad WEBTOON Book Group

Copyright © 2025 Gridiron Holdings, Inc.

Based on the motion picture written by Crystal Ferreiro, © 2024.

Based on the characters created by Tay Marley from the book,
The QB Bad Boy and Me, © 2019.

All rights reserved.

No portion of this publication may be reproduced or transmitted, in any form or by any means, without the express written permission of the copyright holders.

Published in Canada by Wattpad WEBTOON Book Group, a division of Wattpad WEBTOON Studios, Inc.

36 Wellington Street E., Suite 200, Toronto, ON M5E 1C7 Canada

www.wattpad.com

First Wattpad Books edition: December 2025

ISBN 978-1-83411-020-2 (Trade Paper original)
ISBN 978-1-83411-012-7 (Trade Paper edition)
ISBN 978-1-83411-021-9 (eBook edition)

Names, characters, places, and incidents featured in this publication are either the product of the author's imagination or are used fictitiously. Any resemblance to actual persons (living or dead), events, institutions, or locales, without satiric intent, is coincidental.

Wattpad Books, Wattpad WEBTOON Book Group, and associated logos are trademarks and/or registered trademarks of Wattpad WEBTOON Studios, Inc. and/or its affiliates. Wattpad and associated logos are trademarks and/or registered trademarks of Wattpad Corp.

Library and Archives Canada Cataloguing in Publication information is available upon request.

Printed and bound in Canada

1 3 5 7 9 10 8 6 4 2

Illustration by Laura Eckes
Cover photo provided by Tubi
Artwork © 2025 Tubi, Inc.
Typesetting by Delaney Anderson

tubi original

SIDELINED 2

INTERCEPTED

CHAPTER ONE

DALLAS

Morning sunlight poured into the dance studio, casting long shadows over the sprung floors. Gazing up at the high windows, all I saw was blue sky. The colors reminded me of home, the endless Colorado sky. Except beyond these walls, it was Valencia, then the wide cityscape of Los Angeles in the near distance. I often wondered how high I would need to go to see the Pacific Ocean. I still couldn't quite believe that I'd made it here and was living some version of the California dream.

We're not in Kansas anymore, Toto. Or not in Archwood, I guessed.

There had definitely been some culture shock when I'd arrived at CalArts. It felt like a big leap to go from small-town Colorado with one dance studio and a cheer squad to one of the most prestigious dance schools in the country. Everything felt bigger, faster, more demanding. It wasn't terrible so much as different. We were only a week into classes, but it already felt intense. Dancers were vying for the spotlight, and, fair enough, I was also competitive. Classes were ramping up, and I needed to get my head around assignments and figure out how the college library worked. It sometimes felt like everything was coming at me all at once, which was why I'd gotten to dance class early. I needed those extra few minutes to breathe and soak it all in.

This was my favorite room at CalArts. I loved how the barre along the mirrored wall had been worn smooth by years of hands holding on. The floor scuffed by dancers' feet. The room held the stories of everyone who had come before me and the promise of whatever came next. Drayton called me a surprise romantic whenever I got in this mood, and he was probably right. I liked this connection to the past and to a dream for the future.

"I didn't even hear you leave." Miley pulled her dance slippers from her bag before dropping it on the floor. "You're so stealth. You missed your calling as an assassin."

There were a few students drifting in now. Mostly in groups of three or four, carrying water bottles or coffees. I recognized some from our dorm but didn't really know them beyond a few names; I usually relied on Miley to remind me who was who. Scattered around the room, conversations continued as my classmates stretched.

"You don't know what I do with my spare time." I lifted my leg to rest on the barre, feeling the familiar pull and stretch of muscles.

"As far as I can see, any spare time is occupied." Miley pulled her dark, curly hair up into a messy bun, looking as casually stylish as ever. She was a California girl through and through. Grew up in the Valley. Sounded like she only ate granola and wheat germ but lived off coffee, vodka, and tacos. The first question she asked me when we met was my star sign, then she proceeded to tell me why it was fate that we were matched as roommates. "Unless this is where you reveal the QB boyfriend is a front?"

"What are you talking about? You've met Drayton."

"If that even is his name."

"He's the starting quarterback for USC. You've seen him interviewed on sports shows." I switched legs and leaned into the stretch. I'd stayed in the studio late last night to work on a routine, and my body was feeling it. "Do you think I went to all that trouble to trick you?"

"I don't understand all of your spy game ways." She took the spot beside me at the barre. "Who knows what you got up to before I arrived on campus."

"We got up to plenty," I joked and arched an eyebrow. "But we're being more discreet since you moved in."

"Not that discreet. I've seen the snaps."

I was that go-getter who arrived on campus before everyone else. I'd thought it would be a great way to ease into this new life. Nathan, my brother, had wanted to drop me off, but I'd insisted on doing it all myself. The start of the school year was busy for him too, and he didn't need to escort his little sister to college. He finally had time to focus on himself, his job as the high school football coach, and his relationship. I was officially an adult, and he no longer needed to act as my legal guardian. So I set up my half of the dorm room, doing my best to ignore its institutional–slash–prison cell vibe, and wandered around campus.

It was a bit weird. I half-expected to see my mom around every corner. I'd spent so many years dreaming about following in her footsteps and getting into the CalArts program that I was almost disappointed she wasn't actually there. It made me miss home and my brother. I checked in with my best friend, Gabby, but she was already deep into her life at Harvard, and I felt guilty about bothering her. I was on the verge of admitting I'd made a mistake in arriving early when Drayton surprised me. He literally showed up on my doorstep, and it felt like everything had magically come together.

"Enough chitchat, people! Start your warm-up!" Our teacher walked into the studio clapping his hands loudly and shouting across the room. "We have a lot to cover today."

Miley had nicknamed him Oscar the Grouch, which I thought was mostly an eyebrow—as in singular—and attitude thing. He was a hard-ass who wasn't big on words of encouragement. Oscar seemed to think yelling *More!* or *Less!* was constructive feedback. It put me on edge more than I wanted to admit. I'd done some ballet back in Archwood, but I had a lot to learn. I was nowhere near the level of some students who, like my mom, had spent years studying it.

While Oscar talked with our regular piano player, I stretched my other leg on the barre. Then I switched back again, moving through a couple of positions, limbering up.

"You missed a good night. We went to El Coyote for tacos then El Cid to see the flamenco show." Miley dropped her leg from the barre. Her arms went above her head as she arched her back. "Let me guess, you came in to work on the routine."

"For a bit." As long as you considered two hours *a bit*. "Then I studied. You know, because we're in college."

Miley rolled her eyes. "I'll get you out sometime. The school year's just begun."

It had been like this in high school too. Until Drayton and I got together, Gabby was my social convenor. She dragged me to parties, brought me onto the cheer squad. We studied together. She was at my house so much Nathan called her an honorary sister. We even managed to date brothers—Drayton for me, Josh for her—which surprised both of us but was also kind of perfect. It was harder for her now since she was in Boston and Josh was in Connecticut at Stanford, but she was also busier than all of us. She was going to be the scientist who cured cancer, solved climate change, and figured out how to colonize Mars. She'd thrown herself full-force into her studies as soon as she'd arrived, so catching up wasn't easy. We'd had a phone date planned for last night, but time in the lab won out.

"Did you hear the dean's making the rounds?" A tall, blond student—David, maybe?—joined Miley beside me. He crossed his arms over his chest and leaned in like he was sharing high-level gossip. Or maybe he just wanted an easy way to show off his biceps. "She's back from her Juilliard seminar and popping into classes to observe."

"Already?" Miley pulled her leg behind her to stretch out her hamstring. Miley was compact and all muscle. It was inspiring to watch her dance, watch her move. Watching her made me want to be a better dancer, to push myself that much harder. "It's so early in the semester. Doesn't seem fair she's observing now."

"This isn't a wait-and-see program, sweetheart." Maybe-David laughed. "Cut and throat."

"Not your sweetheart, Darius." Miley threw him the stink eye.

Darius! I needed to develop mnemonic tools to remember everyone's names.

"My mom thought really highly of Dean Adams." I sat on the floor to put my slippers on. "Said she was tough but fair."

I had no actual memory of my mom talking about Dean Adams. My parents died when I was nine, and my mom's stories about dancing didn't center around school administrators or teachers. Nathan had told me that when he started his coaching job. He said he was inspired by our mom's comments about teachers who didn't hold back while pushing her forward.

I felt a sudden swell of excitement about meeting Dean Adams. She knew my mom. Knew her when she was my age and a dancer starting out. What if the dean walked into the room and recognized me? Thought, *How do I know that face?* and remembered my mom? It would be the first verifiable crossover. My first CalArts experience where I didn't have to wonder if my mom had been there. Decades ago, my mom stood in a class while the dean, then a teacher, watched her dance, and now it was my turn. The swell of excitement flipped into feeling suddenly overwhelmed. It was coming too fast, too soon, and I needed to process it quickly because class was about to start. I tried manifesting Drayton's voice in my head.

Go in and show no fear. They can smell it. You got this, Cheer. You'll blow them away.

It was the pep talk he'd given me before my first class when I worried about being the small-town kid in the big leagues. That man oozed confidence. No imposter syndrome there. He was a freshman starting quarterback for an NCAA Big Ten team and had no doubts that he was the right man for the job. It wasn't about entitlement or legacy or destiny because his father was a former pro. He'd earned his place through hard work and talent. It was one of the things that drew us together, our ambition to be the best. And if I hit a rough patch where I didn't feel as strong and capable, then I relied on Drayton's words and support to get me over that hump. It was an added bonus that Drayton's voice was on a constant loop through my brain.

Drayton had the best voice. He could do incredible things to my body just by speaking to me in a low growl. He liked describing exactly what he planned to do to me and what he wanted me to do, but honestly, he could read a user manual in that voice and I'd dissolve into a puddle.

"What are you smiling about?" Miley cocked her head. She was sussing me out and clearly suspicious.

"Nothing," I said. "Thinking about how much I'm looking forward to Oscar's class."

"Riiiiiigggghhhht." She nodded her head slowly. "That sounds like a perfectly normal thing someone would say."

As if on cue, my phone buzzed, and when I pulled it from my bag I saw a notification from Drayton.

> Can't wait to see you. Until then, here's a little something to keep you going.

The message was accompanied by a video of Drayton in front of a mirror wearing only a towel slung low on his hips. His wavy brown hair was still damp from the shower, his dark eyes throwing a sexy look at the camera. At me. He was magnificent. He smiled and gave me a small swivel of his hips, and his look told me he knew exactly how I would react. Damn. We'd been together for almost a year, and I still felt a jolt of electricity whenever I saw him. I saved the video to my camera roll because I was going to want that one later before realizing Miley was watching over my shoulder.

"Hot jock boyfriend strikes again."

"Yes, he does." I bit my bottom lip. *Strikes again and never misses.*

"Do you have enough hot jock boyfriend to share with the whole class?" Darius narrowed his eyes. "It's not nice to keep tasty things to yourself."

I wasn't sure if he was joking or if it was a serious threat.

"Who has a hot jock boyfriend they refuse to share?" Another blond who looked like she could be Darius's sister jumped into the conversation.

"Dallas's boyfriend is the quarterback at USC." Miley was only too happy to provide the information. "And yes, she's terrible about sharing. Definitely keeping him all to herself."

"Oh, I know that guy!" the blond woman said. "My cousin goes to USC, and the word is out. The new QB is hot as hell."

I returned to my stretching while the three of them discussed the relative hotness of my boyfriend. And I did what I usually did when faced with Drayton's enthusiastic fans: ignored them.

"We're starting in three!" Oscar held three fingers up in case we didn't understand the concept of three. "If you don't have perfect form, you're sitting this one out!"

"I take it back." Miley sat down and quickly pulled on her ballet slippers. "He's not Oscar the Grouch. He's a troll under a bridge demanding we answer his riddles three before we can pass."

The room grew quiet. And then Dean Adams entered. She was about sixty, with long, sleek black hair pulled into a tight bun, and she gave off some serious Miranda Priestly vibes.

"Class, good morning. I won't take up too much of your time. I'm only here to observe, but I wanted to say a few words first."

She scanned the room to make sure that we were all listening and that she had complete command of the studio. She didn't stop to stare at me. There was no flash of recognition.

"Our dance program is both prestigious and competitive. Congratulations on being here; you are among a select and rare breed. But getting in and staying in are two different propositions. At least three of you will drop out of the program this year. By graduation, only eight will remain, half of whom will go on to grad school for a more 'practical degree.'" Yes, she used air quotes for *practical degree*. "Realistically, only one, perhaps two, will make a career out of dance."

I gave Miley a quick *what the hell* glance before looking around the room. Everyone was stunned. It felt like a strange way to boost morale for a good school year.

"We expect the most of you. We expect each of you to push yourselves to be the best. With that in mind, I will be choosing one freshman to join my master class next semester. Of the freshmen previously selected for this class, the vast majority have become the one or two who went on to have a career as a dancer. I want to see dedication and talent. Perseverance and creativity. This process will be highly selective. And, as I said, highly competitive."

My chest tightened. *Yes.* I wanted to be picked, but so did everyone else in this class. Every freshman in the dance program would be gunning for it. Everyone wanted to prove to the dean and to themselves that they were the one.

"And so, good luck!" Dean Adams held her hands up and smiled. "I'm looking forward to seeing what you have to offer me today."

Show no fear. Show no fear.

With my game face on, I followed the rest of the class to our marks. I wanted that spot in the master class, wanted to make my mom and Nathan proud, wanted to prove I could be the one to make it past everyone else's expectations of me. But I didn't feel so light on my feet. It felt like everything around me had just gotten much heavier.

CHAPTER TWO

DRAYTON

As soon as the ball left my grip, I knew that it was golden. It was muscle memory. Instinct. I'd been doing this long enough—most of my life, really—and knew what I could do. Knew when I was right on target. The ball sailed down the field. Perfect spin. Perfect arc. The guys scrambled into position, and it landed right where I wanted. Zach caught it, tucked it under his arm, and took off into the end zone. Touchdown.

Two women watching from the stands clapped and cheered. For a second, I thought one of them was going to lift her top in salute, but they didn't get that far—only a lot of leaning forward in low-cut tops and short skirts.

"Lahey! I'll catch whatever you throw my way too!" one of them shouted.

There were usually a few girls hanging around during practice. Or waiting by the stadium exits when we were leaving. At parties, it felt like they'd been bussed in. It had been pretty easy to hook up in high school if I was looking, but college football was next level. We were still in preseason, and the offers were already plentiful. Some of the guys kept the girls busy, but I kept my distance. Only had eyes (and hands, and all other body parts) for Dallas. She was way more than enough for me. I gave the women in the stands a quick nod instead of a wave and turned back to the next huddle.

"We might actually get somewhere this year," Marcus said as he took his position beside me. He was small for a linebacker, topping out at maybe 225, but he made up for it with speed. He could block any run and protect the receiver, assuming we got the ball that far. "Good to see Zach having something to do."

"That's what I'm here for."

The team was still a bit of a mess. They'd shit the bed last season, their quarterback had tanked, and the brass had opted to shake things up. New coach, reordered lineup, new quarterback. *Me.* I was also a late addition, which meant it was a tough adjustment for some, mostly the old quarterback.

USC had always been a top choice for me, but it complicated things with my dad. He wanted me at Waco, where he and my grandfather had both gone. Growing up, choosing anything but Waco was never an option. Even when we were little kids, my sister, Abby, used to tease me about being the next appointed prince of Waco. When I told my dad I wanted to go to Los Angeles, it wasn't pretty. He accused me of following my girlfriend, accused Dallas of leading me astray like she was a siren calling a sailor out to sea. The negotiations were so tense that I didn't even tell Dallas in case they fell through. It was also pretty sweet to show up at her dorm wearing a USC sweatshirt, with the news that

I was a short freeway ride away. That made for a damn good reunion night. It was only later that I realized the roads between LA and Valencia were usually a shit show, and my new team was struggling to gel. Still, there wasn't an ounce of regret in me. And I was going to prove to everyone that I'd made the right decision.

Summer training camp had been intense, but now everyone was back on campus, and we were under the microscope. It was like Archwood on steroids. Or whatever they gave Captain America. These were good players, and this could be a great team if we ever found our groove, but there was too much playing at cross-purposes. Guys trying to be the star player. Most of them were juniors and seniors and could see their getting-drafted-to-the-NFL clock ticking. They needed the scouts to see them. Needed to have that one shining moment even if the team was sinking. We needed to pull it together.

I looked over for a signal from Coach Watson, but he only nodded. He was testing me. Seeing what I could do. How I was going to lead us through the rest of this practice game. No problem. Being in charge was my sweet spot. I'd been playing football all my life, watched my dad in the NFL and had him looking over my shoulder for all my games. I knew how to get the job done.

"All right, boys. Let's finish this one off." I waved my hand for everyone to get in tight while I called out the play. We counted down, slapped some shoulders, and were off.

Sometimes Dallas described how she felt when she danced. How it could feel like the music and movement took over, but she was still in total control. That it was like having an out-of-body experience while also feeling like the center of a whirling storm. That was what football felt like for me. It might look like chaos to someone else, but it made sense to me. When I was in the pocket, I felt like the conductor and the musician. I loved pushing my body to new limits and feeling it from head to toe afterward. And yeah, it felt damn good to win.

After a few more scrimmages, Coach sent us back to the locker room. It was a good day. It felt like we'd made real progress. Like I had a better idea what everyone was capable of and how it would be when we hit the field for real.

"You going to ignore that?" Ryan nudged my shoulder, nodding up to the stands and the girls there. They were waving and calling my name. "You scared of college girls, freshman?"

"Not scared." I held my helmet by the cage and ran a hand through my wet hair. Yeah, a hot shower was definitely in order. "Not interested."

"Suit yourself." Ryan picked up his pace and trotted over to the stands.

One of the women booed when I didn't turn around, but I guessed Ryan would have them distracted soon enough. He liked the spotlight on and off the field. He played at being friendly, but I wasn't sure if I trusted him. Ryan had been the quarterback last year, so landing on second string was a blow. Fair enough. I could take whatever trash talk he wanted to throw my way while I got a handle on my new teammates.

Back at Archwood, the team had known each other for years. We didn't all get along, not all the time, but we knew how to push each other to be the best. This USC team liked to push but also spent a lot of time pissing each other off. We needed to put that energy on the field and direct it at the opposing side. We were all here to win, and I was determined to get us a Bowl game by the end of the season. It was a big thing to have a freshman as starting quarterback, and I was going to prove to everyone—the coach, the team, the reporters, my dad—that I was the man to get it done.

On the way to the locker room, I stopped for some photos with a group of schoolkids who were hanging out. It might seem weird that I had fans before playing a single game, but I was used to it. I saw it with my dad when he was he playing and even after he retired. It'd happened to me all through high school. Just how it is with football. The fans are hardcore and devoted. Dallas liked to rib me about it, telling me not to act like I didn't like all the attention.

"I can't help that I'm so charming," I'd say. I loved it when I could make her roll her eyes at me and try to hide her small smile that threatened to crack my chest wide open. "Isn't that what you love about me?"

"That and your humility."

Dallas and I had had a good time in Los Angeles before football and school officially started up. I thought we'd see more of the city, but between practice and her self-imposed rehearsals, we didn't get out a lot. Well, we probably could have, but it was also great being in on our own. My parents weren't the hovering type, and they let me do my own thing, but having them in the house meant they could show up or knock on my door whenever. Nathan was pretty chill for an older brother, but he was still another set of eyes. He was also my high school coach and liked to pull rank. So having a dorm room to ourselves with no interruptions was sweet.

Things had shifted as soon as classes started this week, though. My football schedule was taking over; practice and workouts had ramped up. Our first game loomed, and Coach was moving us into overdrive. It didn't help that Dallas didn't have a car and now had a roommate. Miley seemed nice enough, but sharing a room wasn't my favorite thing. Sleepovers meant staying at the campus of whoever had the earlier class. I never thought I'd be in a relationship that required this much negotiation, but it was worth it. Dallas was worth it.

The locker room was already buzzing by the time I got there. It was big, with labeled spaces for each player around the perimeter. It was decked out with fresh towels, water, energy drinks, and whatever snacks we might want. Side rooms had massage and physiotherapy spaces, quiet spots to relax and meditate, steam rooms, ice baths, and saunas. The equipment team here was first class, so all our gear was impeccable the first time we arrived. I grew up with money, so it takes a lot to impress me, but these USC digs were pretty swank.

I pulled my duffel out of my cubby first and checked my phone. Dallas had responded to my video with several heart emojis and *Can't wait 2 see this IRL*. I had to bite my cheek to keep my smile in check. I was really glad my girlfriend was only technically down the road, but that road sometimes felt really fucking long. But as much as I missed her, I had to hustle, hit the shower, and get ready for class.

~

"Lahey!" Coach Watson walked in with a clipboard under his arm. Along with a windbreaker in USC red and gold, this was his standard uniform. "Great job on that last out route. A second later and he would've been out of bounds."

"That's why they pay me the big bucks." I held my arms out and smiled. I'd just gotten out of an extra-long, extra-hot shower and was still wearing my towel, which was all part of the show.

"They're paying you?" Zach raised an eyebrow as he flung a towel over his shoulder. He was a tough player on the field but basically a puppy dog off it. Dallas called him a golden retriever with pit bull tendencies.

"C'mon, Coach," Ryan shouted from the other side of the room. He was already dressed and ready to go. I was guessing he had some plans. "If you're not careful, we're not going to find a helmet big enough for this guy."

A couple of guys laughed, and Ryan looked pleased with himself, like he'd landed the perfect jab. I really couldn't decide if Ryan pissed me off or if I felt sorry for him. He was like that cartoon with the little dog bouncing around the big one, desperate for attention.

"Yo, at least he can back it up!" Marcus got an even bigger laugh with that one, and Ryan dropped his smile.

"All right, you all got your shots in." Coach readjusted his cap. "Can we focus now?"

Coach was stressed. He was maybe mid-thirties and still pretty fit but looked like he spent more time in the locker room than out on the field these days. There was a lot of pressure on him to produce a winning team. Coach Watson was also a last-minute hire and the one largely responsible for bringing me in. He needed this to work. He was a hard-ass but seemed fair enough. At least he didn't scream at us or throw insults around like they were the key to winning. But he also never pulled punches. He didn't waste time or sugarcoat anything. If he thought practice sucked, he'd tell us. You always knew where you stood with him.

"Preseason's over. From this moment on, you're going to live, breathe, and think about football and only football." He readjusted his cap again. Now I knew Coach's nervous tic. "Everyone here wants to make it to the big show. Well, that dream starts here."

That got a few *damn rights* and cheers from the team.

"Our first game is next week." Coach paced the room as the guys jeered. We were all getting worked up. This was why we were here. To win. To kick ass.

"De Leon ain't shit!"

"DL can suck my balls!"

"Let's go!"

"I hear you." Coach held up his clipboard. "We need to pull it together when it comes to passing."

He did his breakdown, going from one player and play to the next. He listed everything we'd done right and what had been missed. Coach was a details guy. He kept saying that we were playing the long game. I was so used to hearing sports jargon that I sometimes tuned it out. Bring our game to them. Give it 110 percent. I actually wanted to listen to Coach, though. It was only going to help me in my job if I saw what he saw.

I worked on my own playbooks at night. I didn't share them with anyone, but it was a good way to collect my thoughts. Josh got me into it back in high school. He was on the team but didn't want to talk football as much as me. Or our dad. He was more of a science guy, so no surprise when he hooked up with Gabby. Also no surprise when he suggested I treat my rambling thoughts like a school project and put them down on paper. Now it was a postpractice ritual and really helped prep for games. I definitely lucked out in the best friend and adopted brother department.

"And let's get to the final, maybe most important point. De Leon's defense." Coach stood in the center of the room again. "Their linebacker is no joke. All the work we've been doing isn't going to amount to much if we can't push past that line. So I'm adding a film session tomorrow morning, 6:00 a.m."

Everyone groaned, including me. A Saturday film session at six meant getting up at five at the latest, and I had plans that involved not sleeping much before five.

"We've already got practice at nine." Marcus didn't look pleased. I was with him on this one.

"And you now have a film session at six." Coach raised his hands in response to the rumbles and groans. "This isn't up for discussion. We're going into this game with our eyes open."

"Bro, who cares about some linebacker when we got Lahey's cannon?" Zach slapped my shoulder.

This was the kind of team spirit we needed. Faith that I could pull them out of the slump without getting up before dawn.

"Exactly. Let's wait and see what freshie can do." Ryan sounded more like he was mocking my ability than supporting me, but I wasn't interested in arguing the details.

"A whole lot more than you did last season." Marcus high-fived the guy next to him as everyone else laughed. The mood was lighter but not friendly. This team definitely needed work.

"It's not up for discussion." Coach waved the clipboard as he backed out of the room. "See you at six o'clock tomorrow morning. Rest up!"

If I had to deal with an early morning, then I needed to make the most of the time I had.

CHAPTER THREE

DALLAS

"It's a really big deal." I pushed the door open. There were at least a dozen people hanging out in the corridor. I only recognized a couple of them, so I had no idea if they actually lived here. "She went into classes all day making her announcement. Every freshman wants that spot."

It was all anyone was talking about. That and Dean Adams's prediction of how many of us would drop out. Miley said there was already a pool on who wouldn't last. I suspected some were also considering ways to eliminate the competition.

"That's amazing, Cheer." Drayton's voice rumbled against my ear. Even over the phone, the guy gave me the shivers.

I stepped over legs and wound my way around a group playing quarters, careful not to turn over their Solo cup goal posts. I didn't understand why everyone hung out in hallways when they had rooms and there was a common area. This made me sound cranky, like I was about to start shaking my fist in the air complaining about pesky kids, but I didn't understand the need for constant socializing. Most of the time I rolled with it, except when I just wanted to get somewhere private to talk to my boyfriend who I already didn't see enough of and there wasn't a quiet place in the dorm to talk.

"There's a showcase at the end, and she brings in agents and artistic directors," I said. "Almost everyone gets a summer residency out of it."

"Sounds like you have to get into this class. Priority one."

My face flushed at his enthusiastic response. Drayton made me think that anything was possible. That I was capable of doing anything.

"Oh, and I now have a meeting with financial aid tomorrow."

"Why?"

"No idea. The email just said I need to come in to discuss my scholarship distribution." I reached into my bag to pull out my key and, of course, it wasn't in its usual pocket. I put the bag on the floor and knelt down so I could root through it, my phone resting between shoulder and ear. "It's probably some form that I need to fill out again, or they need my maternal grandmother's middle name. Nathan will lose his mind if I have to ask him for more info. Ugh, where's my key?"

My brother was headed for a stroke when I applied for financial aid during the summer. He had to dig up tax returns, death certificates, bank records. Nathan managed to get a lot of things done, and he'd kept a roof over our heads and his kid sister fed and clothed, but he wasn't the best archivist of important documents. The idea that my college experience depended on IRS forms from five years ago that he may or may not have saved did not do wonders for his mental health. But we did it. I got a scholarship for a full ride, and for the first time since I was fifteen, I didn't have to have a part-time job. It was all dance, all the time. Well, dance and Drayton, ideally.

"His head might actually explode." Drayton chuckled, and I felt my cheeks get warmer. Apparently, I didn't need visual stimulus to be turned on.

"Found it." I located my key and unlocked the door. "Anyway, how far away are you?"

"Um, not sure . . ."

I opened the door and there he was. On my bed, stretched out, one arm behind his head on my pillow, wicked grin in place.

"Pretty damn close, Cheer." He jumped up as I shut the door and leaped into his arms, wrapping my legs around his waist.

"Nice catch, quarterback."

It had only been a week, but we were feverish. Desperate for each other. I ran my fingers through his hair and kissed him hard. I squeezed my thighs tighter, my hips pressing against him. God, I wanted him. Drayton had an amazing ability to help me block out the rest of the world. All the stress and the noise outside this room no longer existed. It was just us. Just me and Drayton and the way he made my body feel like molten lava.

He threw me on my bed, and I let out a squeal that would have been embarrassing if I'd cared about anything else in that moment. I jumped up on my knees and yanked my shirt over my head. He did the same, throwing his shirt on the floor beside mine, then knelt in front of me, pulling me in, one hand on my back pressing me close, the other cupping the back of my head. I could feel him already getting hard.

"Sorry! Sorry!" Miley was suddenly in the room with a hand covering her eyes. "Need to grab my wallet."

Drayton and I remained in place, arms wrapped around each other, watching as she dashed to her desk then held up the wallet in victory. In two quick steps, she was back at the door shouting, "Carry on!" before disappearing into the hall.

I dropped my head to Drayton's chest, laughing. I wouldn't say the mood was ruined, but it was definitely dampened.

"What do you want to do tonight?"

"This." He pulled me in again and kissed my neck. Okay, maybe I was wrong about the dampening part.

"Careful." I pulled away slightly. "Not all of us likc showing off hickeys." I giggled—yes, giggled—as he leaned me back onto the bed and kissed down my neck. My collarbone. Down, down.

We both opened our eyes and paused when Drayton's phone rang. He pulled it out of his pocket and showed me the screen: *Josh*.

"I'll call him back."

He didn't have a chance to hit Ignore before my phone rang. I held the phone up to him.

"It's Gabby. That's weird, right?"

"Yeah." He sighed then sat up. "Guess we should pick up."

I pulled myself up to a sitting position and answered my phone at the same time Drayton answered his.

"Hello, Ms. Harvard."

"Hey, bro, what's up?"

"Hey, do you have a second?" Gabby sounded stressed. That couldn't be good this early in the semester. This was usually the stage where Gabby was riding high. Was she already worried about maintaining her perfect GPA? The pressure to be a top student at Harvard had to be tough.

"Yeah, of course." Drayton tossed me my shirt, and I quickly pulled it back over my head without letting go of the phone.

"Shit. What happened?" Drayton shot me a look before walking over to my desk chair. It didn't sound like Josh had called with good news.

"I broke up with Josh." Gabby spit out her words.

Nope. Not good news.

"Oh, Gabby, I'm sorry." I looked over, and Drayton nodded. Yup, we were having the same conversation.

"What happened?" Drayton pulled his shirt back on. The mood was officially over.

"It's okay," Gabby said. "Long-distance was tough, between the time difference and school. We both sort of knew it was coming."

"Sorry, man. Sounds like you didn't see this coming." Drayton raised an eyebrow, checking in with me.

"Sure, that makes sense. I mean, it sounds tough, but sure." I shrugged my shoulders, responding to Drayton. This was super messy. I was in my best friend's corner, always going to be her biggest supporter, but I didn't know what to say.

"Exactly." Gabby sounded positive, but I wondered how much of that was her old cheerleading spirit, smiling in the face of impending disaster. "I'm ready to get back out there. Move on as quickly as possible."

I didn't think this was the time to point out that if you broke up because you didn't have the time, dating someone new didn't seem like the best idea.

"Look, man, it's tough. You need a bit of time. There's plenty of fish in the sea."

Maybe we weren't having exactly the same conversation. Josh didn't seem to have the same feelings about the breakup.

"Is it really over?" Was I mourning the end of their relationship? I wanted Gabby to be happy, that was obviously and one hundred percent the priority, but I was also going to miss all four of us together. Holidays in Archwood just got potentially awkward.

"Yeah. Conceptually, I think if two people want to make it work, then they'll find a way." She sounded thoughtful, almost clinical. "And we didn't."

"Yeah, man. I get it." Drayton was stuck. He liked being the guy who solved problems, and there wasn't much he could do for his brother.

"Is there anything you need from me, Gabs?"

"No, I'm fine." She let out a slow breath. "Nobody actually ends up with their high school sweetheart anyway." It took Gabby approximately two seconds to realize what she'd said. "No, I mean . . . I'm sorry. You and Dray are obviously the exception."

"Yeah, we are." I looked over, and he winked back. As steady as always even when he hadn't heard Gabby's comment.

"Hey, I should go." Gabby was back to being perky. "I gotta get back to the library. I wanted to fill you in before Dray gets the news."

"Thanks for telling me."

I waited as Drayton told Josh he'd check in with him soon and to keep his chin up. As soon as Drayton ended the call, I straddled his lap in the desk chair.

"I'm happy you chose USC," I said before I wrapped my arms around his neck and kissed him.

"You okay?" He kissed my nose and leaned his forehead against mine. I nodded maybe a bit too vigorously because Drayton stood up, holding me close to keep me steady. "Let's go outside. Change of scenery. We could use a walk."

It was the right move. Whatever was happening in the corridor had amped up. More people, louder music. Someone was handing out bottles of beer. Drayton took my hand and led me out into the quad.

Late-summer evenings in California were basically perfect. It was cooler once the sun went down but not too cold, and the humidity didn't linger. It might only last a week or two before it was properly fall, but it was glorious. We wandered along the path through the mostly deserted quad.

"I didn't see it coming." I looked up at him as he slung an arm over my shoulders. "I haven't talked to Gabby much lately, but she didn't let on at all. Not even in texts."

"Me neither. She and Josh were like perfect for each other."

"And I know we're not technically long-distance, but . . ." I didn't finish the sentence because Drayton understood.

"Yeah, I get it. LA is way bigger than Archwood."

"And I don't have a car."

"And there's always traffic."

I leaned my head against his shoulder. "But we're not long-distance?"

"Is that a question?" He laughed then shook his head. "No. No. We're . . . short-distance."

"Okay, you might be joking, but it's kinda true." I nudged his shoulder while we walked. It was such a Drayton thing to say. He usually went for the joke, something to cut the tension and make me laugh. It was almost romantic except for the fact that neither of us really did romance. We weren't into grand gestures like some rom-com, but we needed to spend time together. We fed off it. It was our fuel. Gabby said it was our love language, but even thinking the phrase *love language* made me uneasy.

"I thought being in the same city . . . I thought we'd see each other a lot more," I said.

"Me too."

I sat down on a bench under one of the oak trees, and Drayton took the spot beside me.

"But sometimes when you're on the field, you gotta switch up the play." He grabbed my legs and pulled them across his thighs. "Doesn't mean the game's over."

"Oh, God." I shook my head slowly, feigning disdain. "Are you only going to talk in football metaphors now?"

"Only if it's working?" He pulled his head back to look at me, raising an eyebrow. When I laughed, he kissed my forehead. "Would it make you feel better if we made a plan?"

"You know it would."

"Okay." He got that look like he was going through a mental playbook to find the perfect setup to get us out of this mess. I really did love my quarterback jock boyfriend. "Let's promise to see each other every weekend."

"Who goes where?"

"We can switch off."

Acceptable so far. We went through the list like we were negotiating a high-stakes contract until I was crying from laughing. The number of texts allowed per day, if punctuation was acceptable and under what circumstances, which emojis were out of bounds. We established appropriate milestones, deciding we would start with a houseplant, but negotiations broke down when we couldn't decide who had naming rights.

"Okay, what happens after college?"

"We live happily ever after." He shrugged like it was the most obvious and inevitable outcome. Like how could I possibly consider that there might be another version? "Unless, you know, I get rich and famous."

"Oh, I see how it is!" I swatted his chest. "You're going to big-time me?"

He grabbed my hand, kissing my palm, then wrist, then forearm. "Never."

"Do you really think we're the exception?" My voice was low, almost a whisper. My eyes felt suddenly hot. "That we're the high school romance that makes it?"

"I know it."

His kiss confirmed his words and sealed the deal. We held on tight, and the rest of the world drifted away because we already had everything we needed.

CHAPTER FOUR

DALLAS

I've never been a morning person. I get up early if I have to because I am a responsible adult, but I'm not really awake until I have a couple of coffees in me. I'm a hit-the-snooze-four-times person if I have the option. So being startled awake by Drayton suddenly sitting up and exclaiming, "Fuck!" was more than a little discombobulating.

"Fuck! Fuck! Fuck!" He threw the covers off and jumped out of bed.

My first still-basically-asleep thought was, *Wow, you're cute.* His hair was a mess. There were lines along his right cheek marking where he'd been asleep on my pillow, tucked in close, only seconds earlier. Thankfully, my brain snapped to attention before I spoke because Drayton didn't look like he wanted to hear about his level of hotness. He looked pissed.

"Shit! This can't be happening." He grabbed his pants from the floor and yanked them on.

I turned as I heard a groan from Miley's side of the room. Everything was coming into focus. Drayton in a panic. My small dorm room. Roommate who had left us alone until well past midnight a few feet away. She rolled away and pulled her pillow over her head. "Too early."

Drayton found his shirt then started the search for his shoes.

"What's going on?" I blinked a few times and looked at the clock: 7:42 a.m. *Fuck* was right. "Oh no. What happened?"

"Phone's dead." He sat on the bed to put his shoes on. The veins in his neck were bulging. His jaw clenched. It had been a while since I'd seen stressed Drayton. "Can you check the traffic for me?"

I was wide awake now. His anger or frustration—I wasn't sure which one was winning out—was palpable. Drayton stood up again and had grabbed his bag by the time I had the maps app up.

"Fifty-seven minutes to USC."

"Fifty . . ." It was almost a deer-in-the-headlights moment. I couldn't remember seeing him look so suddenly helpless. "Coach is going to murder me." He muttered a quick, "Talk later" and rushed out the door.

I looked at my phone again—7:44 a.m.—then flopped back down on the bed. My pillow was still warm and smelled like him. I curled into it and tried to hide from the world for a little while longer.

Unfortunately, my brain had other plans. It started running through my list of assignments and errands, replayed my conversation with Gabby, wondered why Nathan hadn't called me back. I needed to schedule time to do laundry, book one of the rehearsal rooms, email my History of Design group to discuss our upcoming assignment.

Lying on my back, I looked around the room. Miley's side was decorated with travel posters from the 1920s and '30s: couples drinking wine at Italian ski resorts or sitting on deck chairs on luxury liners. Her desk was messy with dance outfits and shoes, makeup, and a wet suit for surfing. Basically anything other than school-related items. We'd put up a corkboard that was considered common ground. She'd filled a good half of it with photos of friends, including a surprising number taken since moving in. My side had one of me and Drayton, another of me and Nathan, and one of me, Drayton, Gabby, and Josh taken just before leaving Archwood. It was amazing how quickly a photo could be considered out of date. After thirty minutes of no sleep and no hope of relaxing again, I headed out for coffee. If I was lucky, I could cross a few things off my list before my meeting.

It was upsetting to see Drayton so rattled. He was always the rock, the glue, the guy who seemed unflappable. He'd held steady against his dad when pressured to go to Waco. Didn't waver when I struggled to commit to a relationship. Came up with a plan to maintain our short-distance relationship despite conflicting schedules. Then the first morning of our new regimen went to hell, and Drayton left without a proper goodbye. I made the conscious choice to not take this as a sign of anything more than one of us forgetting to charge a phone.

I grabbed a substandard coffee from the cafeteria and headed toward the library. I'd spent so much time looking at photos over the years that I'd thought I knew what to expect, but the CalArts campus was more beautiful in person. Unfortunately, I'd been too busy rushing from building to building as I learned my way around to take enough time to enjoy it. There were tons of people on the lawns, playing Frisbee, hanging out. My mom would have walked this path. My dad too.

All of the pictures we had of Mom from her college days had been taken by Dad. He'd followed her here. Went to school at a community college so he could be nearby. She always looked so happy, almost glowing. Maybe Nathan could send them to me. They should be on my corkboard. And maybe I could figure out where they were taken. I could ask around to see if anyone remembered her. But considering how little time I had to explore on my own, doing a deep dive into my mom's college years seemed unlikely. I headed into the library instead and found my way into the stacks. Daydreams were better suited for someone not on a tight schedule.

~

I arrived for my meeting just as a student exited the financial aid office. He didn't look happy. That was probably the case for most of the people who came in here after the start of the semester. I stood by the open door, watching him push past people in the hall, until I heard my name.

"Dallas?" The financial aid officer waved me in. She looked mid-thirties with a perfect bob and a bright blue blazer. "Come in, come in. Have a seat."

The office was decorated with slogans designed to convey positivity and a can-do attitude. They were one step away from declaring, *Live, Laugh, Love*. The only thing missing was a kitten hanging from a branch proclaiming, *Hang In There, Baby!*

"Did I ever tell you my ex-husband is from Dallas?" She reached across her desk to shake my hand. I felt immediately grateful that she hadn't gone in for the hug. "Spent a lot of time there."

"I've never been." I sat in the chair opposite her. Prayed the ex-husband wasn't a big topic for the day.

"Some would say I gave that city the best years of my life."

"That's . . . nice?" I should have arranged for Miley to call me with a fake emergency. It was a mistake to come here without a proper escape plan.

"It was until it wasn't." She picked up a file from her desk and flipped through the papers. "I called you in because I wanted to warn you that next year's tuition is increasing to adjust for inflation."

"Okay, but I'm on a full ride."

It still gave me a small thrill to say it. It was as close as I was going to get to being a trust fund baby.

"Yes and no." She clasped her hands together and rested them on her desk. I sensed this was her signal that things were about to get serious. "You were generously granted the Great Pacific Media scholarship, but it's a fixed amount."

"What are you saying?" I swallowed and hoped my eyes didn't suddenly look like saucers.

"You have this much money." She held her hands, palms facing each other, about a foot apart. "But you need this much money." She moved her hands further apart. Did she think I wouldn't understand simple math without a demo? "The remaining balance is roughly thirty percent. Plus living expenses."

"What!?" I almost jumped up from my chair. "That's like eighteen thousand dollars!"

See? I could do math very quickly when circumstances demanded it.

"Plus living expenses."

My mind moved into overdrive. Eighteen thousand dollars! Eighteen thousand plus! My budget didn't allow for an extra $1,800, forget $18,000.

"I don't have that kind of money."

I had some savings thanks to working throughout high school. There was a small education fund from my parents, but they'd died when I was nine, and it wasn't like Nathan, who was only seventeen at the time and dealing with the fact that an injury had ended his own plans for a college football scholarship, was able to add much to it.

"You could take out a private loan." She was back to being cheery. Sure, that was the solution to all my problems! *Crippling* financial debt. "Which frankly isn't that much compared to what other students borrow. You're actually pretty hashtag blessed."

She literally said *hashtag blessed.* My financial aid officer thought her Pollyanna attitude was going to fix everything.

"Right . . . so, besides a predatory loan, what are my other options?"

She blinked twice at my predatory loan comment. Computing . . . processing . . . processing . . .

"You could always get a job and start saving." Her voice went sickly sweet. She thought that was the best method to soothe me. Like I could be distracted by a shiny object. "And the good news is that you're eligible for federal work-study. However, most students applied weeks ago. So a lot of those positions have been filled."

Motherfu— I took a deep breath and bit the inside of my cheek to stop myself from screaming at her. She wasn't to blame, and it couldn't be easy spending your day ruining the lives of undergrads, but her delivery needed some work.

"But again, you can always look at our many loan options." She slid a brochure across her desk like she was making me an offer I couldn't refuse. "Let me know if you need any more help."

I took the brochure because clearing her desk and flipping it over didn't seem like the best idea. This was nuts. Fifteen minutes ago, I'd thought my biggest problem was finding time to hang out with my boyfriend. Now my CalArts dream was potentially slipping through my fingers if I didn't find a way to bank at least $20,000 over the next year.

I moved quickly until I was outside and could take a few deep breaths of fresh air. It didn't calm me down, but I felt fairly certain nothing would. I could get through this year, but next year was screwed if I didn't earn that extra money. I needed to spend any free time rehearsing to get that spot in the dean's master class, and now I was going to have even less time to spare. I pulled my phone out and texted Drayton.

I hope your morning was better than mine.

I gave up on my plan to go back to the library. I headed back to the dorm instead. Time to look for a job.

CHAPTER FIVE

DRAYTON

Google Maps was right. From Dallas's dorm room to the USC stadium, it took me fifty-four minutes. Unfortunately, there was an additional ten minutes to park and run like I had the New England Patriots line on my tail to get to the athletes' lounge. Then maybe another thirty to sixty seconds to stand outside the room while I tried to calm my heart rate. I needed to look like everything was perfectly under control when I walked in. *Don't let them see you sweat.*

I was late, sure, but mistakes happen. It wasn't like I hadn't already proven my commitment to the team. I could catch up. It was more important to get out on the field and work through the plays. I had a few ideas we could try. I was on top of it.

Everyone in the room, except Coach, looked my way when I opened the door. A few of the guys were slumped down on the couches and armchairs looking like the 6:00 a.m. call had been a struggle. Zach waved, and Marcus gave me a *what the hell* look. Ryan wore a smug expression that immediately pissed me off.

The video review room was decked out with expensive and surprisingly comfortable furniture and all the accessories. USC football spared no expense for its athletes. There were empty plates scattered around the room, coffee cups, and water glasses. They'd all been there for hours, enjoyed breakfast, made themselves comfortable. I sat down beside Zach and leaned back in the chair just as Coach shut off the video.

Shit.

"You good?" Zach whispered. "Coach is pissed."

"Yeah, good." I kept my eyes on Coach with the vague hope that when he looked my way he'd think I had been there for a while. "Minor mishap."

Zach didn't look like he believed me but didn't ask anything else.

"All right, guys!" Coach shouted across the room. "Let's hit the field. We'll start with your positional groups before we go seven on seven."

Everyone stood up and grabbed their things. I did the same. If I was lucky, I could slip into the stream of players exiting the room.

My heart was still pounding a bit too fast, though I was pretty sure I was holding it together. I'd gone into complete panic mode when I woke up and realized the time. I should've checked that my phone was actually charging before crashing. I'm usually good with those details, but it was a late night, and Dallas and I did a good job of tiring each other out. Sleeping next to Dallas had seemed like the right choice at the time, but I should've come back to my dorm instead. Her bed was too small for both of us. The party in the hall was raging for a little too long. Miley woke me up when she stumbled in. And, most importantly, there was no margin for error if anything like a dead phone messed with the schedule.

"Look who decided to show up." Coach stood in front of me, hands on hips, as I made my way to the door. Zach was right. Coach was pissed.

"I'm so sorry. I had car trouble—" Yeah, that wasn't technically a lie since freeway traffic could be considered trouble.

"You missed the film session."

"I know. It was a mistake, and—"

"Oh, a mistake! Well, that's fine. Mistakes happen. What can you do?" Apparently, Coach did sarcasm. Good to know. "I assume you mean mistakes like when you don't expect the defense to fake cover two, roll the safety late, and disguise the weak-side blitz." Coach was standing close. Leaning in to really get into my face. He knew I recognized all those words but not the context. He was trying to mess with me. "The kind of mistake that if you don't see it coming until it's too late, your ass will be on the ground, and that means a lost opportunity for the team. Is that the kind of mistake you're talking about?"

I didn't respond. I'd had coaches yell out orders and thrive on intimidating players. Some of them went for this same up-close-and-personal tactic like they were drill sergeants. I'd seen my dad get riled up like this a few times when dealing with refs. Football was a high-tension sport, and the stakes were big in college ball. I got it.

But I didn't respond because Coach was partly right. I'd screwed up, so he had to take a strip off me, especially in front of the team. Make sure no one thought they could get away with it, including the star quarterback. The part I didn't get was why this session was so damn important. Why was he acting like this had been entirely for my benefit? I'd take the licks if I deserved them, but we needed to get out there and get to work.

"Ryan's running the first team." He pointed his finger at my chest. "You're with the twos."

"Coach, come on. Please." Our first game was a week away. How was it going to help putting me with the second string? "It was one—"

"Get with the twos or get out. Those are your options."

His voice was calm. I'd say it was soft, except his eyes told a completely different story. I didn't need to look around the room to know that all eyes were on us. I nodded once, and Coach stepped back. He blew his whistle to snap everyone to attention.

"On the field and ready to go in ten minutes."

Coach left first, then the team followed. Zach squeezed my shoulder as he walked past to show solidarity. Everyone had been on the receiving end of some coach's fury, and everyone was always relieved when it hit someone else and not them.

I fell in line. Got changed and on the field in record time. Took my place with the second string and worked hard. Ran plays. Led scrimmages. Threw the ball and landed it on target. When the assistant coach told us to run laps, I went harder than anyone else. Every time I checked out the first string in action, I wanted to jump in. I spotted the misses, knew what I would've done differently. It was frustrating, but I'd dug my own hole.

This was a new feeling for me. At least a new feeling where football was concerned. I'd screwed up by being late and hadn't fulfilled my role as a team leader. I'd let my team down. Let Coach down. It would've been a drag to drive home at 2:00 a.m., but that was life. I'd chosen USC because it was my best option for an NFL draft. Yeah, having Dallas close by was a bonus, but we'd been willing to do long-distance. If I'd come here to play football, then I needed to focus on football. Dallas would understand. She had the same determination about dance.

I felt a familiar rush of guilt, something I hadn't experienced in a while. It'd happened to me a lot after my younger twin sister, Abby, went missing. I blamed myself for not being there to get her home safely. And when she was found dead, it felt like losing half of myself. Everything I did after was marked by her loss. Everything I did had to be for Abby as well as for me. If I succeeded, so did she. If I failed, I let her down. There were so many things she never got to do, so I was doing it all for both of us. I didn't realize how heavy a weight I was carrying until I admitted it to Dallas. She helped me see that I couldn't live for both of us.

Focus. Stay in the game. Keep your eye on the ball.

I gave my head a few shakes then moved on to the next play. There was only the game in front of me. That was all I needed to focus on.

~

Practice ended, and everyone headed to the showers. The mood was lighter, lots of joking around and banter, but I kept mostly to myself. When everyone was gone, I went back up to the lounge and put the video on. I sat on the couch and tried to make up for lost time.

I was deep enough into it that I didn't notice Ryan until he plopped down on the couch beside me. I didn't give him more than a sideways glance, hoping he wasn't there to bond.

"Sorry Coach was being a dick today."

Ryan playing nice was suspicious, further proving my luck continued to suck. Maybe I should have stayed in bed. Dallas had sent me a text that sounded like her day wasn't going much better.

"It's fine. I can take the heat." I rewound the video to catch a play.

"Sure, but who hasn't been late?"

Ryan wasn't picking up on my fuck-off signals. He did a quick shoulder check around the lounge, making sure no one was within listening distance.

"Coach is just salty because he was fired from DL."

That got my attention. "I thought he was headhunted?"

"Nah, dude." Ryan shook his head and smiled. I hadn't pegged him for the team gossip, but guess you never know. "Fake news."

I wasn't sure what to do with this information, and I definitely didn't trust the source. If Coach was in a grudge match with De Leon, wasn't that the kind of thing Dad would've picked up on? He did a full workup on Coach Watson before I signed with USC.

"I don't want it to be awkward between us." Ryan looked sincere but kept his voice low. He wanted to keep this conversation private. "It's not your fault I played like ass last year."

"You didn't—"

"I did." He held up a hand to interrupt. "I was dealing with a lot, and I let it affect my game. It was my chance, and I screwed up. I had a good run."

"It's not over." I might not trust the guy, but part of my job as quarterback was team morale. The team worked, won games, when everyone felt like they could contribute.

"Yeah, it is. I blew it. It's senior year, and I'm running out of chances to get the scouts' attention." He smiled again, but it didn't reach his eyes. "Now I'm the butt of the joke for every douchebag with a podcast mic."

"Sorry, man." I remembered everything my dad had to put up with when his career ended. He was at the top of his game when he was injured and had to listen to endless talk about what could have been. "That's tough."

My phone buzzed with a text notification from Josh. The screen lit up, and a photo of Dallas popped up. It was our first week in Los Angeles, and we drove up to Malibu. She was on the beach with Point Dume behind her. That was a good day, and my girl looked beautiful, radiant, smiling into the camera.

"That's your girl?" He nodded to the phone. "She's cute. DG?"

"No. She's not in a sorority." Did Ryan ever say full names? Why go with DG instead of Delta Gamma? It felt like he was always trying to test if I was cool enough to understand the lingo. "She's a dancer. Goes to CalArts."

Ryan looked genuinely confused. "Where's that?"

"In Valencia."

"Damn." He laughed. "That's a long drive. You could get up to plenty of other activities instead of spending all that time on the freeway."

"She's worth it." I looked at the phone screen one more time before putting the phone down beside me.

"I hope so because you're about to have a lot of options. You've already got fans in the stands for practice. Wait until the season actually starts. Up to your eyeballs."

I was getting tired of hearing how I wouldn't be able to keep it in my pants. Like there was nothing I could do to resist the lure of willing partners. I had no interest in anyone other than

Dallas. Definitely didn't find the promise of an easy lay enticing. I wasn't one of those guys who liked a challenge or chased women who made me work for it. But I also didn't see the appeal of sleeping with anyone simply because they were available. I did that in high school, and everything changed with Dallas. Loving someone made everything better.

"Right. Anyway." I picked up the remote again, letting Ryan know I was done with the conversation. "Appreciate the olive branch."

I meant it too. I still didn't trust him, but it took guts to come over and check on me. And to admit he'd had a bad run last year. Maybe this was something we could actually work out.

"Any time." He stood up and lightly slapped my shoulder before heading to the door.

I pressed Play on the video and leaned back. The De Leon wide receiver had some surprisingly good moves. I decided to check in with Coach to go over some ideas. Mend some fences. Hell, if Ryan could extend a branch, so could I.

CHAPTER SIX

DALLAS

The common area in our dorm had definitely seen better days. The furniture wasn't old so much as well-used. A lot of bodies had passed through, sitting or sleeping on these couches, eating a meal while stuffed into an armchair. It was the kind of room you should never do a black light test on. Otherwise, it was perfectly comfortable and a great place to whine away my sorrows while Miley made her dinner.

"Library? Dining hall?" She opened the microwave when it beeped and took out a plate of mac and cheese. "Oh! Or a tour guide. You'd be great at that!"

She let the too-hot plate slide onto the counter, shaking her hand to cool her fingers. There was yet another party tonight, and Miley was dressed up as a sexy pirate. She wore a skintight shirt as a dress. There was a ruffle down the front, and only a few buttons kept the shirt closed. The outfit was topped off with a pair of thigh-high boots and a wide belt cinched tight around her waist. I had no idea if it was a costume party or if Miley was simply in the mood to express her inner pirate.

"You think I would be a great tour guide? In what world?" I'd never looked into the qualifications, but surely one of them would be "likes to talk to people."

"Dorm cleaning staff? Chief photocopier in the admin office?"

"Filled and filled." I scrolled through another page of closed job postings. It felt like I'd been sitting in front of my laptop for hours because I had. I should have spent my afternoon in the dance studio. Or back in the library to find out how much or how little William Morris had influenced modern stage design. Instead, I'd spent hours trolling for a job that didn't exist. "At this point, I'll need to start doing OnlyFans."

"I looked into it when I got into NYU, but it's like a full-time job, and it's such a saturated market."

"You got into NYU?" I completely ignored the OnlyFans part. It was a lot harder to shock me these days. Living with Miley had clearly already changed me.

"Yeah, but my parents were very clear. Out-of-state tuition was out of the question."

She carried over her plate in one hand and a bottle and two shot glasses in the other. She sat down opposite me. Even when relaxed, Miley had perfect posture. One of the side effects of spending years in ballet classes.

"But it's fine. I got over it. New York might be the dance capital, but there's plenty going on here. I'm constantly going to open calls. I'll get there eventually."

How did I not know Miley was going to open calls? Had she

gone to many—or any—since we'd met? I filed that one away for a later conversation.

"Is New York the dream?"

Funny how I'd never even considered going to New York. It was always CalArts for me. I knew I might have to settle for Colorado, but not until I'd exhausted all possibilities and auditions with CalArts.

"Isn't it for all of us?" She poured herself a shot of tequila and drank it.

"To attend NYU?"

"No. To dance. Anywhere." She filled the other shot glass and pushed it across the table toward me. "NYU has a good program, but it was a way to get closer to the action and not have my parents completely freak out."

I drank the shot then winced at the taste. Tequila was always harsher than I remembered. Miley didn't offer a lime wedge with it, so I guessed that wasn't a California thing. Or a Miley thing.

"Are your parents protective like that? They'd worry about you being in New York on your own?"

I lifted my foot onto the chair, wrapped my arms around my bent leg, and rested my chin on my knee. I was dressed for comfort, or maybe depression, in sweatpants and an oversized hoodie. I had no desire to dress up like a pirate, sexy or otherwise.

"Sure. They're parents. That's what parents do, right?" She was about to take a bite of her mac and cheese when her words registered. "I'm sorry! I wasn't thinking. I forgot."

"Don't worry about it." I waved a hand to dismiss her concern. Miley didn't have a mean or inconsiderate bone in her body. I knew she didn't mean it as a slight in any way. "My parents would've probably been the same. They weren't, like, overly protective when I was a kid, but they always knew where I was. I always felt safe."

Things were obviously different after my parents died, but it was never a question of me not feeling safe. Even when my grandmother died a few years later, I had Nathan, and we had each other. It wasn't perfect, but we were good.

It was probably why I had such a strong sense of independence. I was used to doing a lot on my own. Nathan was my legal guardian, but he couldn't do everything. It was crazy to think he'd been younger than I was now when all that responsibility was dumped on him. He went to college for a bit, though it didn't last, then had to work. He was barely an adult and trying to figure things out while also packing a lunch for his little sister and helping her with math homework.

I *had* to pull my weight. I did laundry. We both cleaned and cooked. I got a job as soon as I could for pocket and gas money. Saved for school. Sure, I sometimes had to go to Gabby's mom with help braiding my hair for a dance, and there were a lot of sleepovers. Neither of us enjoyed Nathan's attempt to inform me about menstruation or sex, but we survived. And we were close. It was always going to feel like a tragedy to have lost both parents so young, but I was grateful for the relationship I had with my brother.

"My parents would prefer if I went into engineering or accounting." Miley poured another shot for herself. "They always talk about wanting me to see the world and follow my dreams, but they'd prefer if I stayed in the Valley and came over for Sunday dinners."

"Cute."

"No, that's my definition of hell."

I understood that too. I looked forward to visiting Archwood for holidays, but it already seemed like an alternate reality. I couldn't see myself going back there permanently.

"Wait! I know this junior who manages a coffee shop." Miley pulled her phone out. I had no idea where or how a phone could be stored in that outfit but chalked it up to one more Miley mystery. "Let me text and see if there're any openings."

"Miley, you goddess! Thank you!" I watched as she typed on her phone. "How long is this text?"

"I need to fill them in on the background."

"Do you?" I wasn't sure I wanted a stranger knowing about my financial difficulties. "Can't you just say a friend needs a job? That's a fairly common problem."

"I'm not revealing your deepest, darkest secrets." She glanced up from her phone. "But that's mostly because you have yet to share."

"I'm an open book." I held my hands up. "Dead parents. Jock boyfriend. Knows way more Steely Dan songs than a nineteen-year-old should."

"It is a disturbing amount. Sure, you blame your brother, but that's still no excuse for playing them in our room." Miley finished the text with a flourish then stuffed her phone back into whatever secret cavity it came from. "You can thank me by being my plus-one."

"In general, or do you have something specific in mind?"

"The drama kids are throwing a party." She pushed back her chair so I could see more of her outfit. "The theme is worst movie musicals of all time."

That information didn't help me. I should probably brush up on musicals if I wanted a job dancing in one, but right now I was drawing a blank.

"You thought I was dressed as a pirate for no reason other than being dressed as a pirate, didn't you?"

"Sexy pirate didn't seem so far-fetched for a Saturday night." I bit my bottom lip and laughed. "Sorry."

"Oh, I take that as a compliment. I prefer the element of surprise."

"Like the Spanish Inquisition."

"What?"

"Never mind." I laughed again. I needed to remember to keep my Monty Python jokes to myself. Especially since I'd never seen a single episode and was only channeling what Gabby would say.

"What's your answer?" Miley leaned forward. "Wanna come to the party? It promises to be strange and unusual. There may or may not be a magician."

"I'd love to, even with the threat of a magic show, but I can't." I closed my laptop. There was no point in torturing myself any longer. "I have a date with Drayton. Rain check?"

"Sure. Of course." Miley stood up and turned around. "If I bend down, can you see my ass?"

I tilted my head to the side and gazed perhaps a bit too intently at her ass. "A little."

"Great!" Miley spun back around with a huge grin. "Okay, I'm off. Have fun with your hot jock."

And just like that, she was gone. Like the wind. Like a lit bomb or a stick of dynamite. Everyone needed a Miley in their life.

CHAPTER SEVEN

DALLAS

No one had ever accused me of being a patient person. I was not a fan of waiting. Hated standing in line. Fast food was never fast enough. It wasn't that I always had somewhere more important to be—though, yes, that might often be the case—but that I didn't know what to do in the meantime. It all felt like busywork.

Drayton was supposed to have picked me up hours ago.

A high school guidance counselor once told me that I was too goal oriented. "Everything doesn't need to be a stepping stone to the next achievement. Try to enjoy the journey as much as the destination."

And yes, he did have that on a poster in his office.

I could relax. I was, in fact, a big fan of doing nothing. Gabby and I could sit for hours over burgers and fries. I'd even sat with her while she got her nails done for the sole purpose of keeping her company. Nathan and I had some of our best conversations while tossing a football together. Or all the times when Drayton and I would curl into each other—literally and figuratively—and exist on the tiny island we built for ourselves. My point was, I wasn't a tyrant about my time, but waiting for something to happen that I shouldn't have to wait for drove me mad.

I was ready. I'd changed into my date outfit, a red dress that was maybe a bit too short, and done my makeup. Then I'd waited. Organized my desk. Read a few chapters from my economics textbook. Tried a handstand because I was bored and wanted to prove to myself that I still had the cheer skills. Waited some more. Changed into another date outfit, a green dress with more of a skirt but a lower neckline. Redid my makeup. Reorganized my desk. I would have taken a nap, but I was running on coffee and adrenaline after our late night, and if I put my head down, there was no way I'd get it back up. Plus, after the brutal $20,000 problem, I needed him. When I'd finally gotten back to the dorm at the end of the day, I'd sent Dray the longest text known to humanity. It had felt good to get it all out, but I needed to hold him right now. To feel him solid, with his arms around me. To let him tell me it was all going to be okay and offer to pay for all four years of my schooling. Not that I'd ever accept it.

When there was finally a knock, I was feeling so agitated that I pulled the door open with a bit too much force and opened with, "Everything's closed by now."

Drayton stood on the other side looking tired and maybe a bit sheepish. That was a new look for him, and I almost gave in.

"I'm sorry. Had football homework, then class ran late, traffic was bad, *and* I caught every red light." He gave me a couple of seconds to respond then powered through. "Are a you a little hangry?"

"No." The answer was clearly yes.

He stepped into my room, wrapping his arms around my waist and pulling me in close.

"Come on, I'm trying my best. It was a long day. Let's not fight?" He kissed my forehead then my nose, pausing just before reaching my mouth. "You look beautiful."

I made a move to pull away but actually wriggled up against him. I heard his sharp intake of breath.

"Stop smiling at me like that." I still had a lot of pouting to do, and his smile was distracting me.

"Why?" He didn't listen to me. He continued with that smile. "Because it's working?"

I tried not to smile back and failed miserably. "Maybe."

As suspected, kissing Drayton erased my anger. Kissing Drayton only made me want to kiss Drayton more.

"Okay, there has to be somewhere open." Drayton let go of me long enough to pull his phone from his pocket. "This is a college town next to one of the biggest cities in the world. There's food somewhere."

"I will literally eat anything."

"If nothing else, we can do a drive-through then go for a beer."

I stepped away to grab my bag and coat when something caught my eye. A pair of cowboy boots I'd bought on a whim while thrifting with Miley. They were cute, but I hadn't found the occasion to put them to use.

"Dray?" I threw him a wide grin when he glanced up from his phone. "I have a suggestion. Do you trust me?"

~

Sally's Saloon was a Valencia institution. I'd never been before, of course, but Miley had plenty of tales to tell. It was a Western-themed bar that brought in locals and students, and the floor was usually full of line dancers. Drunk line dancers who didn't understand the concept of a line, or maybe dancing. I wore my cowboy boots; Dray wore dark jeans and a just-tight-enough T-shirt. We both had hats provided by the bar. It was hot, the music was loud, and the night was starting to feel perfect.

"You've been holding back on me." I had dragged Drayton out on the dance floor, expecting him to fight me tooth and nail, but he was a natural.

"I'm just getting started." He tipped his hat at me then tucked his thumbs into his jeans pockets like he was walking through a rodeo.

I loved that I was the only one who saw this side of Drayton. No one from high school would believe that the quarterback bad boy had a goofy side. Or that he was willing to put himself out there if it made me smile.

He grabbed my hand and spun me around. I threw my head back laughing as he pulled me in and dipped me. It was quick and breathtaking. The couple beside us clapped while another glared as we bumped into them. I realized we were being the obnoxious couple on the dance floor, but it was hard to stop. If only there was a way to bottle this feeling. I would never have a bad day again, never feel like life was crushing me, if I had access to this feeling whenever I needed it.

Drayton pulled me back upright and kissed me. I felt light-headed and happy. Apparently, I was a sucker for country and western and Drayton in a cowboy hat.

"Now, food."

He took my hand, and we went off to find a table.

I recognized a few people around the room but no one I knew well enough to talk to. We gave each other brief nods after making eye contact and that was it. If Miley were here, we would all be doing shots together by now.

Was it strange that Drayton and I never really spent time with other people? I'd met a few of his teammates—Zach and Marcus—but only because they were in his room when I arrived. He knew Miley, but they were ships passing in the night. Or, more accurately, ships asleep at night in a shared dorm room. We used to spend a lot of time with Gabby and Josh, but that was over now. Drayton might be my refuge in a chaotic world, but our lives were separated. Two silos along the 405.

Nachos and beer arrived at our table, and we dove in. Maybe it was because I was starving, but I felt certain I'd never eaten anything more delicious in my life.

"These might be better than Nate's." I was talking with a full mouth, and thankfully it made Drayton laugh. That was a sign of true love. "Don't tell him I said that!"

"Calling him now." He wiped sauce off the side of my mouth with his thumb. How did he make that move sexy?

"Traitor." I narrowed my eyes at him. "You'd throw all this away for my brother's nachos?"

"He's an expert at cheese distribution. Layering is an art with that man."

My phone buzzed. I picked it up and let out a woot when I saw the notification.

"Listen to this." I leaned in so Drayton could hear me over the music. "'Hey, Dallas, this is Skyler, the manager at Emmy's Coffee. Can you come in for an interview this week?'"

"That Miley's girlfriend?"

"Not girlfriend. Girl who is a friend."

"Whatever. Glad she texted." He raised his glass of beer. "See, Cheer, things are looking up already."

An interview! It almost seemed too good to be true. I had dropped off dozens of resumes and filled out as many applications hoping for a bite. As it turned out, it was all about who you knew. That didn't mean I had the job, but it was the best shot I had.

"Yeah, it's great." I put my phone back down on the table. "But I'll also probably have to work weekends, which kind of sucks. That was sort of our time for . . . all the little moments."

"Little moments?" He rested his elbows on the table and leaned toward me.

"You know what I mean. We're already stretched thin."

"I could pay you to come with me to my away games?" He lightly ran a finger along my arm. It tickled in the best way. "Call it a boyfriend tax."

"I'm not ready to put 'sugar baby' on my resume."

Drayton had the best laugh. His whole face reacted. Wide, open smile. Wrinkles sprouting around his eyes. It was contagious. I felt lighter than air when laughing with Drayton.

A server came to clear away our dishes as Drayton tapped my phone screen to check the time.

"I gotta get going. Tomorrow's a two-a-day."

"Already? Nooo." Didn't we just get here? It was supposed to be a date night, but we were cut short thanks to traffic and a class schedule. "Just one more dance."

"I can't be late again, Cheer. Coach will skin me alive."

"One." I took his hand. "More." I walked backward toward the dance floor, pulling him with me. "Dance."

He spun me around so my back rested against his chest, then leaned in and whispered in my ear, "Fine. One dance."

We continued walking with his hands on my hips.

The line dancers were gone, and the DJ played a slow song. We swayed to the music. One of his hands clasped mine, and he held it against his chest. His other hand rested on my lower back. I closed my eyes and nestled my head into the crook of his neck. I knew the dance floor was still packed, but we might as well have been the only people in the room. Where was that bottle for these feelings when I needed it?

CHAPTER EIGHT

DRAYTON

I knew I was pushing it. I'd been smart enough to not sleep over at Dallas's this time, but it was hard to cut out after only one slow dance. We got out of the bar and made out for a bit in the car in the parking lot. Then when I dropped her off. In my defense, she was wearing a short dress and cowboy boots. What's a man to do?

Then I was too wired to sleep when I got home. Stopped off for a beer with some guys down the hall. Played a few rounds of *PGA Tour* on the Xbox. It was a laid-back hang but still late, so I was a bit slow getting moving this morning.

But I wasn't late. Nope. In fact, I was right on time. The session had been called for eight, and it was exactly eight. On the dot. I knew everyone else would already be there and Coach had probably started talking at 7:57, but I wasn't late. I was willing to die on that hill.

Once again, the room turned to look at me when I opened the door. I walked in and dropped onto the couch beside Zach. I noticed Ryan watching me but chose to ignore him. Let him stare if he wanted. I couldn't care less about what he had up his ass today.

"Cutting it close." Coach checked his watch then turned back to the whiteboard. "Now that everyone's here, let's get started."

He drew his plays on the whiteboard, all Xs and Os with lines joining them. Everyone had their own language and style when drawing plays. Nathan's were perfectly designed and laid out, labeled. When my dad coached my flag football league, his plays looked like hieroglyphs that no twelve-year-old was ever going to decipher. It was all laid out in his head, but it was impossible to explain to anyone else. Leroy was a great football player, a great dad for the most part, but he was not a great coach back then. It caused a lot of friction between us. He couldn't understand why I didn't just get it. I couldn't understand why he wouldn't just say what he wanted. That part wasn't new, though. We'd always butted heads. Abby was the go-between for us, interpreting and smoothing things over, until she wasn't. Then Dad and I had to relearn how to talk to each other, which was still a work in progress.

"Let's go through some scenarios." Coach tapped the marker against his hand. "Drayton, if the linebacker drops into coverage, what do you do?"

"Easy. I throw over the middle."

"No!" Ryan practically shouted from his spot across the room. "That safety's a ball hawk. He's gonna jump the route."

"Okay, what then?" Coach nodded toward Ryan.

"You should check the flats or hit the tight end on the out

route." Ryan flashed a smug smile my way. "You missed the film sesh, so you didn't see how tight their defense is."

What the fuck? Ryan had seen me watching the clips. He sat beside me on that couch and gave me the sob story about ruining his chances.

"I've watched the tapes." I leaned back further, stretching my legs out in front of me. "And maybe you can't complete it in that window, but I can."

There was a chorus of *oohs* around the room. Ryan tried to keep his expression neutral, but it was obvious his jab hadn't landed like he'd wanted. He was trying to get me going, but I wasn't going to bite.

"Let's take it again." Coach went back to the whiteboard. "First one, Drayton sees single coverage, what route should the receiver run?" He drew a line from one X to the end field.

Coach liked conversation, asking a lot of questions and getting people talking. It had annoyed me the first few weeks during our preseason practices because it seemed like a waste of time. Why go through all these scenarios when we could be on the field? But now it made sense. I hadn't known any of these guys coming in—same as Coach—and all this talking helped me see everyone's thought processes. We got to know how they worked out a problem, their instincts when things got messy. It ramped up the trust because there were fewer unknowns.

Not Ryan, though. He was a good player. It made sense he'd been starting quarterback last year. He had a good arm. Strong runner. But he was also erratic. Changed the play too often. And he had a temper when things didn't go his way. I couldn't read him—was he trying to be my friend or gather enough information to bring me down?—and that meant I didn't trust him. We all wanted to win, but most of us understood that we needed to work together to get there. Ryan seemed like the guy who'd put himself first if that got him the spotlight.

My phone buzzed, and I pulled it out of my pocket. A good-morning text from Dallas. She was in bed, her arm held up to get a photo of her head still on the pillow. Dark hair messy around her. Dark eyes still only half opened. Her cheeks flushed a soft pink. This was one of those little moments she was talking about. It was hard to drag my eyes away. Hard to believe I'd turned down the option of staying over. I could've experienced that in real life. Real time.

"Are we distracting you, Lahey?" Coach was staring me down. "Got something more important on your mind?"

"Nah." I stuffed the phone back into my pocket. "I'm all yours."

I didn't bother looking at Ryan. I knew that smug smile would be back.

"All right, we've hit the wall with their defense." He circled a line of Xs representing De Leon. "Let's draw them out."

Everyone joined in. We hadn't played a game yet, but I knew we had a good team. Practices were less disjointed. Everyone was having fun and still kicking ass. We were getting a rhythm. Liked spending time together.

Team friendships could be strange. It had been fine in high school because most of us were there for all four years. But I'd barely been playing with these guys a month, and there had already been cuts and replacements. Injuries, poor performances, and line switches. You got used to playing with someone one week, then they were gone or moved the next.

Dad talked about former teammates like they'd been on combat missions together, blood brothers. But as soon as one of them got traded, it was over. Out of sight, out of mind. Next time they met, they were the enemy. Their friendships were intense, loyal, for as long as they were on the same team, but they didn't exist in one another's lives off the field.

"Why don't we go run all our options and find out." Coach blew his whistle, and everyone jumped up. Finally, we were going to see some action. "Drayton, hang back."

Everyone filed out, but Ryan was dragging his feet, moving slowly to catch whatever Coach wanted to say. Coach wasn't falling for it, though. He waited until everyone was out the door.

"I've been in this business a long time, and I know you've worked hard to get here, but nothing is guaranteed."

"I know."

"No, you don't." Coach crossed his arms over his chest. "This is the time to put in your ten thousand hours."

I was past that number already. I'd already put in the time. I was here to put in more. But those hours weren't going to add up in an office. This was all important, but I needed to play. That was what mattered.

"If you want to go pro, you need to keep your eye on the ball. And that means all of it. Not just the parts you think are important."

Coach didn't wait for a reply. He walked toward the door and shouted over his shoulder, "Get on the field, Lahey. If you're a minute late, you're back on second string."

CHAPTER NINE

DALLAS

I checked my phone again: 10:45 a.m. This interview was supposed to start thirty minutes ago. I was already cutting it close, and soon it was going to be impossible. I'd told Drayton I would be there before the game to wish him luck. It was his first game of the season. I redid the Google Maps calculations. If I left in the next ten minutes, I would make it in time. Assuming I could get a car that quickly.

The coffee shop was cute. If I were in a better mood, I would call it cozy. It was small with only a few tables. Everyone seemed laid-back, sipping coffee with laptops or books open. Definitely the kind of place I might linger in, do some schoolwork, when I wasn't on edge and anxious to get on the road. I picked up my phone again and called Drayton. As expected, it went straight to voicemail.

"I'm running late, but I'll be there as soon as I can." I tried to sound upbeat and present a can-do attitude.

The plan had been to have this interview earlier in the week, but Skyler was sick for a few days, and this was the earliest we could meet. Which, in the end, was good since my schedule went haywire all on its own. I picked up extra studio time to prep for a performance and was assigned the dreaded group project in economics. That was on top of duties like laundry, errands, and food, plus the constant worry about my impending financial crisis. I didn't want to tell Nathan until I figured something out because I didn't need him worrying too.

It was slowly dawning on me that being an adult sucked. I couldn't believe I'd spent all that time wishing for it to happen when I was in high school. It was so much easier when I only had to worry about dance and cheer and cleaning up after Nathan cooked.

I needed to do something to keep busy, so I sent Gabby a check-in text. I'd tried to call a few times since her big reveal, but she always replied with, "Busy, talk later." If we were still in Archwood, I could show up at her door with Oreos and ice cream—the only proven remedy for heartache—but Harvard was on the other side of the country, which might as well have been a different planet. Plus, she insisted she was fine. Scientist Gabby had treated the breakup as a logical and practical response to distance and a heavy workload. But it was my sweet, push-her-feelings-aside friend Gabby who worried me. I wasn't sure if she would admit it if her world fell apart.

I might have considered this past week a complete chaotic mess if it hadn't been for a surprise delivery yesterday. I'd been in my room studying when Miley had arrived with a package.

"Picked this up at the porter's desk for you." She handed me a small box sealed with tape.

"I didn't order anything?"

"Is that a question for me?" Miley laughed.

"Yes. No." I bounced the package in my hands, checking the weight. I considered shaking it. "I've never received a mystery package before."

I used a pair of scissors to cut open the box, removed the packing materials, then stared at the contents for a few beats. It was a Polaroid camera.

"What the . . . ?" I lifted it out and turned it over in my hands. There was a note attached to the bottom.

"What does it say?" Miley jumped onto the bed beside me. "Do you have a secret admirer? Someone obsessed with 1970s technology?"

I read the note and bit my lip to slow the smile, then held it up for Miley: *To capture all the little moments. Love your short-distance boyfriend.*

"It's like he's speaking in code."

It *was* a code. Our code. Our language. And this was one of the little moments. I held the camera up to capture a selfie, and Miley popped into the frame, throwing her arms around me, just as I clicked the button.

We collapsed on the bed, laughing. Once again, I felt very grateful for winning Miley in the roommate lottery.

Miley put her hand on mine as I shook the Polaroid. "I don't think you're supposed to do that."

"It makes it develop faster."

"No, it doesn't. Have patience, my friend."

"Says the person who can't wait to microwave a Hot Pocket."

I put the picture on the bed in front of me, watching as the image slowly emerged.

"By the way, a few of us are hiking tomorrow." She rolled on her side to look at me. "Want to come?"

"I can't. I have my interview and then Drayton's game."

"Ah, yes, the fabulous life of a WAG." Miley batted her eyelashes then flopped back down on my bed.

"Still friends?" There was going to come a time when Miley lost interest in asking me to join in. Everyone other than Drayton and Gabby eventually grew tired of my isolationist streak.

But instead, Miley flashed me a bright smile. "Obviously."

I looked down at the photo to reveal the two of us slightly off-center and laughing.

"Hot!" Miley grabbed the photo. "Definitely worthy of the corkboard."

She jumped up to pin the photo to the board. Our collection of mementos and pictures had grown over the past few weeks. Looking at it, you might actually think I had a life at CalArts.

~

"Hey, can I get you a coffee?"

I jumped in my seat, banging my knee against the table leg. The guy standing in front of me screamed artist. Bad T-shirt and jeans. Slightly shaggy but still styled light-brown hair. In another lifetime, I probably would've thought he was cute. Possibly cute enough to share a coffee with and ask all those small talk questions. But that was definitely not in my present timeline.

"Thanks but no thanks." I turned back to my phone, hoping that would be enough to dissuade him.

"Do you not like coffee?" He sounded like he was laughing. When I looked back up, he had one eyebrow raised.

"I love coffee." I leaned forward on my elbows and somehow refrained from sighing. "But I'm already super anxious because I'm running so late for my game, and more caffeine might just set me over the edge."

"What do you play?" Now he seemed intrigued. Why did he seem intrigued? He wasn't picking up on any of my signals.

"Not me. It's my boyfriend's game."

"USC?"

Whoa, that was weird. "How did you know that?"

He waved a hand at me, indicating my outfit. I looked down, and, yeah, I was wearing a USC sweatshirt. Dead giveaway.

"Anyway, my point is I should be there, but instead I'm here. Waiting around to interview for a job I don't even want."

It felt good to let it out, but it didn't solve anything. I checked my phone again: 11:03 a.m. That wasn't good.

"My apologies for keeping you waiting." He pulled a chair out and sat down opposite me. "I was dealing with a pastry fiasco in the back."

I stared at him. What the hell was a pastry fiasco?

He leaned back and crossed one knee over the other. "But we can start the interview now."

Shit. Definitely not good.

"You. You're Skyler? I thought you were a girl." That wasn't exactly how I'd intended to respond, but there was no turning back now. Maybe I wouldn't make a terrible *second* impression.

"Happens all the time." He shrugged. It was possible he was being charming.

"Maybe it was all the emojis?"

"What?" His voice rose in mock outrage. "I use an appropriate amount of emojis." Yeah, he was definitely trying for charming. "Anyway, I know you're in a rush. So, let's see . . ."

He nodded—*May I?*—then pulled my resume toward him. My resume actually wasn't too bad. I'd worked at the dance studio in Archwood for years and had some volunteer experience, mostly teaching dance for school musicals or at the community center. So not a lot of variety, but it proved I could work with people, despite my not-so-stellar start to the interview.

"Freshman. Dance major. Impressive GPA." He put the resume back on the table and looked up. "No prior barista experience?"

"I'm a very fast learner."

"I'm sure you are." He looked at me for a couple seconds before speaking. He was considering something. "I guess I only have one question. Why do you want the job?"

"Ha. Funny. You're funny." It took me a moment to realize he wasn't joking. He took this barista business seriously. "As I said earlier, I love coffee."

"You said coffee made you anxious."

"I said *too* much coffee made me anxious. There's a difference. That only proves that I'm human." He continued to stare, which wasn't helping my nerves. I needed to get this job and then I needed to get the hell out of here. "And I'm good with people. Usually."

"Obviously."

"Look, I can't take back what I said." Desperate times called for desperate measures. "I don't want this job. But I need it."

He clasped his hands in his lap like he was relaxing into a story. He wanted to know more. I felt my jaw clench. I needed to convince him to hire me, but I also had no desire to bullshit or suck up to him. If we had to work together, he needed to know that I pulled no punches and said what I meant. Even if it rushed out of my mouth in an anxiety-fueled stream.

"Financial aid is a joke, and my full ride is turning into 70 percent next year, so I need to work now to prepare for later. So if making oat milk lattes is how I get to stay at CalArts, I'll show up to every shift, on time, with a smile."

Skyler laughed, a boisterous, drop-his-head-back kind of laugh, which I did not expect.

"Did I mention I love coffee?" For some reason, I was laughing too.

He took a moment, staring me down, long enough that I was sure he was finding a way to say *not a chance* when he nodded once.

"Can you start tomorrow?"

I didn't have to reply because my wide grin said it all. I couldn't believe I'd managed to pull this off after such a bad start. Maybe things were finally starting to look up. All I needed to do was finish with the paperwork, get an Uber, and then turn back time so I could get across the city in time for kickoff.

CHAPTER TEN

DRAYTON

A flash went off, and I had to blink a few times to clear my vision. There were a dozen reporters gathered in the stadium hallway. Enough that it felt like a wall of faces and cameras. I'd been on this side of the press before but only a couple times with me as the focus. Mostly, I'd watched my dad from the sidelines as he answered questions. When Abby and I were small, he brought us with him to face the press a bunch, though that was probably to distract the journalists. No one wants to ask the hard-hitting questions when faced with two big-eyed twins. Dad was always so calm, collected, and smooth, even when the reporters were giving him hell for a bad play. And if things were going well, he turned on the charm. Today was no exception.

"This game's exciting, to say the least." Dad put a hand on my shoulder and smiled at me. More flashes went off. "It's just the beginning for Drayton, and I'm ready for the world to see what he can do."

"No pressure, though." I put my hand on his shoulder, mirroring his stance.

The journalists laughed, and my muscles relaxed. It was one of those moments I hadn't realized I was tense. I was wired about the game, anxious to get back in the locker room and start the pre-game ritual. Shower, get dressed, pep talk, a few minutes to clear my head of everything but football and our playbook.

"How does it feel to have your son following in your footsteps?"

Most of the questions were directed to Dad. He was the former NFL star, after all. He was the one with the Super Bowl rings. A Leroy Lahey quote was going to get picked up a lot faster than one from the nepo baby quarterback. Plus, my dad looked damn proud, and he'd put a lot into getting me here too.

"As a father and former quarterback, it's an honor to shepherd my son into this next phase."

He threw an arm over my shoulder and hugged me. It was a tight hug, and for a second I wondered if Dad was thinking about Abby too. It still surprised me when and how much I missed her. Even though she'd gone missing years ago, sometimes it felt like it was only yesterday. We let the reporters take a few more shots before heading through the door to the locker room.

It was a whole other level of busy back there. Players were getting dressed, calling out to each other, getting the energy up. Team staff moved around equipment and uniforms. Towels, water, and protein shakes were being delivered. The physio team was setting up in case anyone needed support during the game. I loved this part. Seeing everything come together. Everyone pumped and ready to take on the world.

"Remember, don't try to be a hero on the first snap." Dad put his hand on my arm, so I turned to him. He had his serious game face on. "Let the play develop. You can stay ahead of it by watching."

"Got it."

"You need to react as much as act. Follow the play then see where it lands."

"Dad."

"And don't forget to—"

"Dad. I got this." I put my hand on his arm. "Don't worry so much. We did it, I'm here. Your job's done."

That might have been the wrong thing to say. He didn't quite wince, but I think it hit him harder than I'd intended.

"My job is never done."

"I know, I know." Dallas and I talked about this a lot. How it was hard for my dad to let go. His NFL career had ended with an injury, then he'd put all his energy into me. None of this had been forced on me–-I wanted this as much as he did—but it could be a lot. "And I'm glad you're here. But maybe just try to . . . chill a little?"

He let out of a puff of air and laughed. "Less coach, more dad?"

"Exactly." A year ago, my comment wouldn't have gone over so well. We were both a bit more tightly wound before I got to USC and asserted more control over my life. "Listen, I gotta head back with the guys. But grab a beer, relax, I got this in the bag."

"Right, yes." Dad nodded a few times before giving me another hug. For sure he wished there was a playbook for being a father. Maybe I should return his advice. Follow the play and see where it lands. Then react.

I checked my phone before dropping it in my locker. There was a voicemail from Dallas saying she was running late because of the interview. She sounded nervous. In her mind, this job was her last chance. If she didn't get it, there was no way she could stay at CalArts. I'd tried telling her we'd find the money somewhere without actually saying that I could take care of it. She'd never let me pay for it outright, but I'd be a better option than a loan. Better interest rate. Better benefits. Yeah, that was the kind of joke I needed to use sparingly with Dallas. I wasn't really joking, and she was never going to take something she hadn't earned on her own.

I checked the time. There was no way she'd make it for kickoff, which wasn't ideal. Back in Archwood, it was good to look at the sidelines and see her. I could feed off her energy, her excitement about the game. I was looking forward to seeing her in the stands today and making a new game ritual. There might be fans and boosters cheering us on, but there was only one Dallas.

~

The stadium was packed. A sea of red and gold filled the stands, surrounding us. It was the biggest game of my career so far, the start of the next chapter, and it felt great hearing the crowd roar when we stepped onto the field. This was exactly where I was meant to be. Everything in my life up until this point had led to this very moment. I did a quick check of the VIP section—my dad was there, but no Dallas—then got down to business. We were going to win this fucking game.

De Leon University was a tough team. They had some killer players, and it was a challenge to stay on top of them. Control of the ball went back and forth. Coach Watson was right about their linebacker. He was quick for a guy built like a literal wall. I should have seen him coming and switched up the play. I took a few steps back, trying to hand off to our fullback, but I didn't hit the pivot as fast as I should have, and the De Leon linebacker smacked into me, knocking the ball loose. There was no time for a scramble. He scooped up the ball and was off. Tied game.

My dad looked pissed. Maybe not at me, but I understood. I'd had control of the ball. I hadn't fumbled it—an opposing player swiping it was part of the game—but I could have made other choices. Maybe one that would've had us in the lead instead of neck and neck.

"Time-out!" Coach signaled the ref then called us all back to the bench when the whistle blew.

I gave another quick glance into the VIP. Still no Dallas.

"The run game isn't working." Coach leaned into our huddle. "Let's try to open it up with the pass. Lahey, you think you can fit it in a tight window and avoid the safety?"

"Absolutely." That was my specialty.

"Okay. Zach is going to run a ten-yard button hook." He pointed at Zach then me. "Drayton will hit him on the curl."

We all clapped, slapped one another on the back, then ran out to take our positions.

"Come on! You got this!" Dad's voice was loud and clear from the stands.

It was a make-or-break moment, and the crowd was going wild. The cheerleaders chanted, getting everyone even more keyed up until the action started.

Things moved quickly. I had the ball and made eye contact with Zach. He was completely covered by De Leon's defense. My mind quickly spun through all my possible moves. Zach was going to hit his mark, but so would the DL players. I had to make the call, and I stuck with Coach's play. Threw, perfect arc, perfect catch, and Zach was down two seconds later.

"What an interception!" The announcer's voice boomed through the stadium.

Shit. De Leon was on the move. I took off, darting to the side to block their path. I was acting on instinct, muscle memory. My body felt electrically charged. Alive. On fire. I ran on an angle so I would meet them only a few yards back. They wouldn't make much ground, and we could push them back. We were going to take this game.

I hit the ground. Hard. With my leg underneath my body and a 250-pound linebacker on top. The first thing I felt was a sharp pain in my chest. The wind was knocked out of me, and it took a couple seconds to get my breath back. Then the pain hit me hard. My knee. I heard the ref's whistle going. Felt the linebacker get up. There were suddenly feet all about me. Players' cleats, then Coach Watson.

I rolled onto my back thinking that would relieve the pressure on my knee and the pain, but it only made it worse. *Fuck, fuck, fuck.* People were talking to me, but nothing was getting through. It was all pain.

I needed to get up. Stretch it out. Walk off the pain. I pushed myself up but didn't get to a sitting position before wanting to throw up. I think I screamed. I know I swore. I really didn't care. I just wanted this god-awful pain to stop.

"Lahey, can you hear me?" It was Coach. I knew the voice, but he sounded strange. Like he was moving further away. "You need to stay still."

The pain wasn't slowing down, and my vision was messed up. Blurred. I dropped back down onto the turf. Heard Coach call for the doctors. Tried to make out who else was there, then . . .

CHAPTER ELEVEN

DALLAS

I could feel the panic in my throat. I felt my blood pounding in my chest, heard it in my ears. My body was running on adrenaline and fear.

Drayton's dad led me down the stadium corridors. I'd arrived in the VIP section just in time to see the tackle. The play was intercepted, then Dray was down. It happened so quickly that I didn't believe it at first. He was running to stop De Leon's advance, and then everything came to a crashing halt. When he didn't get up, I just stood there in the stands, barely breathing, repeating, *Please, please, please.*

I had to wait while Leroy went onto the field to talk to the coach. Wait while they put Drayton on a stretcher. Wait as I watched him carried out unconscious. I was having flashbacks to my parents that had been in a car accident, and I was kept at a distance since I was only nine, but it was the same helpless feeling. Someone I loved was injured, in pain, and there was nothing I could do.

"The doctors are worried about his ACL." Leroy pushed through another set of doors on our way to the parking lot. "They're not sure if it's a sprain or a tear. We'll learn more as soon as he gets to the hospital and is evaluated."

"But he's going to be okay?" My voice sounded shaky. I could still hear the announcer in the stadium. It seemed surreal that the game was back on when Drayton was hurt and in an ambulance. Didn't they know that the world had stopped turning?

He pressed the button for the elevator. "Yeah, he will, but . . ."

"I should have been there," I said. I didn't need him to finish that sentence to know the truth.

"Hey." He looked over at me. "It's not like you could have stopped a linebacker from tackling him to the ground."

It wasn't about physically stopping a linebacker. That was impossible. But I hadn't missed a game in more than a year, and he'd been fine. Maybe me not being there meant a twist of fate. The elevator opened, and we both stepped inside. Leroy turned to me again.

"Injuries like this, especially so early in your career, can take a toll." His voice was surprisingly gentle. I didn't know Drayton's dad very well, but I'd really only seen two speeds: angry or enthusiastic. This was my first encounter with a less intense Leroy. "Both physically and emotionally."

"What do you mean?"

Leroy let out a slow breath. "Drayton's . . . I suspect that he won't be totally himself for a while. This is going to be a tough adjustment for him, especially if he can't play for now."

I didn't have a chance to reply because the elevator doors

opened, and we were back to moving at full speed through the parking level. Leroy said that while the doctors were worried about Drayton's knee, he possibly had a concussion too. It made sense considering how hard he'd hit the ground. Was that what Leroy had meant? Drayton was the strongest, surest, most reliable person I knew. I couldn't quite comprehend what not being himself might mean.

We hopped into Leroy's rental car, and we were on our way.

"I might be speaking out of turn." Leroy kept his eyes on the road. "But be patient with him. This is going to be hard on both of you."

I glanced over at him and swallowed. "I will."

"I'd move in, but something tells me he didn't picture me as his freshman-year roommate."

"Probably not."

Leroy took the streets with some Fast & Furious moves, taking tight corners and maneuvering around traffic. I couldn't imagine what he'd been thinking when Drayton was injured. Tackles happened all the time in football—they were an integral part of the game—but it must have been hard to watch his son crumple under a linebacker and not get right back up. Leroy looked calm now, though. Clearly, this was a man comfortable in chaos.

"Look, I haven't always been the most supportive of you two." He shifted gears again as we approached the hospital. "But I was wrong. I'm grateful you have each other. Hold on to that. I made it through a lot of tough times thanks to Dray's mom."

I held my breath and refused to blink to keep the tears at bay. I knew that Leroy's anger toward me had been misdirected. He and Drayton had fought because Leroy wanted him to play college football at Waco, a Lahey family legacy, and Drayton wanted to decide his own path. He wanted USC, and Leroy had blamed me, saying I was dragging him to Los Angeles. It wasn't true. I was willing to go long-distance to stay together, but Drayton wanted USC.

"Thank you." I didn't know if that was the appropriate response, but it was how I felt—grateful that Leroy could see what Drayton and I had. We were good together.

~

I waited while Leroy talked to the doctors before I could see Drayton. I had my backpack with me and could have pulled out books to study while I waited, but I'd never have been able to concentrate. Instead, I spent the time watching the others in the waiting room. We were in the fancier wing of the hospital, so there was no emergency room drama. No patients rushing in and out. It was nothing like television.

When a nurse told me I could see Drayton, I followed her instructions to his room. Leroy was in the hall talking on the phone. From his tone, I guessed it was Dray's mom. When Leroy ran a hand through his hair, I finally understood his stress. His shield came down, however slightly, talking to his wife, and I was reminded how much the Lahey men were alike. They were made of steel but melted with the right woman.

I pushed open the door and silently stepped inside. Drayton was in bed, hooked up to an IV and staring at the TV. If he heard me, he didn't turn. He was caught up in the broadcast showing the game and his injury. It wasn't Joe-Theismann-breaking-a-leg bad but definitely not something Drayton should be watching on repeat.

"Why would Lahey make that play? Morgan was so obviously covered." The sportscaster sounded appalled. The play was rewound, and they went through it again, step by step.

I knocked on the doorframe to get Drayton's attention. He looked over, and my heart leaped into my throat. He looked so fragile—dark circles under his eyes, pale skin, body sunken into the hospital bed—and I had no idea what to do. This didn't seem like something a hug could fix.

"Hey, how are you feeling?"

"Been better." He turned back to the TV.

I took a few slow steps toward him. "I'm sorry. I wish I'd been there sooner. But my ride—"

"It's okay." He still wasn't looking at me.

"And my interview took forever and—"

"Dallas, it's fine." He shifted slightly in his bed, trying to get comfortable. "I don't want to talk about it."

I was at his bedside, not sure if I should hold his hand or brush his hair back from his forehead. I could care for Drayton during the times he opened up to me. I'd offered support when he fought with his father. Comfort when he talked about Abby. I'd even played nursemaid when he got food poisoning. It wasn't easy for either of us to show vulnerability, but we could do it for each other. Or so I'd thought. But right now, Drayton wasn't just shutting me out. He was shutting down.

I picked up the remote and muted the TV. He didn't look pleased but also didn't argue with me about it.

"Sometimes talking is good." That was a new one for me too. A year ago, I would have said that talking was exactly what I didn't need. That talking didn't help anyone. "You know, a very wise QB once told me that sometimes you gotta redirect." His jaw twitched, which was enough of a reaction to keep going. "Doesn't mean the game's over."

Still no response, so I grabbed his hand. I was not backing down. I was going to be patient and kind and supportive whether Drayton liked it or not.

"And if there's one thing I know, it's that you, Drayton, are tough." I squeezed his hand. "And stubborn. And when you set your mind on something, it's happening. What did the doctor say?"

He took in a slow breath then squeezed my hand back. When his gaze reached mine, his eyes had softened.

"Did you get the job?"

"I did." I tried for a big smile but suspected it wasn't entirely convincing. I wanted to find a way to distract him. Maybe make him laugh. "I start tomorrow. Early shift, so you know how well that will go."

A corner of his mouth turned up, the hint of a smile, and it broke my heart. This was a man who'd line danced because it made me happy. Sent me a camera so I could capture all those moments we couldn't share together. He looked so lost and confused.

"But I can spend the night and leave early—"

"No, my dad's here." He squeezed my hand again. Slid down a little more in the bed. "He's staying the week. You should go get some rest."

"Are you sure?" I couldn't fake the positive attitude. Drayton was setting a firm boundary. "I'm happy to—"

"I sort of want to be alone." He cut me off. Let go of my hand. "I'm pretty tired. But I'll call you tomorrow, okay?"

I brushed the hair back from his forehead and kissed the top of his head. He was warm, like maybe he had a fever, but I put that down to stress.

"Okay, sure. If you say so."

He gave a small nod but wouldn't look my way.

"I'll talk to you tomorrow."

He had already turned back to the TV, volume on, before I reached the door.

CHAPTER TWELVE

DALLAS

The first thing I learned at my new job was even access to bottomless cups of coffee wasn't enough to wake me up for the ass-crack of dawn. It was brutal. People were still stumbling home from parties while I stumbled to work. The only plus was the café was just a short walk from my dorm. The downside was being fully aware of exactly how close I was to my bed. I decided to focus my attention on emptying the dishwasher because I couldn't do much damage if I fell asleep while working.

Drayton hadn't texted. I'd sent a few—okay, more than a few—messages last night and this morning, which was technically the same thing, but nothing. No reply. He was on pain meds and probably asleep. His dad was there, and staff were probably in and out of his room. I came up with plenty of reasons why he hadn't called or texted despite saying he would. The one I feared the most—that he didn't want to talk to me—I did my best to push aside.

"Any preference on music?" Skyler came in from the back room carrying bags of coffee beans.

"Why are you so perky? It's unnatural at this hour."

I was scowling and couldn't be bothered to try for a more neutral expression. If Miley were here, she would offer her mother's sage advice: Scowling, furrowing, squinting, basically anything that involved brows and moving one's face beyond the bare minimum was a bad idea. *You'll need Botox by the time you're thirty!* Hearing that always made me want to scrunch up my face even more, encourage all those laugh lines.

"We're up, we're here, we might as well make the most of it." He put the bags on the counter and pulled his phone out of his pocket. "Let me try again. Do you have any music preferences? We have to play white girl pop once the doors open, but before then it's dealer's choice."

"I don't care." I put away the last dish and closed the dishwasher. That third coffee might finally be kicking in.

"Suit yourself."

A couple seconds later, the café was filled with the sound of thrash metal. Very loud, very aggressive thrash metal. There may have been actual saws involved, gears scraping against each other. It was music that should accompany Mad Max being chased across the desert. I looked over at Skyler. He was smiling. A mischievous, shit-eating grin.

"What? You said you didn't care."

"Can you at least lower it?"

"What?" he shouted to be heard over the noise.

"It's too loud!"

"I can't hear you." He shook his head and pointed to his ear.

He paused the music just as I screamed, "*This isn't funny!*" I glared at him, and he shrugged his shoulders.

"It was a little funny." He laughed, eyes twinkling a bit too much as he turned on a far less aggressive song at a very reasonable volume.

Maybe I wouldn't need caffeine at all if this was how mornings with Skyler were going to go.

"Okay, next on the list." He pulled a wrapped ball of dough from the fridge and put it on the counter in front of me. "We make our own cinnamon buns here. Meaning they send all the parts, and we assemble and bake."

He took off the plastic wrap and tossed some flour on the counter.

"You need to knead this until it softens a bit but not too much. Roll it out till it's a quarter-inch thick." He stopped me before I picked it up. "You're going to want an apron. This is a messy job."

Kneading dough didn't sound like a terrible job. It might be a good way to work through some frustration. Like starting my day at 6:00 a.m. at a job I didn't want. The dough was cold and not very pliable, so I used the heel of my hand and pressed down with as much weight as possible, but I barely made a dent.

I was never big on—as my grandmother called them—the domestic arts. She baked and did her best to keep us stocked with cookies and cakes after Mom and Dad died, but I wasn't interested in learning. I understood the basic concepts of baking, and I watched *The Great British Bake Off* like anyone with a heart. I'd helped Gabby with her endless bake sales for cheer squad and science clubs, but I'd kept my involvement to the bare minimum. That was all to say that the learning curve here was going to be more than figuring out how to make an espresso without spraying hot water everywhere.

The music caught my attention. It was catchy even though

there wasn't much of a beat. There was an acoustic guitar and a cello, and the singer had a slightly rough but still melodic voice.

"This is a nice song. Who is it?"

"Thanks. It's my band."

"Really?"

"Okay, the double take was a bit much." He finished replenishing the coffee beans then walked over. "Here, let me show you. The dough can be a bit tricky."

It seemed like only seconds later that he had the dough worked in and rolled flat. Either I was confused by the passage of time or Skyler was very good at his job.

"Have you been playing music long?"

"Yeah. Forever, really. Been in a few bands, but I think we've got something with this one." He handed me a container from the fridge. "We're like Noah Kahan meets The National."

"Which one is Noah Kahan?" I opened the container. Cinnamon roll filling. "I'm not up on my singer-songwriters."

"That aren't Taylor Swift, you mean."

"Hey, don't stereotype me. Not every young woman is a Swiftie."

I made a mental note to never wear my Taylor Swift concert shirt to work.

"Fair point." He gave me a quick demo on spreading the filling then passed me the spatula. "His songs are folky pop and sound sort of happy, but he talks about important things. Mental health. Personal struggles."

"That's what you do? Your songs?" I wasn't as fast or precise at spreading the filling. These might end up being cinnamon blobs instead of rolls.

"Sometimes. I hope so." He leaned against the counter beside me. I realized what I'd thought was his cologne was more likely vanilla from all the baking. "But let's be honest, most of the songs are about the woman who did me wrong."

"You can't go wrong with heartache. At least with songs. I hear it's not great in other circumstances."

"Guessing that means you've never had your heart broken."

"What can I say? I'm very picky and have exceptional taste."

He laughed that big throw-his-head-back laugh again. I wasn't really in a laughing mood, but smiling felt good.

"Actually, you might like this." He snapped his fingers. "Hang on."

He scooted around the corner and grabbed a flyer from the community bulletin board. The café positioned itself as a hub, so the board was covered in flyers. Upcoming events and art shows, calls for actors and crew for short films, submissions for poetry journals.

"We're auditioning dancers for a music video we're shooting next month."

Yup. Right on point.

"There's literally no budget, but everyone's super talented."

"Sounds great." This was one more reason why I avoided talking to people. I didn't want to have this kind of conversation or be put in this position. "Sounds like it'll be fun."

"I'm suggesting that you, the dancer, come out." He handed me the flyer. "Might be a cool way to meet new people and get some footage."

"Wow. Thanks." There wasn't much to the flyer. It had a photo of the band, a date, and a location. They weren't big on marketing, apparently. "That's a nice offer, but I'm a pretty busy between class and rehearsals for my showcase."

“On top of moonlighting as a barista.”

“Exactly. But your band sounds very cool.” I put the flyer on the counter and slid it back toward him. He watched me with a slightly tilted head.

“Thought you’d be into a chance to dance.” He pushed the flyer back toward me.

“It’s more that I’m not sure I’m what you’re looking for?”

“Isn’t dancing dancing?”

“Is music music?”

“We’re looking for dancers. You fit the bill.”

“But I’m more . . . I prefer elevated dance. Like ballet.”

“Wow.” He nodded a few times and did not look impressed. “That was a very snobby thing to say.” He held a hand up. “Sorry, I meant pretentious. You being so high art and all.”

Okay, that was taking it a bit too far.

“This isn’t a comment on what you do. I’m trying to say that I’m not a backup dancer.”

“Yeah, not helping your case.” He pushed himself off the counter and walked toward the back room. “You’ll need to get those in the oven so you can mop the floor before opening.”

I watched the door close behind him before picking up the flyer again. I’d come to CalArts to become an artist, to learn more about ballet and improve my craft. I didn’t see how that fit in with a music video. Still, I folded the paper and put it in my pocket because leaving it on the counter felt too much like evidence at a crime scene.

YouTube was going to have to help me figure out what to do next with the rolls. Then I’d have to take my punishment and find the mop. The job I didn’t want had just gotten that much worse.

CHAPTER THIRTEEN

DRAYTON

A week later, I was standing on the field, and I was not enjoying myself one bit. I tried to keep my anger in check, but I wasn't doing a great job. I hated being on the sidelines watching my team run through plays and scrimmages. Hated that I was wearing a T-shirt and shorts, this stupid leg brace and crutches, instead of my gear. And I really hated that my ACL sprain was keeping me off the field. I couldn't even pretend there was a chance I could jump in. I hated watching my team run plays I should be leading. Really hated watching Ryan drop back, wind up, and unleash a bomb downfield. The doctor said I'd be sitting on the sidelines for the next couple weeks. Never, in the history of my football career, had I been injured like this, forced to be an observer and not a top-tier participant. My ego was bruised, sure, but it was more than that—this wasn't in the plan. This was never part of the plan.

Ryan took off his helmet and let out a loud, arrogant whoop. He pointed toward me and shouted across the field.

"Hey, water boy!" He smirked at me. An honest-to-god smirk. "At least make yourself useful and throw me a bottle."

Yeah, fuck that guy.

I was tempted to throw the bottle with enough precision and force to crack his skull—that would serve him right for taking his helmet off so quickly—but I held it together and tossed the bottle so it arced high and he easily caught it.

"See? Knew you were good for something." There was the smirk again as he jogged over to talk to Marcus on the other end of the bench.

I needed to get the hell out of there and burn some of this energy off. I needed to get back in shape and on the field. Enough of this sideline bullshit.

Coach nodded when he saw me head out. He was giving me space, which was probably smart. I wasn't much fun to be around.

The workout room at the stadium was top-of-the-line, like everything else connected with USC football. Even the benches felt plush and padded like they didn't expect their athletes to suffer the indignities of hard surfaces. I focused on weights. Being out of commission for even a week meant muscle loss. It was my Bionic Man moment. I was going to be bigger, faster, stronger when all this was done.

I left the crutches and brace to the side and got on the machine. Worked my arms, proving to myself that I hadn't lost any ground. Pushed myself past the pain. Paused just long enough between sets to catch my breath.

My dad had stayed in Los Angeles for a week after my injury. Long enough to make sure I didn't need surgery and I was set up with doctor's appointments and a follow-up. There wasn't much for him to do since the team was basically in charge, and I could tell he was frustrated. Dad liked to have control. And Dad being frustrated made me frustrated, so I told him to go home.

"Nothing's happening here. It's just me going to the gym. Me getting back on track."

"It's not going to happen overnight." He repeated that like a mantra. "Trust me, it takes time."

Dad was on the verge of giving me the speech about what he should have done when he got injured. How he should have taken the time to recover instead of pushing it too fast and doing permanent damage. I had to avoid that conversation, but I didn't want to point out the obvious. He was years into his NFL career when he got injured. Retirement had been in the cards sooner than later for him anyway. If I didn't stay on track now, there wouldn't be a career at all.

"I've got this, Dad. I know what I'm doing."

"You don't have all the answers, Drayton. Listen to people who've already been through it. We see the big picture."

It was stuff like this that made me miss Abby. She'd been young when she went missing, so there was a lot we didn't get to experience together, but we understood things without having to explain them. Maybe it was a twin thing. I knew when she felt overwhelmed with school or some friend drama. She knew when I felt pressured to be a mini version of Dad. We'd hang out, distract each other, find some little-kid trouble to get into. For a long time after she was gone, I didn't know how to be on my own. I felt like I had to solve every problem. It was a good mindset for a quarterback but a tough place for a kid figuring out the world.

I'd pushed a lot of that stuff down before Dallas. Refused to even say Abby's name. Held on to all those memories like I'd lose them if they were exposed to the outside world. But talking to Dallas about my twin sister had made those memories grow. Made them stronger. It was like Abby was real again. Sharing her with Dallas had made Abby come alive. Dallas understood because she'd lost her parents. Watching her and Nathan tell stories, laugh about things, and feel sad when they needed to helped. It was good opening that door.

Moving to the next machine was a bit of a struggle. It was probably a mistake to leave the crutches and brace behind, but I wasn't going to improve if I didn't push myself. No pain, no gain. I set my usual weights on the bench press and got to work. I felt it right away. My muscles straining, tearing, as I grunted the bar up then lowered it. My hands were already getting sweaty. I could feel the beads forming on my forehead.

I needed to call Dallas. She'd sent me dozens of texts and voice notes, and I'd only replied with some combination of *I'm fine, I'm good, talk to you later*. It wasn't enough—for her or for me—but I also didn't want her to see me like this. Injured, in pain, angry. Besides, she had more than enough going on without me showing up asking if I could lay my head in her lap for a few hours. That wasn't going to help anyone.

"Need a spot?"

I held the bar above me for a second longer as I looked up at the speaker. The blond I'd seen a few times with the physio team. She was tall, or tall from my angle on the bench, and looked fit in a USC shirt and leggings. She was watching me, hands on hips.

"Nope." I lowered then raised the bar again. My arms wavered slightly, shaking more than expected. She moved in quickly to secure the bar, guiding it back into place.

"You shouldn't be lifting this much."

"I know how much I can lift."

"You know how much you *could* lift. A week following trauma changes things."

"I hurt my knee, not my arms." I didn't point out that my injury was something the physio team should know about.

"Trauma affects the whole body. You're in recovery mode."

"I know what I'm doing." I sat up and grabbed my towel. I wasn't interested in hearing another lecture.

"And yet you still almost dropped it."

"You distracted me."

"Says the person who won't admit he needs a spotter."

I wiped the towel over my face and neck. My arms felt a little more rubbery than I would've liked. "Who are you?"

Before she could answer, Coach Watson walked in. He was carrying his clipboard because of course he was.

"Lahey, meet Charlotte Carlisle," he called out as he walked across the room. He was a man on a mission with a million things to do. "Your new PT."

"Technically I'm a physiotherapy assistant, but I work closely with your general practitioner." Her hands were still on her hips. She didn't look as tall now that I was sitting up, but she still maintained a commanding presence. Charlotte didn't look like she took shit from anyone. "I'm also graduating top of my class—"

"Great. So how soon can I get back on the field?" I was going to test that *not taking shit* theory.

"Our first priority is getting you healed." Coach used the clipboard like a pointer, directing it at me. "Ryan can always finish out the season if we need."

"The season?"

What in the actual fuck was he talking about? If he thought I needed any more motivation to get back out there, he was insane. Threatening that I'd lose the whole season was unnecessary.

"We're talking worst-case scenario." Charlotte held up her hand like I needed to be calmed. Like I was a bear ready to charge. Okay, she might not have been too far off the mark on that one. "In general, we like to err on the side of caution."

We didn't need caution right now. We needed action. We needed to move.

"It's just a sprain."

"Right." She nodded like we'd come to some sort of agreement. "And it would be dumb to let it become a tear and jeopardize your entire career by pushing you back onto the field too quickly."

I bit the inside of my cheek to stop the stream of expletives. *Do you know the best way to jeopardize my career? Getting stuck on the sidelines. Doing nothing.* I wasn't going to let my career, my life, my job as a quarterback slip through my fingers. This injury, this sprain, wasn't going to slow me down or push me off course.

"What Charlotte says goes. Trust her and trust the process." Coach pulled his phone from his pocket, frowning at whatever notification had popped up. "I gotta go. But you're in good hands."

Charlotte stared at me for a few seconds, maybe waiting to hear whatever threat or excuse I was going to throw at her, before speaking.

"We're going to take it nice and easy. Lots of rest."

I held her gaze, half-expecting it to soften or for her to look away. It didn't. She didn't.

"Google said it would take two to four weeks to heal."

"Oh, you Googled it? Never mind then. Those two minutes on the internet have got you covered." She picked up a towel from the rack and threw it at me. "Avoid extraneous activity on your knee, especially running. You'll need to wear the brace. Crutches if you want to be cautious."

"I'm done with the crutches." Relying on the crutches meant I wasn't working on the muscles in my legs. Plus, I hated being that guy who needed them. It made me feel weak when I needed to prove I was strong.

"Brace it is. Take it easy for the next two weeks. Try not to stand too much. Binge a show this weekend and elevate your leg. Only take pain meds if you really need to. And if it gets worse, we can talk about a cortisone shot."

"Anything else?" I stood up and realized I was much taller than her. She actually wasn't much bigger than Dallas.

"Yeah." One side of her mouth went up in a small almost-grin. "Stay off Dr. Google."

She walked back out of the gym, leaving me alone.

This wasn't how my year was supposed to go. I'd been riding high. Starting quarterback at a top-tier school. Dallas close by. One step closer to my NFL dream.

How the hell had it all gone so wrong?

CHAPTER FOURTEEN

DALLAS

"How have I never been here before?" I stopped in front of a photograph of two young girls on a dock. They were wearing life jackets over their bathing suits, their wet hair slicked back over their heads. The camera captured their joy so perfectly that I felt like I was right there with them. "This place is incredible."

The art gallery had a mix of past and present CalArts student works lining its walls. Photographs, paintings, some fabric art. I hadn't even known that fabric that wasn't fashion on a runway could be considered art. This afternoon had been eye-opening. For me, CalArts was only about dance, but I had clearly been missing a lot. I'd been so reluctant to come—Miley had practically had to kidnap me to get me out of our room—but I was so glad that I had.

"Not a lot of galleries on the farm?" Miley nudged me with her shoulder and smiled. She never passed up an opportunity to remind me I came from the Colorado sticks while she was a California girl through and through.

"I've never been on a farm." I moved on to the next photograph. "But yeah, Archwood definitely didn't have anything like this."

Archwood had stores that sold art, but it was mainly of the tourists-like-mountains variety, which was somewhat surprising since Archwood didn't get a lot of tourists. I had nothing against pictures of mountains, and no issue with people who liked them, but it was very different from this.

The truth was I'd only been in one art gallery before. We took a class trip to Denver in eighth grade that included a visit to a gallery. The art was abstract expressionism—the first time I'd heard that phrase—and I didn't get it. Giant canvases with paint in colorful swatches and no discernible shape. I'd expected paintings of trees and flowers or women wearing floral dresses and carrying parasols. Gabby was mesmerized. She got up close and talked about brushstrokes and color palettes. She had obviously done the prereading before the visit. But I didn't really feel anything while looking at the pieces. I was happy that Gabby connected with the art, but I was left feeling a bit numb to it all.

This gallery felt different, though. Maybe it was because I was older and had a different perspective on the world, or maybe I'd found more to connect with here. It was also possible that I was more willing to let myself feel something when looking at the art. I was more open to asking rather than ignoring something simply because I didn't understand. Letting myself feel uncomfortable in order to learn was a new thing I was trying.

I wasn't used to talking about art—mine or anyone else's. I always felt a lot while dancing because I was so connected to my body and to my mom. Dancing had always been my special place, my safe space, so if I was hitting my marks, doing everything right, what else was there to do? I only really started talking about it when Drayton wanted to understand. I was shy about it at first, thinking his eyes would glaze over and we'd go back to talking football. But he asked questions, sometimes requested a demonstration, and I was going on excited rants before I knew it.

And it made me a better dancer. Opening myself up to someone freed me as an artist. There was a vulnerability in loving someone but also in letting myself be loved. Knowing he supported me and my dreams, believed in me, made me stronger. Understanding that I could try and fail and he would still be with me was the clincher. I wasn't as afraid to try. Watching Drayton at practice, working through plays, working at his throw over and over until he got the result he wanted, felt like art to me.

"He needs to know." I'd spent the weeks since Drayton's injury worrying about him and the distance between us. He was on edge and ricocheting between needing me and pushing me away. I was trying to be supportive and attentive, but we seemed to be struggling to get on the same page. Maybe it would help if I said something out loud. Something other than *I'm worried* and *You need to take care of yourself.*

"Who needs to know what?"

Miley stood beside me, smiling. I hadn't meant to say that out loud, and Miley knew it.

"I didn't say anything. You must be hearing things."

"Sure." Miley narrowed her eyes at me. She was suspicious but decided to let it go. "Play dumb then."

We walked in silence for a few minutes, taking everything in, then stopped in front of a large photograph. I was immediately drawn in, my breath catching in my throat.

It was shot from above, looking down on a grand staircase. Two dancers were lying on the stairs, reaching toward each other but not touching. The man was higher, resting on one knee with a leg stretched out behind him. The woman was almost on her back, one leg bent, the other straight, toes perfectly pointed. She was wearing a white gown or slip, and the whole thing had a dreamlike quality. It reminded me of pictures of the Sistine Chapel with hands reaching across clouds in the heavens, except the stairs looked like they were in an opera house or palace. I leaned in to read the label—*Departure* by Justin Wu—then stood back to snap a picture with my Polaroid. The photo popped out of the camera with a satisfying whir.

"Hey, no flash photography."

Miley and I turned to see Skyler walking toward us.

"Ah, look, if it isn't the work husband." Miley reached over to give him a quick hug.

"What? I've never said that." I said that more loudly than expected. I turned back to Skyler. "I've never called you that."

I wasn't sure if he heard me, though, since he was speaking at the same time. "That's not appropriate."

I couldn't tell if he was kidding or not. Skyler was always very careful with his words. He wasn't shy about sharing his opinions, and we definitely disagreed on a lot of things, but he would never say anything just to be offensive. He and Drayton were so different in that regard. I loved Drayton's ability to cut through any moment, any tension, and say the most intense things. I'd seen many people, including his mother, cringe at the things that came out his mouth. It never bothered me. In fact, I usually enjoyed it. Also, if I needed him to not be that guy, he dropped it. He was always honest, and I loved him for it.

He *was* always honest, but I wasn't sure that was still true. He was holding back. Possibly lying to me and probably lying to himself.

Miley's phone rang. She smiled at the notification and walked away without saying anything.

"Okay, so tell me what you're thinking." Skyler put his hands behind his back and leaned in like he was hoping for a secret or something special. "Surprises? Delights? Or something that you hated. Doesn't have to be positive."

I laughed. "Well, that's a relief. I'd hate to have to be positive."

I took a step back to look at the photograph again, taking a few breaths to give myself time to take it all in. I wasn't sure why, but I wanted to give Skyler a thoughtful answer. I had no interest in impressing him, or anyone, but I wanted him to know that I took his question seriously. I wanted to have this conversation.

"Visually, it's stunning. The technique from the dancers, I'd kill for his arch." I looked at the muscles in their legs. Their shoulders. The looks on their faces. How they both seemed to be suspended in midair. I didn't know how they'd achieved that in the photograph. Somehow, it didn't look two-dimensional. "But it also feels so . . . tragic. Like they're being pulled apart. They were together but couldn't hold on."

"Hmm."

"What?"

"I see the opposite." He smiled at me. "Like they're reaching out to each other. I think it's hopeful. It will happen, they're just not there yet."

The only response I could think of was to smile back.

"Did you take many shots?" He nodded toward my camera.

"Yeah, a few." I pulled a small stack of Polaroids from my bag. "I took some shots of the art, but there's also a lot of Miley."

"Miley is the queen of the photobomb." Skyler flipped through the photos. "What are you going to do with all of them?"

"Some will go on the all-important corkboard of inspiration and regret." From the look on Skyler's face, he needed more of an explanation, but I decided to leave him hanging. "Not sure about the rest. Guess I need an album or a shoebox. Seems weird to throw them out."

"My mom told me about an exhibit she went to in Manhattan. I think it was by a graphic designer or something. There were chairs attached to walls you could sit on then look down over Broadway. Music you could play by stepping on tiles."

I had no idea if my parents had gone to art galleries. If my mother would have enjoyed an exhibit with chairs attached to walls. In my mind, she was so often trapped inside the photos we had of her. Two-dimensional. For an instant, my mood dipped, and I wanted nothing more than to share this moment with her.

"The part that really got me as a kid was this shelf where you could leave something behind for the next person and take something for yourself." Skyler was looking at the photograph of the dancers while he spoke, occasionally glancing my way. "So my mom and her friend took a selfie with her Polaroid and left it on the shelf. I was obsessed with the idea that someone somewhere had a photo of my mom. It sounds kind of creepy when I say it now, but as a kid I loved knowing my mom's smiling face made somebody's day."

It was a sweet story. Was Skyler secretly a sweet guy? When he wasn't forcing emo rock on me and trying to convince me that my life needed more Bon Iver.

"Okay." Miley returned with a bounce and a giant smile. "Who wants to go to the *La La Land* screening at Street Food Cinema!?"

Once again, Skyler and I talked over each other as I said, "No way! I love that movie!" and Skyler said, "I thought they were sold out!"

We shot each other a quick look then let Miley take over.

"They are sold out. But my friend owns one of the food trucks and offered us comped tickets."

"That's amazing!" Skyler looked ready to give a fist pump. "Glad I showed up when I did."

"Don't worry, baby. I've always got you covered."

"Not falling for it. I'm invited because I was the one standing in front of you."

"That's hurtful." Miley shrugged. "And also true."

"Are you in?" Skyler nudged my arm with his elbow.

"I want to, I mean it sounds great, but I can't." I looked between the two of them. "It's my first date with Drayton in weeks."

"Bring him!" Miley threw her arms in the air. "The more the merrier."

"I would, but he wants to go show his face at some frat party. It's his first outing since . . . you know."

Miley didn't sigh or clench her jaw. She didn't even roll her eyes. She really did have a lot of willpower when she wanted it.

"You'll be missed, but you'll have fun. What's the theme of the party?"

"Probably something elevated," Skyler said.

Miley looked between us then linked her arm in Skyler's and walked away. It was a solid burn on Skyler's part, and maybe he wasn't so sweet after all.

CHAPTER FIFTEEN

DALLAS

"Blondie hos and G.I. Joes." I stopped on the walkway before entering the frat house. I needed more than a minute with this one. "Glad feminism is alive and well."

Drayton didn't respond. He was too busy staring at the house, maybe trying to psych himself up to go in. He was dressed in camouflage pants that hid the tension bandage around his knee and a tight green T-shirt. Gorgeous, as per usual, but not the normal carefree version.

"You with me?" I asked.

He looked down at me, took a beat, then smiled. "Yeah. Of course. Just taking it all in."

It was a lot. The party was already in high gear. Music was blaring from open windows. The front lawn was already littered with beer cans and empty bottles. I didn't really want to be here. Parties had never been my thing, and I didn't particularly want to spend a night with drunk USC frat boys. But Drayton needed it, and I was here to support my boyfriend. He wanted to make an appearance to prove he wasn't out of commission. His injury was only a temporary setback. So I'd raided Miley's closet for a hot-pink minidress and shoes that I already regretted and repeated tonight's mantra.

Do it for Dray. Do it for Dray. Do it for Dray.

A group of blondies came up the walkway behind us. They must have been pregaming because they were already weaving as they passed us. One of them stepped onto the grass in high heels, wobbled, and tumbled into Dray. He winced, almost doubling over as he grabbed his knee, but she only noticed enough to say, "Hey there, QB," before her friends pulled her away, laughing.

"Are you okay?" I put my hand on his arm, leaning in so he looked me in the eyes.

"I'm fine." He spoke through gritted teeth and definitely didn't look fine.

"I really wish you'd worn your brace."

"I said I'm fine." He stood up straight and put a hand on my upper arm in what he probably thought was a reassuring gesture.

"We can ditch this." I stepped in closer, pressing myself lightly against him. The heels meant I was at the right height to kiss him on the chin. "Miley invited us to a movie. Or we could go back to your place and have our own party."

I missed him and our quiet nights together. We were both so stressed out and could use a battery recharge. Some time to reconnect. It was one of the things we'd promised to do when we made our short-distance relationship rules: make time to be together. Even if we couldn't be in the same place, we could talk or watch a show together. Over the summer, we'd made it through entire seasons of *So You Think You Can Dance*. We'd watched old seasons of *LA Ink* because he'd insisted I needed to research my new city. I wanted to have him all to myself. To have him relax and be my sweet goofball instead of the guy who thought he had to perform for his team.

"Tempting offer." He took my hand and smiled at me, and I felt like I could see my Drayton for a moment. The one who'd been my rock throughout the last year of high school and the summer before moving west. "But all the boys are here. Gotta go in."

We both took a deep breath then laughed. We could do this as long as we stuck together.

As predicted, the party inside was crazy. Loud, crowded, already edging toward out of control. He kept my hand in his as we wandered into the living room, weaving our way through the sea of blondies and G.I. Joes. More than a few looked our way, and all of them recognized Drayton. I squeezed his hand to remind him that I was there and with him all the way.

A few guys clapped him on the back and said, "Good to see you, buddy," and some girls bit their bottom lips and tried for a sultry look as we passed. But I knew he was paying more attention to other looks—sympathy or pity—and those comments instead.

"Is that Drayton Lahey? Brave to come out."

"I can't believe he's here."

"Heard he's transferring."

"Can't play at this level."

I looked around the room to see who was talking, but no one would own up. Cowards. Drayton kept his eyes focused forward and his hand in mine.

"Way to fumble the sack, Lahey!" The voice came from

somewhere in the back of the room, loud enough to overcome the music.

"That's not an expression, dumbass!" Drayton yelled back.

A few people snickered, and another guy clapped him on the shoulder in a dude acknowledgment. I saw Dray's expression change, softening slightly. He could feel the support of a few people around him, and that seemed to bolster his spirits.

I'd been to a few USC frat parties but was still amazed by the amount of money these kids had. Designer everything. Even their hair extensions looked expensive. If there were scholarship and student loan kids in the house, they were cosplaying as trust fund babies.

Suddenly, there was a guy beside us that I quickly clocked as Ryan. We'd never met in person, but I'd heard enough about him. It was also immediately obvious that he wasn't to be trusted. He was the kind of guy I would tell my friends to swipe left on.

"Someone get that clown out of here!" He made a big show of pointing toward the corner where the voice had come from then smiled at Drayton like they were best friends. "Good to see you, man. Didn't know if you'd be up for it."

"All good." Drayton was being cautious, waiting to see how this conversation played out.

"You the girlfriend?" Ryan nodded toward me and took a slight step back to get a better look.

"This is Dallas." Drayton's hand went to my lower back in his protective mode. "Dallas, this is Ryan."

I nodded back. "Ryan."

He took a second to check me out—not long enough that I could call him out or kick his shins—then quickly returned his attention to Drayton. This asshole was up to something.

"Down for a game of darts? Your arm still works, right?"

Drayton narrowed his eyes. He wasn't going to back down from a challenge, especially one from Ryan.

"Sure, I'm in."

Drayton turned to me as Ryan walked off, but I didn't give him the chance to check in. I put a hand on one cheek and kissed the other one.

"Kick his ass."

He winked at me then followed Ryan. I made sure to give him a pat on his ass for good luck.

I decided to do a circuit, keep busy, and maybe I'd find a friendly or familiar face. The house was big, like a mansion you might see in a movie, with lots of interconnecting rooms. One had a keg, with the requisite keg stands happening, while another had dancing. One had foosball and Ping-Pong. The kitchen was a mess of Solo cups and crushed beer cans. The guys were dressed in camo but still wore Rolexes and expensive gold chains. The girls wore Louboutin and Jimmy Choo shoes. Designer dresses and spray-on tans. I noticed a few checking me out, usually with a *look*, but I was comfortable in my borrowed vintage dress and returned the gazes with steady defiance.

Do it for Dray. Do it for Dray. Do it for Dray.

Eventually, I gave up on my exploration. I'd hoped to come across Drayton's dart game, but I needed a break from the onslaught. I tucked myself into an armchair and went with every introvert's favorite pastime: scrolling through my phone.

Miley had sent pics of her and Skyler eating tacos while waiting for the movie to start and posted more on Instagram. Shots of people lined up in front of a row of food trucks. People sitting on blankets on the grass. There was a video Skyler must have taken of Miley dancing. I was experiencing some hardcore FOMO. I wanted to be outside, sitting under the night sky and strung-up fairy lights.

It hit me that I was in one of the greatest cities in the world, but I was living in my own small bubble. It wasn't that much different from living in small-town Colorado. I should be exploring LA. Going on hikes. Going for brunch. Sure, brunch might be a waste of time and money, but that wasn't the point. My free time was spent going from Valencia to USC and back again. If we went out to dinner, Drayton picked me up and dropped me off. I knew the USC campus better than my own.

I hadn't come to college with a Hollywood movie vision of what it would be like. I certainly wasn't a *these are going to be the best years of my life* person. I'd come here to dance. That was my entire plan. I was excited when Drayton ended up at USC, and I thought that would be a bonus. And it was—truly—but I was also sitting at a frat, alone, with no Drayton in sight while the few friends I had were sitting under the stars watching one of my favorite movies.

My phone rang, startling me from my pity party. Miley. I was starting to think she might be psychic. I put a finger in my ear to block out the room and answered.

"Hey, girl. How was the movie?"

"Soooooo good. So much fun. I'm sorry you missed it!" Miley sounded tipsy, leaning into drunk, and very happy.

"Yeah, I bet. I saw the pictures." I tried to sound upbeat, like I was also having the time of my life.

"We're heading to a bar in Silver Lake!" Miley's voice was muffled. She must have been in a car. "You and the hot jock boyfriend need to join!" She said something else but was drowned out by the voices and laughter around her as well as the music and chaos around me.

"I can't really hear you. Hello?" The phone cut out. "Dammit."

If nothing else, Miley could've kept me company until they got to Silver Lake. I sent her a text saying the call was dropped and I'd see her tomorrow. She replied with a single tear emoji, and I sent back a heart. I was tempted to request no more update photos because I didn't want to know what I was missing, but that felt too vulnerable. Or like I was betraying Drayton.

Instead, I texted Nathan and Gabby, though I didn't have a lot of hope either would reply. It was almost three in the morning at Harvard. If Gabby was up, she would be studying, and that meant phone off. Nathan was being weirdly shady lately and not quick with his responses. Archwood football would be in full swing, so he was busy. Plus he had his boyfriend, so any free time was probably spent with him.

"I didn't think it was possible, but he's sooooo much hotter in person."

Three girls stopped by my chair. They all looked drunk and wore skintight minidresses. I wouldn't have been able to tell them apart except one was blond, one brunet, and one redheaded, like they'd been ordered from central casting.

"The team Insta account has kept me and my vibrator very busy, but in person is next level." The blond fanned herself like she was overheating, and her friends laughed. They all slouched on the furniture around me, crowding into my space.

"I bet he needs a lot of extra attention with that bad knee. Some extra-special care." The redhead giggled and bit her lip. "You'd have to be careful."

"So, I'm on top. Works out for both of us."

"I heard he has a girlfriend." The brunet wasn't defending me or my relationship. She presented the information with disdain, not concern.

"I don't see her here tonight. If she's dumb enough to leave her man unattended, there's nothing I can do."

"Oh, I think there's plenty you can do." The redhead nudged the blond's knee with her foot.

"But I haven't heard anything about him hooking up." The brunet was so earnest. Under other circumstances, I might have liked her. Circumstances that didn't involve women discussing fucking my boyfriend. "So maybe he's loyal."

The blond and redhead both laughed.

"Early days. They all start out loyal to the high school chippies." The blond adjusted her dress so her boobs popped more. "Besides, I like a challenge. You saw how he looked at me when he went to the back room with Ryan. Only a matter of time, girls. Only a matter of time."

That was my signal to get out. This was supposed to be a date night. It was supposed to be a way to support Drayton through a difficult time. But this was me stuck in a room with the cast of *Vanderpump Rules* and no Dray in sight. I pushed through the sea of blondies and tried to retrace my steps to get the hell out of this house.

CHAPTER SIXTEEN

DRAYTON

Darts was more evenly matched than I'd wanted. Or expected. I knew Ryan could throw and hit a target, but I didn't think he had the easy touch that darts required. I'd figured he'd lay it on too hard for darts and not make the landing. I'd been wrong. We were on our fourth game in a best of seven and tied all around.

I sipped my beer and watched him. Ryan was as much a showboat here as he was on the field. He strutted, raised his arms in victory, high-fived his frat buddies on the sidelines. He was trying to get under my skin, but the best way to deal with guys like Ryan was to stay calm. Don't let them see any jabs land. Let them spin in circles and wear themselves out. And then strike.

He threw his dart and hit the twenty. It was a good shot. One of the girls watching whooped. She was definitely on Team Ryan.

"Getting nervous, Lahey?" Ryan swigged from his Solo cup. "Need to rest up? Wouldn't want you to overdo it."

"All good, pal." I aimed, lined up my shot, and got a twenty. I was pretty sure he mumbled *fuck* under his breath.

My arm was feeling good, strong, but it wasn't the problem. My leg ached. Throbbed. I knew I should sit down, but that wasn't happening anytime soon. I was here for as long as Ryan wanted to fight it out over darts. If I couldn't face him on the field, this would have to do.

I didn't trust this guy. I'd seen Dallas's expression when they met and knew she didn't either. Dallas had no game face. The first thing I'd noticed about her—well, other than her face, body, tight ass, and strong thighs—was her unwillingness to take bullshit. Dallas was honest and blunt but never rude. She wasn't intimidated by anyone. She wasn't impressed because someone drove a luxury car or had a designer bag. She could see through Ryan's blowhard personality immediately, and I loved her for it. I didn't have to explain the background or my issues. She understood.

Where was she, anyway? I'd thought she'd find her way back here to watch the game. I had a cheering squad. A few guys I recognized from campus and the frat. A few girls in barely-there pink outfits. A blond who was making the most of sipping her drink from a straw so I could see her full, pouty lips. I looked over a few times because it was hard not to. She was trying so hard it almost hurt to watch. It was the opposite of Dallas and what I wanted.

My phone buzzed in my pocket. Josh. We were checking in on each other at regular intervals but never mentioning what was really going on. He didn't ask about my knee. I didn't ask about life without Gabby. Tonight's text was telling me to watch *Fallout* because it, quote, *rocked harder than the game*, whatever that meant.

Ryan and I kept up the back-and-forth, alternating taking the lead while taunting each other. This wasn't how I'd planned or wanted to spend the night. But it had to be the smart move. We were teammates. We needed to find a way of working together. If I was going to suit up anytime soon, we needed to work through this tit-for-tat crap. I'd played with difficult people before. It was about finding some common ground then building from there.

Ryan shot again and whooped even though he hadn't quite made the point he was aiming for. My next shot wasn't better.

It had been a hot topic for Dad and me over the past couple of weeks. It helped with the drowning feeling that took over sometimes when my leg hurt and I was exhausted from working out and didn't seem to be any closer to getting off the bench. Dad knew football, and he knew how to deal with arrogant teammates. He told me stories about butting heads with linebackers who didn't want to follow his plays. Running backs who wanted to take all the glory and lost the team the ball and yards.

"Most of us are a bunch of hotheads with something to prove. And the simple truth is sometimes we're the arrogant assholes."

I didn't want to talk about my injury or recovery plan. Didn't want to deal with sympathy and concern. Dad compared what had happened with his injury, Dallas talked about dancers getting hurt, Josh was just Josh. I didn't need any of it. Action was the only thing that would help. I went to the gym first thing most mornings. Ran sprints then laps. Ran the bleacher steps like I was Rocky. Raced up then back down. Did some going backward. It killed. Sometimes the shooting pain was so strong I had to stop to catch my breath as it sent my heart rate through the roof. I could feel it in my hips too, likely because I was compensating for the bum knee. I didn't let any of it stop me, though. I had to push through if I was going to get anywhere. And I made sure to do everything, *everything*, that Charlotte told me to do. I hadn't missed a physio appointment.

"Your girl's hotter in person."

"What?" I threw the dart while turning to look at him and missed the board. The dart bounced hard off the wall and onto the floor. He'd finally done it. Ryan had gotten under my skin. "What the hell did you say?"

"Dude, relax." He laughed as he aimed and threw. His dart hit a double ring. "It was a compliment."

"How do you figure that?"

"Your home screen's a cute pic in that hometown, high school girlfriend way. But in real life, she's hot. Got that dancer body but curves."

For a split second, I thought he was going to cup his hands over his chest to indicate a nice rack, and I almost tackled him. If he wanted to know how well my arm worked, he could feel how fast and hard it came at his face. He smiled because he knew that jab had landed. I decided to wait it out and see where he thought this was going. Instead of responding, I stepped to the side for a drink and took a slow sip of my beer.

"Sunday's a big game." He stepped in closer, trying to invade my space. "Third win in a row would be great for morale."

"Can't argue with that." I put my cup down on the table. Every move was methodical. Careful. I was sizing him up like I would any opponent. "Winning's the idea of the game."

He was in close. Where was Dallas? She'd give me total shit if she was witnessing this showdown. She made fun of sports fights, claimed she couldn't tell if they were going to kiss or fight. I always found her reaction ironic since she would be right in the mix if she thought someone was insulting me or Gabby. She would never back down if a friend was in need of support.

"It's good, you know," Ryan said. There was that smile again. Did he think he looked charming? Threatening? That he was tricking me by putting me at ease? "I feel like order has finally been restored."

"Let's see how you do here before you make big promises for on the field."

We went back at it and didn't waste any time. One dart after another. Our crowd had thinned out during our brief standoff, but the ones left cheered and booed as our scores went higher.

"Like I said, Ryan. Don't get too comfortable." I had my arm raised. Ryan was a couple points ahead, but I had the last throw.

"Look, Drayton, you're a great player. But face it. It was too much pressure too soon, and you choked."

"Excuse me?" I turned to him, slightly pissed that he was messing with my concentration again.

"It's not your fault. I should've been first-string. That was a bad call on Coach's part. And most of the guys agree with me."

The little shit. I didn't let my eyes veer from his face. Didn't want to know if any teammates nearby had heard him. Definitely didn't want to know if any of them were nodding along.

"After last year, you're lucky they didn't revoke your scholarship." I turned back to the board, threw the dart, and hit the bull's-eye.

It didn't matter if anyone had heard or agreed with Ryan because they were all cheering now. A few clapped me on the back so hard I could feel it in my knee. I kept my expression steady, though. It was all *fuck you, buddy*.

"Guess my arm still works."

Ryan was trying to brush it off, acting like it was no big deal, when I caught a flash of pink moving quickly past the door. I didn't have to see Dallas head-on to know it was her. And that she was pissed. I gave chase without looking back at Ryan and knew that only pissed him off more.

She was already out of the house and heading down the walkway by the time I caught up with her.

"Dallas! Hold up."

She stopped, turning to watch me walk toward her and pretending not to notice my limp.

"What's wrong? Why are you taking off?" *More like why are you taking off without telling me?*

"Nothing. Nothing's wrong." Her jaw clenched. "I'm tired, and I want to go home."

"Okay." Being outside and away from the chaos made me realize I was feeling done too. "Let's head back to my dorm."

"Do you want me to call an Uber?" She pulled her phone out from her purse.

"We can walk. It's not that far."

"Drayton." Her eyes had softened. Whatever had pissed her off had passed, and she was back in take-care-of-Drayton mode.

"Dallas." I matched her tone and hoped she understood this wasn't up for discussion. We were both stubborn, and neither of us liked to back down.

"Isn't all this a lot for your knee?"

"I feel great."

"That doesn't mean you won't exacerbate your injury."

"I got this, Cheer. Stronger every day." I turned her around and gently pushed her in the right direction. "Let's go."

We took it slow, my arm slung over her shoulder, Dallas

tucked into my side. I wasn't sure what I'd wanted to prove by coming here, but it didn't feel like mission accomplished. Ending the night with my girl was the best outcome, though, so I knew I'd gotten something right.

CHAPTER SEVENTEEN

DRAYTON

"I heard the dean decides who gets into her class by Christmas break." Dallas added more hot sauce to her breakfast burrito. "Now everyone's trying to book the studios to get in extra rehearsals."

"You've got plenty of time to work on it." I pulled a chair closer then lifted my leg to rest on it. It was throbbing way more than usual, and the brace wasn't helping at all. "You figure out what you're going to do?"

"I've got a few ideas." She had her legs up on her chair, crossed in front of her. Her hair was pulled back in a messy bun, and she wore one of my USC T-shirts. I always felt lucky getting to see morning Dallas. "But it's got to be perfect, you know? Everyone in the program is a great dancer. I need something that makes me stand out."

"You'll stand out because you're the best."

She smiled. "Now we just need to get you on the dean's selection committee."

A couple more players wandered into the athletes' lounge. They were carrying gym bags and comparing notes on their workouts, discussing how many calories and milligrams of protein they needed to replenish. I reached across the table to grab the hot sauce, and even that small motion sent a shooting pain through my knee.

"Are you okay?" She held her burrito in both hands and stared at me.

"Yeah. I'm okay." I didn't feel okay. "My knee's just acting up a little. I did some track work yesterday. It's not a big deal."

I'd gotten up early this morning, leaving Dallas still sound asleep, to work out. The morning workout was all informal, but a few of the guys did it. But it was entirely possible I'd gone a bit too hard this week, and with the late night after the frat party, I was a bit off. I'd done my usual routine running the track, but I'd needed to stop a couple times. I'd walked it off, breathing through the pain, but I didn't let it slow me down. And I sure as hell wasn't going to let the guys see me vulnerable. So I ran faster and harder. Took the bleacher steps. Cranked it up to pass everyone and get to the top first. I made it, but my knee also popped. The pain hit me so hard I thought I was going to vomit.

I couldn't hide that one. Everyone, including Ryan, saw it.

"What?" Dallas hadn't moved. She still held the burrito and stared at me, though she was getting that crease in her forehead that indicated she was pissed. "I'm sorry, what are you saying? Did physio approve you doing track work? Should you be running on your knee?"

"I promise, I'm fine." I could barely walk by the time I got back to my dorm. After I took a shower, I put on my brace before waking Dallas up for breakfast. "I'll just take a muscle relaxer."

I focused on my own burrito. Added salsa and hot sauce. Played nonchalant until I couldn't take it anymore.

"What?"

"Nothing." Her face was not hiding her frustration.

"Nothing? Really?" I leaned back in my chair. "You're telling me that look means nothing."

"Fine." She pushed her plate away and leaned forward with her elbows on the table. "You're pushing yourself too hard."

I put my burrito down. I was losing my appetite, and that said a lot.

"Not this again. We've been through this."

I looked around the lounge. No one was close enough to hear. I had an ego and liked the spotlight, but this wasn't the kind of attention I was after.

"You have to take it easy, Drayton."

"No." I held a finger up. "I have to keep my eye on the ball."

She'd told me about her dean's special class and needing to put in extra hours in the studio to prepare. Dallas knew success only came with hard work. She knew how much football and getting off the injured list meant to me.

"But you can't force yourself to get better. It's going to take time."

Time. Right. Why did everyone think I had infinite time? We were several games into the season already, and it wasn't that long. Our team was doing okay, which was great, but a winning season wouldn't do me much good if I didn't play. I wasn't in front of NFL scouts. I wasn't getting the stats I needed to get noticed. They were only going to see me as Leroy Lahey's kid who'd flopped during his first year of college ball.

"You don't understand. The longer I'm on the bench, the more time Ryan is on the field."

"Wow." She shook her head. "Who knew football was Machiavellian."

It was way too early for this shit.

"What does that mean?"

"Machiavellian means—"

"No, I know what Machiavellian means." Had she actually just played the dumb jock card?

Dallas's expression changed again, and I could tell she regretted that last comment. In another context, in a less heated moment, we would've laughed about it. We'd always ribbed each other about those things. Jock versus dancer. Opposites attract. Oil and water. We both loved that we weren't precious with each other. It didn't feel like either of us was in the right headspace, though. It felt like every word was dynamite and might blow up in our faces.

"Can we just change the subject?" Her voice was quiet but still had an edge.

"Gladly."

I guessed it wasn't surprising that a crap morning followed a crap night. Not that our time together was all bad, but nothing had turned out as planned. I'd been proud to have Dallas on my arm going into the party. Glad that I put Ryan in his place. I understood that things would be different in college, but my life felt off. I didn't know how to explain it except that it felt like something more than my knee.

There was a lot more that we needed to say, but we didn't

talk. Dallas scrolled through her phone and didn't look at me. I could see her pausing on Miley's Instagram posts. They looked like shots from the outdoor movie last night. There were more at a restaurant or bar after. Had Dallas wanted to go? She'd mentioned the movie thing as an option if I didn't want to do the party. If Dallas had wanted to do something else, something with her artsy friends, she would have said. Right?

"'Sup, lovebirds." Zach plopped down on a chair beside me. "Dallas, nice to see you as always." If he'd had a hat, he would've tipped it toward her. "Heard I missed a rager last night."

"Yeah." Dallas looked at me with a mix of sadness and love. "You certainly did."

CHAPTER EIGHTEEN

DALLAS

Miley and I had taken over a corner of the common room. We were both going stir-crazy sitting in the tiny jail cell known as our dorm room and needed a different set of four walls to stare at. She was stretched across one of the couches, looking far too relaxed for someone supposedly studying for a test, while I was curled into the opposite end. I had my laptop and a stack of books while Miley was armed only with an iPad and a stylus to make notes. Unsurprisingly, we were already distracted from our purpose and focused on more immediate concerns.

"He's hyperfixated on his beef with Ryan." I kept my voice low. There were enough people around that someone could pick up on the gossip. I wasn't sure how many CalArts kids cared about the USC quarterback's love life, but I wasn't taking any chances.

"It sounds like this Ryan guy is being a dick." Miley, of course, was happy to learn all the details. She wasn't one to spread rumors, but she loved being up on it. "And Drayton probably has too much time on his hands. Do they make football players take classes? Don't they give them an automatic 4.5 to keep them playing?"

"He goes to class." Drayton didn't talk about it often because football stole the show, but he did well. His GPA wasn't 4.5, but it wasn't far off.

"My point is, he has a lot of time to stew about Ryan if he's not playing games."

"Or it's what he wants to tell me."

Miley put her iPad down to look at me. "What does that mean?"

"I don't know." I really didn't. I'd spent the days since the frat party trying to work it out, but my brain was running in circles. "He's stopped telling me how much he's working out or if he's in pain. He knows I think he's pushing himself too hard."

"But he's doing physio, right? They must know what they're doing. They're keeping an eye on him."

"All I know is that his physiotherapist's name is Charlotte and she's a senior." It was painful saying any of it out loud. Drayton and I weren't like we used to be. A couple of months ago, I would've been able to tell you everything he was up to, and now I had no idea where he was on any given day. "I don't know . . . everything just feels off."

"Yeah, I've noticed the FaceTimes are getting shorter and shorter."

"Ouch." The truth hurt.

"Sorry." Miley nudged my thigh with her foot. "Was I not supposed to notice when I sleep five feet away?"

"No. It hurts because it's true." It was a dull ache. A constant reminder that we weren't living in our own little world anymore. "And now he's leaving for Florida. Days on the road and even less contact."

I'd tried talking to Gabby a few times. Sent some texts, left a few voicemails even. I didn't leave any information, only said that I missed her, so I couldn't really blame her for not responding. She didn't know I was in crisis. But I also knew that if I told her, then it was more truth I couldn't ignore. It would be making it real. And rehearsal, dance practice, and training could only take up so much space in my brain. All of it combined with work and, ugh, Skyler meant I was teetering toward overwhelm.

There was also a part of me that didn't want to hear Gabby say, *I told you so*. She wasn't that kind of friend, but she had literally just broken up with her high school boyfriend because dating and college weren't a great match. I didn't want her reminding me that I'd avoided having a high school boyfriend for this very reason. Still, I'd gotten swept away, and he was all the things: attentive, special, strong. But maybe our romance had clouded our judgment and distracted us. I didn't want to admit that I wanted to break up with Drayton, but maybe Drayton wanted to break up with me. He was pulling further and further away. And our lives were moving in completely opposite directions right now.

Leroy's words echoed in my head: *He won't be totally himself. Be patient with him. This is going to be hard on both of you*. And all of it had turned out to be true. But what I never saw coming was that truth splitting us apart instead of keeping us tight.

"Why does he have to go to the games if he's not playing? That seems like a waste of resources and time. It's not like he's an understudy."

"He says it's because he's 'on the bench but still a part of the team.'"

"Why did you put that in air quotes? Is some of that not real?"

"No. All real. That's what he said to me." I grew more frustrated. "He's pissed about being stuck on the sidelines but then goes to sit on the sidelines. He doesn't really have a choice, and it's how teams work, but I don't know how to help him or help him help himself."

Or help myself for that matter.

"Look, you can't change a man. That's twenty-first-century dating 101 for women. Or at least it should be." She sat up and flashed me the *I've got a plan* smile. "But you can scream-sing Taylor Swift at a karaoke bar tonight. I have it on very good authority that it's pretty therapeutic."

"On whose authority?"

"Okay, anecdotal personal experience, but I stand by it."

I hadn't sung karaoke since Josh's birthday in the summer. Drayton and Josh's mom had rented a machine, and we all took turns belting out tunes. As it turned out, I was enthusiastic and terrible at it, which is a dangerous combination for everyone else. I'd had a great time.

Skyler liked to threaten to host a karaoke night at the café, but I'd called his bluff. He would never want to risk letting a better singer into his domain. Thankfully, Skyler laughed whenever I said it.

We spent a lot of time talking about music. I didn't know half the bands he mentioned. Apparently, Skyler had a thing for early-2000s bands, the more sensitive the singer-songwriter the better. The Weakerthans, Bonnie Prince Billy, Richard Swift, FemBots. We didn't always agree, but it was a fun way to pass the time. I was never going to be keen on any job that required mopping, but I didn't mind dealing with customers. I had a job to do with assigned tasks, and I was behind a counter, so interactions were limited.

"You know what, that sounds like fun."

"What?" Miley's eyes went wide. "Have the stars finally aligned? Will the intrepid and elusive Dallas Bryant come out for a night on the town?" She put a hand to her chest. "Oh my stars!"

"Okay, okay, take it down a notch." I laughed. "I leave the house on a regular basis."

"That's absolutely not true. Don't try to gaslight me."

Then, as if on cue, my phone rang, and Drayton's name popped up on my screen. I barely got my hello out before he started talking.

"I don't want to leave like this." He sounded tired, maybe out of breath. Like he had been through the wringer. Another wringer. "I'm sorry I've been a dick lately. I'm feeling so much pressure." I looked over at Miley, who was politely pretending not to eavesdrop. "And I hate that things are off."

Knowing that he could feel it too, that it wasn't just me being paranoid or anxious, was a relief. And it was also a bit sad because Drayton saying it out loud made the feelings true.

"What if we meet up in the middle? I'll buy us dinner. No parties, no football. Just us."

I looked up at Miley, and she smiled, gave me a thumbs-up, and mouthed, *Go for it*. What would I say to a friend if the situation were reversed? Would I tell them we needed to have some real talk?

"That sounds nice."

"Great. I'll call you a ride."

I ended the call and looked over at Miley. "I'm sorry. If I don't see him tonight then maybe we'll never clear the air."

"Girl, you do not owe me an explanation! But you can make it up to me by going with me to an open call tomorrow? I don't want to do it on my own. Plus I think you'll ace it."

"Open call?"

"It's for a movie musical! They need background dancers, but honestly everyone has to start somewhere."

"Why not? It'll be good experience."

"Great. Now go and have fun, because makeup sex is the best sex!"

CHAPTER NINETEEN

DALLAS

According to Google Maps, the halfway point between CalArts and USC was a Del Taco off the 405 in Van Nuys. When I arrived in the parking lot, Drayton was waiting for me, sitting on the front bumper of his car, looking like cool perfection. I'm not going to lie, I ran from my Uber into his arms. Being wrapped in his warm embrace felt like home.

"God, you smell good, Cheer." He took a deep breath with his face buried in my neck. "I'll never get enough of you."

It seemed loopy that an hour earlier I had thought we were doomed. Apparently, the answer was being in his arms. That solved any and all problems.

We picked up our food and parked on a nearby residential street. It was dark, and the street felt deserted. We sat in the front seat eating our tacos and laughing like we hadn't in a long time.

"No, trust me. The only way to describe it is extra. All three of them." I turned in my seat to face him as I grabbed my last taco from the bag. "The blond one was making some serious claims. Full-on bragging she could seduce you away from me."

"Guessing I had no choice in this scenario." Drayton had his seat slightly reclined so he could stretch his legs out. He wasn't wearing his brace but was still careful how he moved his leg.

"Nope. Powerless. You're lucky you got out of there in time. Who knows what could have happened."

"Thanks for taking one for the team and bailing on that awful party." He picked up my bag from the console and started looking through it.

"I'm a hero." I crumpled up the wrapper and threw it back into the Del Taco bag. "Anyway. It was a lot to take. Then her friends were all, 'You're such a villain!' Who says that? It made me so mad."

Drayton snapped a photo of me with my Polaroid, the flash momentarily illuminating the car. I covered my eyes, but it was too late. I was blind.

"Sorry, I had to capture it." He pulled the photo from the camera, laughing. "I've never seen you so jealous before. I kind of liked it."

He stuck the photo on the dash facing forward so we could watch it develop.

"Well, I hate it." I rubbed my eyes a few more times, trying to clear away the spots. Admittedly, it wasn't the most efficient method. "There're so many women throwing themselves at you."

"It's not just women." He waited for me to laugh then put a hand to over his heart. He put on his serious look. "But unfortunately for them, I'm deeply and madly in love with my girlfriend."

"Yeah?" I bit my bottom lip.

"Yeah." He nodded slowly, put a hand on my cheek, and leaned in.

It was a quick, soft kiss. A gentle confirmation after saying he loved me. My hands moved through his hair as the kiss deepened. His arms went around my back, pulling me in closer. His tongue found mine, and I let out a soft moan. He growled in response.

"I think I left something in the back seat."

I kissed along his jawline. I felt the scratch of his stubble as I moved my cheek along his. "Oh yeah?"

Drayton moved his hand to my thigh, slowly pushing up my skirt. He whispered in my ear, "Want to help me find it?"

"Drayton." My voice was breathy. Desperate.

"Do you want to?"

His hand went higher up my thigh. He kissed my neck. My breath, and my heart rate, sped up.

"What if someone sees us?"

We'd spent plenty of time in cars back in Archwood. Nathan was pretty lax when it came to rules as my legal guardian, but he didn't necessarily approve of me bringing boys home for sex. Drayton's parents didn't stop us either, but I wasn't crazy about his mom always knowing what we were up to. So cars and country roads often won out. A residential street in Van Nuys was a completely different story, though.

"Let them watch."

I chuckled against his neck and felt my warm breath against his skin. "Why does this feel like a porn fantasy come to life?"

"Your porn fantasy?" He traced his fingers up and down my thigh. "Happy to help."

He knew every one of my buttons. Recognized every twitch, every response. It was one of his superpowers. Drayton was a great listener. He listened and reacted then pushed for more. I tried to keep my cool, remember where we were, but then his fingers moved over my inner thigh, and I was done.

"C'mon." I pushed him back to get some space then slid between the seats into the back. Grabbing his hand, I pulled him back with me. "Now."

For a man with a bum knee, he moved quickly. He sat back and pulled me onto his lap so I was straddling him. Our kisses were no longer gentle. We were desperate, hungry for each other. I ripped his T-shirt over his head because I needed to feel him, his skin, against me. His hands moved quickly under my shirt and up my back.

I'd missed this. Missed him. The gulf between us had been growing, and no amount of texting was going to fill it. How did we keep forgetting that we needed time together? Our energy was maintained by this. By us. Sex, yes, but also being physical period. Touching. Connecting. His beautiful, firm body. The way he made me feel. Fuck.

In the moment it took me to pull my shirt over my head, I noticed the car windows were fogging up. I only had enough time to note this was good so no one could see in before my nipple was in Drayton's mouth and I forgot about everything else in the world. The back seat wasn't built for two people in this position, definitely not for this type of activity, but it was so fucking hot. Bruises and leg cramps were tomorrow's problems.

There was a loud bang beside me, a slap, and I let out a short scream. What the hell was that? We both froze.

"Open up!"

The shape outside the window was blurred but recognizable. Police. A flashlight shone inside, and I jumped off Dray's lap.

"Oh my god." It was still hard to catch my breath, which might or might not have been Drayton-related. I scrambled to find my shirt on the car floor. "Shit. Shit. Shit."

"It's okay. Don't worry." He tried to sound calm, but his whisper was more of a rasp, and his eyes looked slightly panicked.

"Drayton. This could affect my financial aid." I quickly readjusted my bra then pulled on my shirt. "I can't afford—"

"Don't worry, I'll take care of it."

Drayton opened the back door and stepped out slowly. He smiled at the cop as I slipped back between the seats. I looked though his window to see a woman, maybe in her forties, with short dark hair.

"Officer, we know what it looks like. But I can assure you this is a misunder—"

"Whose car is this?" She leaned down to look around. She saw me but didn't nod in acknowledgment. Having had little to no interaction with the police, I had no idea if that was a good sign or not.

"Mine." He didn't sound quite as confident when she didn't immediately fall for his charms.

"ID and registration. Now."

I did my part and pulled the registration from the glove box while Drayton pulled his ID out of his wallet. We both watched the cop read it over, and then I saw a flash of recognition. Oh, c'mon.

"Drayton Lahey?"

"Yes." Confidence rising.

"You messed up my fantasy football league."

Was that a joke? Was *she* trying for the charm now? I watched for any sign of a smile, but she held her mask steady. I had a sudden fear that recognizing Drayton wasn't going to be the advantage he thought it was.

"Sorry about that."

"It's a shame what happened." She nodded once, and I started to relax. She made a note in her book then handed his ID and registration back. "Seeing as I didn't technically see anything, why don't I let you off with a warning for loitering? Now get this nice young lady home. Don't do anything stupid like this again."

"You got it." Drayton handed me the papers as I leaned over to give a slight wave.

"Thank you, officer."

"Get home safe." The cop tapped her ticket book on the car door as a small salute. "Good night."

"Thanks again for understanding."

We took a few seconds to catch our breath and recalibrate as she walked back to her car. Had that really happened? We'd avoided getting a ticket because the police officer followed college ball. Drayton slid back into the driver's seat, and once the window was rolled back up, we burst into crazy laughter.

"Is that what your life is like? The secret life of college athletes?"

Drayton was about to respond but checked his rearview mirror. The police car was still there, headlights homed in on his car.

"We need to get moving."

I put my hand on his thigh as Drayton put his car into gear.

We got back to the Del Taco parking lot, and I ordered an Uber. Neither of us had much to say, but it wasn't an uncomfortable silence. We waited outside, getting some night air, as he leaned against the hood and I stood between his legs. I wasn't ready for the night to end, but Drayton had an early morning, and he couldn't be late.

"I hope you guys win." I put my hands on his chest, reassuring myself with his presence. "Unless that makes Ryan look good. Then I hope you lose? Whatever you want to happen, I hope that happens."

"Is it bad that I want us to lose?" He put a hand on my cheek.

"No. I understand." My phone started to vibrate in my hand. "Shit. My car's here."

We didn't have time for much more than a quick kiss, and that didn't feel like enough.

"Promise me you'll wear your brace."

"I promise." He kissed me a few more times, his hands holding my face in place. "Text me when you get home."

I waved once as I walked quickly to the Uber. Why did I feel like crying? It had been a great night, other than the almost-ticket. Why did it feel like our short distance was about to get a lot longer?

Halfway back to Valencia, the tears fell in earnest. The pressure of it all was getting to me. Squeezing each other into the corners of our lives wasn't working. Being so far away was impossible. It wasn't that we'd gotten interrupted tonight—it was that interruptions were the norm. My classes, his classes. His injury, my financial situation. We'd promised each other nothing would get in the way of being together this year. But it felt like the whole world was forcing us to break our word.

CHAPTER TWENTY

DALLAS

My mind was in overdrive, still buzzing from the open call that afternoon. I was pretty sure as soon as the adrenaline left my body the exhaustion would sink in, but until then I was riding high.

"That was amazing!" I threw my bag down and sat on my bed. My dance clothes were probably a bit stinky, but I didn't care. "You didn't tell me it was for Edgar de la Luna! He's like a legend. A choreo genius?"

Miley shut our dorm room door behind her then flopped on her own bed.

"And kinda hot. He's old, and a man, but hot."

"Okay, that wasn't my takeaway, but sure." I'd expected the audition to be filled with too many people and for everyone to be treated like cattle. I'd thought it would be cold and impersonal, that I would suffer through it for Miley's sake. "Do you think I should be auditioning more?"

"Absolutely." Miley jumped up from her bed and stuck her hand down the sides. "But you need a reel. Goddamn it. Where's my ID?"

I laughed. Miley was proving herself to be a loyal, fun friend, but damn she was easily distracted.

"I've tried out for shows but nothing this big." I leaned back on my bed, resting on my elbows. "I've never thought about it. Auditioning more. I'm not sure how to go about it."

When we got there and saw the literal hundreds of people who'd answered the call, I'd thought I would be intimidated. There were professionals in the crowd. People who auditioned all the time. How could I compete?

But I loved it! I fed off the energy in the room. The excitement. Learning the routine and pushing myself to be seen outside the crowd. Connecting with some of the other dancers. We were fighting for the same spots, but we were in it together. I felt energized by the whole process. It felt different from school, where it was all budding egos and trying to prove our worth.

"But I think you need to focus first on getting a reel together if— Found it!" She held her ID up in triumph then raised her eyebrow at me. "What was I saying?"

"You were saying I need a reel."

"Yes, exactly! I knew I made a very good point." She threw her ID onto her desk, and I felt certain it would soon be lost again in that chaos. "You need a reel if you want to be taken seriously." She put on her best, and astonishingly good, Dean Adams voice. "Because art is hypercompetitive."

"And highly selective."

"But of course."

We both burst out laughing. I had a lot of respect for the dean as a teacher and a dancer, but she was the poster girl for pretentious artist.

"Do you have a reel?" I sat up again and crossed my legs.

"Of course." Miley kicked off her shoes. "Any time I do a show or a student film or whatever, it goes on the reel. It helped growing up around LA. There's way more opportunity than in farm country."

"Again, not from a farm."

"And it's super easy to edit together. You just need the clips."

I thought about what I could include. My audition tape for CalArts. Some shows back home. Next to nothing. Amateur, really. If today's experience was typical, then I was going to have to up my game to compete.

Notifications went off on both our phones.

"Ah, crap. Tomorrow's rehearsal is canceled." I held up my phone for Miley to see even though she was reading the same message on hers.

"Why do you sound upset? Are you really that freaked out by possible free time?"

"Funny." I placed my phone back down on the bed. "I have nothing against free time. It's an unfamiliar concept is all."

Coming down from the audition high also gave me space to remember that I hadn't heard anything from Dray since he'd left for Florida. I knew travel days could be like that—early hours and tight schedules—but I'd hoped for something. Especially since last night had felt like we were back on track. So, yes, maybe I liked the idea of staying busy so I didn't think about the lack of messages.

"I don't want to miss rehearsal because our showcase is around the corner and the dean's going to be there, and that'll factor into her master class decision."

"Bitch, please." I'd only looked away for a minute and Miley had already stripped down and pulled on her cover-up. "You could do that choreo in your sleep. Plus, you got the opening solo!"

"Ergo, I need that rehearsal."

Miley jumped and landed on her knees on my bed and shook me by the shoulders. "Come on! We got our Sunday back. That's good news."

"True." I closed my eyes and let her shake me a few times. It felt strangely good. "I can't remember the last time I had a day off."

"That's so sad." She stuck her bottom lip out, pouting and making puppy dog eyes. "What are we going to do with you, Dallas?"

"Yeah, it's been a lot." It was easier to ignore when in the middle of it. It was only when I stopped that I could see how much noise was usually around me. "It's been a lot with school and work."

"And the hot jock boyfriend?" She tilted her head. Miley was going full-force puppy dog with this one.

"Yeah, exactly." I laughed because, no, I hadn't forgotten my hot jock boyfriend. "If he were in town I'd probably run to see him."

Miley shot me a look that said, *Yeah, I know*. Suddenly I felt awkward, exposed. Was I being a pathetic, can't-do-anything-without-her-boyfriend cliché? Boyfriend snaps his fingers and I come running? That was not the feminist ideal I was pushing for. I could almost hear Gabby's voice telling me that I needed to put myself first sometimes too.

The problem was that I didn't understand how to find the middle ground. Before Drayton, I was entirely focused on what I wanted and where I wanted to go. Then it was great to have someone to share it with. We could support each other. Enjoy each other. But we couldn't seem to find that balance anymore. It was all one or the other.

"I wouldn't literally run . . . " Yeah, even my big defense sounded pathetic.

"No, I'm not judging you." Miley sat up straight, again with the perfect posture. "It's just that . . ."

She paused, and that didn't feel like a good thing.

"You should spit it out." I sat up straight to match her posture. "Hearing you say it won't be as bad as whatever I'm imagining right now."

"Okay, look. I've never had the big romance. I didn't have one in high school, and I doubt I'll have one here—mainly because there's no one who interests me beyond a hookup—but I also know I'm going to take whatever chance I might get." She offered a half smile and a sly look. "And I mean that for relationships and dance."

"I get it. That's how I did things before Drayton."

"But I'm also here—at CalArts, in this dorm—and I want to get everything I can out of this experience. Look, if this de la Luna audition goes anywhere, I'm out of here. I'm going to grab the shit out of the opportunity. But until then, this is the place to be. People to meet. Adventures to discover."

"It's not like I don't want to do that stuff."

"My point is that it's obviously hard to build your own life here if you always have one foot in USC."

"You think I'm too available?"

"I didn't say that. Or maybe I don't know. Like I said, I'm not in a relationship, so I should probably mind my own business." Miley looked like she was about to end the conversation then decided there was one more thing to say. "I'm maybe a bit worried that you're taking shelter in all this too. Not making that leap when you need to."

"I'm not hiding with Dray." What the hell?

"Maybe just a . . ." She held her fingers close together to indicate *a little bit*. "But that's something most of us do. At some point. Especially when it's about big stuff like what you're going to do with the rest of your life."

"Sure." I laughed. "No pressure there."

"I don't want to upset you. Honest. I like Drayton and get why you're with him. I think he seems like a dream. Dreamy." Her smile was sincere, kind, and thoughtful. "But he's not your only dream."

Shit. It was hard to argue with that logic. I looked over at my bedside table and noticed a folded piece of paper.

"I know what we should do tomorrow."

I unfolded the paper and held up Skyler's flyer for Miley. She snatched it from my hand.

"You've been hiding the goods, Bryant! What's up with that?"

Rather than answer her, I picked up my phone and called Skyler. It went straight to voicemail.

"Hey, do you still need dancers? Because I might have two for you."

"Hot dancers!" Miley pulled my arm so she could shout into the phone. "Two hot dancers for your video!"

CHAPTER TWENTY-ONE

DRAYTON

The mood wasn't good as I followed the team down the ramp and into the locker room. We were down fifteen at halftime with seven of those points clocked in the last five minutes. It was tough to watch. Florida wasn't a better team, but once they broke through our defensive line we crumbled.

No one was talking. The only sound in the locker room was equipment being tossed around and the occasional grunt. Someone kicked a random chair. Someone else dropped their helmet, and it landed with a loud crack on the floor. Definitely not good. There were times when being behind energized a team, pushing everyone to get back out there and crush the opponent. But silence told a whole other story. That meant morale was in the toilet and rallying for the second half wasn't going to be easy. Right now, the game was lost.

I felt a bit like an intruder. I was wearing my jersey, but I'd spent the whole game on the bench beside Coach. I wasn't sweaty and dirty from a tackle. My knee brace marked me as the guy on the sidelines. But I still took my job seriously. Despite admitting to Dallas that I wouldn't mind Ryan failing, I wanted this team to win. I was in the mix as much as I could be. I shouted onto the field as loud as anyone. Pumped the players up before they ran out for their shift. Talked through plays and strategy with Coach.

"Come on, boys!" I clapped my hands. A few of the guys looked over and shot me a death glare.

Zach looked defeated. It had been particularly harsh for him out there. One of his strengths as a player was predicting where a throw was going to land. He was the master of the quick pivot. When he got hold of the ball, he locked on. But something had rattled him early on. He'd missed one, then two, throws. Spun the wrong way on another and ended up on his ass fast. He was the kind of guy who wanted to win, obviously, but he also put a lot of pressure on himself to not let the team down. I could tell that was doing a number on him.

I raised my hands like I was about to give a sermon and shouted loud enough no one could ignore me. "We're only down by—"

Ryan pushed past me, stomping into the room. He threw his helmet down so hard it bounced along the floor. He went straight for Zach and got right up in his face.

"What the hell are you doing out there? What's with all the drops?"

Ryan was ready to chest bump him. The tension in the room spiked. It was also obvious that no one else wanted to be in the firing line of Ryan's rage. Zach wasn't backing down, though.

"Maybe if you weren't off your first read we'd be up right now."

Zach was usually a gentle giant. A monster on the field and capable of taking on the biggest mountain of an opponent, never one to back down from a tackle or an interception, in real life the guy was all about the charm and good vibes. But he was not so calm when faced with Ryan playing the blame game.

"Yeah?" Ryan moved a step closer. "Maybe if you got your head out of your ass you'd be able to see the ball coming at you!"

I wasn't sure if Ryan was going in for a bump or just trying for extra intimidation, but I moved quickly to get between them. Maybe not the smartest thing with my knee brace, but I didn't give myself time to think that part through. I pushed them both back so my arms were fully extended.

"Why don't we stop bitching and focus on turning this game around?"

Zach still looked pissed but nodded his head then turned back to his locker. Ryan, on the other hand, decided I was the new target.

"Get back on the bench, rookie." Ryan knocked my arm back and stepped closer. "This is a conversation for players. Spectators got no say."

I stood my ground. Didn't flinch. Held his stare. Pushed my chest out like a damn gorilla getting ready to fight it out for dominance. I wasn't going to throw the first punch, but I was ready if he did.

"At least I handle problems like a man." A dozen things ran through my head, recapping everything that had happened during the first half. Ryan was erratic, trying for the big plays when the team needed an anchor during a storm. This guy thought he was in *Friday Night Lights* and everything was a Hail Mary pass. "Instead of playing the blame game like a little—"

Coach's whistle cut in. Out of the corner of my eye, I noticed everyone else in the room stepping back, but Ryan and I took a few more beats because neither of us was backing down by choice. I wasn't interested in getting into a physical fight, especially with the bum knee, but I also wasn't going to give Ryan the upper hand.

"Simmer down." Coach didn't yell. He kept his voice calm but assertive to make sure everyone heard and understood. "It's bad enough that we're losing to the Miami Glades."

He moved into the center of the room and crossed his arms, keeping the clipboard close to his chest. Coach gave everyone a minute to get to their places. Ryan stood by his locker looking like he wanted to rip the door off. Zach and Marcus both sat on the bench with elbows on knees. I wasn't sure what to do so stepped to the outside of the circle.

"USC has more Heisman winners than any other school. Those men didn't get there by squabbling at halftime. They got there by treating each other like brothers."

I saw Zach nod his head, looking a bit guilty when he shouldn't. A few others looked around the room, shifting in their seats. We'd all had the coaches who screamed. The ones who threw out insults, told the players they were nothing, would amount to nothing, like that would inspire them to greatness. That kind of speech could work a team up, but it also created division and added to the tension and hostility in the room. There were more fights. More injuries. Less teamwork.

"I want you all to look around the room. These are your teammates. Your brothers. Their legacy is your legacy. You are carrying on the legacy of everyone who's played for USC, everyone who played before you." Coach circled the room, trying to catch everyone's eye. "You need to honor them. Honor each other."

"Are we going to talk about something real, Coach?" Ryan wasn't having any of this pep talk. He wasn't into the bigger picture. "'Cause this inspirational talk isn't going to fix anything. The passing attack clearly isn't working."

"Clearly." I surprised myself by speaking. It pissed me off that Ryan felt the need to jump in and complain without actually contributing anything. "So what *will* work? We've watched the tapes. We know we can run circles around these guys. We know their weak spots. So how do we hit them where it hurts?"

I wasn't looking at Coach or Ryan when I spoke. I looked around the room instead, checking for a spark from any of them.

"They've watched all our game tapes too." Coach threw me a look I didn't understand. Maybe he was pissed that I'd taken over for a bit. Maybe he thought we needed answers and not more questions. "Ryan's right about our passing not working. They're anticipating our next move, and we're walking right into it."

"We could go no huddle." I faced Coach directly and ignored Ryan. "Get the defense off rhythm."

"That's not a bad idea." Coach pointed at me. "Speed things up."

Coach moved to the whiteboard and worked out some plays with a few of us jumping in. He took some of my ideas, scrapped others. I was seeing Coach in a new light. I still thought he was a hard-ass, which he was, but he wasn't sadistic. I kind of liked the idea that he wanted us to give our all even if we were stuck on the bench. A team was a team. And I needed to prove my worth more than ever. Keep that front of mind. If I had to do it from the bench right now, then that was what I had to do.

CHAPTER TWENTY-TWO

DALLAS

"Hey, take a shot of me." I handed Miley my camera. "I want to show Gabby proof of me living this glamorous Hollywood life." I struck a red carpet pose standing next to the craft services table. "Make sure you get all the Twizzlers and corn chips in the shot."

"Say prune." Miley snapped the shot. "Do you want one of you munching on a Twizzler? For the full experience."

"Nah, too suggestive." I took my camera back. "Now that I'm on my way to being famous, I need to keep it family friendly."

The music video shoot was in an old train station. It wasn't entirely run-down, but the space had definitely seen better days. Our dressing room was a corner blocked off by a folding screen and a couple of bedsheets. Makeup and hair, which we were doing ourselves, was two stools and a handheld mirror. Craft services was bags of chips, cans of La Croix, and the aforementioned Twizzlers. There had been a promise of ordering in some pizza, but whoever was in charge of that task never quite got around to it. Skyler apologized a few times about everything being so low-budget, but I didn't care, I loved it and was having an awesome time.

The crew was so *into* what they were doing. They had so little to work with, but the set looked great. We'd watched the morning shots on a monitor, and I couldn't believe how professional it looked. Sure, there were next to no amenities, but as a student with a strict budget, I wasn't going to say no to free food no matter what form it took. Miley obviously felt the same way since she was swiping granola bars from the table.

"Smile for the camera!"

Miley posed with her bounty held high, smiling wide, then stuffed them into her bag.

"Who knows how long we'll be here? I'll need that sustenance later."

We'd already been there for a few hours. It was busy when we were shooting, but there was also a lot of standing around. We hadn't seen much of Skyler. He was with his band a lot or talking to the director. I'd spent most of the time working out the dances. It was mainly Miley, me, and Darius, whom Miley had recruited at the last minute.

It helped that I had heard the song dozens of times in the café, so I had some ideas going in. Darius had a different vision for the dance, so it took some negotiating. Not fighting. More collaboration. We worked it out by trial and error, and I was feeling pretty good about what we'd landed on. It was a mix of ballet and contemporary that told a story that was true to the song.

"Thank you for coming with me." I smiled at Miley. "It means a lot."

"You know me, ready to dance anywhere and anytime." She leaned forward, grabbing her ankles to stretch. "I've been watching the monitors, and you look gorge. You're going to have a great reel in no time."

"Yeah?"

"Absolutely! We can start editing whatever you have now. Get ahead of the game."

"Aw, you're the best." I watched as she widened her stance then grabbed one ankle then the other. "So, out of curiosity, how much are you auditioning?"

"Not a ton." She stood up again, shook out her limbs. "But as much as I can. I'm hoping I can get an agent this year and start working full-time."

We both turned at the sound of a crash. A light stand, thankfully without a light, had been knocked over. The gaffer and set decorator exchanged a few quick words about whose fault it was and who needed to be more careful, then everyone went back to work.

I looked back at Miley, who was already scrolling through her phone. "But what about school?"

I didn't want to say, *But what about me?* Miley was my one friend in LA, other than Drayton, so really the only person I interacted with on a regular basis.

"Don't get me wrong, I love CalArts. But it isn't the be-all and end-all."

Miley sounded so casual about everything. Like any option was fine. She was so confident that her dream of being a dancer would come true that it didn't occur to her to be anxious about any of it.

"That's . . . so healthy." And also strange and foreign. "Like I understand what you mean theoretically."

"Theoretically?" Miley cocked her head to listen.

"I'm not sure what life would or could look like without CalArts. It's always been the destination. My only dream. I haven't really considered, well, after or instead."

Miley knew all about my mom. That she'd gone to CalArts. That so many memories I had of her revolved around her telling me CalArts stories.

"Right. But what happens after? You won't be at CalArts forever. Unless you're vying for Dean Adams's job."

I didn't know what to say because I honestly had no idea. What did the life of a dancer entail? I knew CalArts because that plan had been set out when I lost my mom. But what would happen when I didn't have a story to follow? I had no interest in retuning to Archwood, and there was no other Mom template. Leaving CalArts behind meant more than breaking the dream Mom and I had shared. It would mean doing something that my mother had no part in.

My phone buzzed, and I dug through my bag to retrieve it. Drayton's name popped up on my screen. I held the phone in my hand, momentarily paralyzed.

"It's okay if you need to answer." Miley grabbed a Twizzler. "It's not like there's millions riding on this shoot. They can wait."

"No, no, I'll call him back. I'm working. It's not like he answers when he's playing a game."

"Exactly. You've got a life too, boo," Miley said.

I sent the call to voicemail quickly—so I didn't change my mind—then put my phone back into my bag. I vowed to leave it there for the rest of the shoot.

"I thought you only did classical dance." Skyler smiled as he walked toward us. "However have you managed?"

The faux upper-class accent he'd put on was pretty spot-on.

"Guess I'm full of surprises."

"Can't argue that." He had changed into a pair of dark jeans and a T-shirt to get ready for the next shot. "And thanks for coming. You're crushing it."

Had he just complimented me? Thanked me? Said I was doing a good job? I wasn't sure how I should respond. Saying something smart-ass didn't seem appropriate, but it was also how we spoke to each other most of the time.

"Um, thanks. And you really surprised me. You're, like, actually talented."

I couldn't resist it.

"I think that's a compliment?"

"Surprise!" I raised my hands in a jazz hands gesture, and he laughed.

I looked over at Miley, who was watching us, eyebrows raised. I mouthed *What?* as the director called us over.

"All right, everyone. Let's get to our places." He was very nice but also occasionally grumbled that he wouldn't have to do all this yelling if he had an assistant.

We all moved back to set.

Darius and I had a quick chat about what we wanted to do and where to start. The director and band were letting us make it up for the most part. They had a story in mind, and we decided what would work. Well, mostly I decided. I signaled to the director that we were ready.

Miley took her place on the other side of Darius. "Don't forget to track the light on that last spin."

The music started, the director yelled, "Action," and Darius and I moved across the floor. We'd tried to pattern the choreography to match the story of the song. In our version, Darius and I were in a struggle, a relationship caught in a bad cycle. I tried to escape, he pulled me back in. Darius spun me a few times then let go as I almost crashed into Skyler.

Then it was all Skyler and me. We hadn't rehearsed this part because it wasn't supposed to look polished, so I tried to quietly lead him across the floor. I half-expected him to fight me on it, but it was easy. He trusted me. We had to shoot this section several times, and each time it got easier—because, of course, practice—and we got closer.

It was the song. It had to be the song. I knew it so well now that it was like a second skin.

Finally, the director called cut, and everything stopped. Skyler and I stood stock still, staring at each other, until I pulled away.

CHAPTER TWENTY-THREE

DALLAS

It was one of those slow workdays where we could listen to whatever music we wanted and putter around the café. It was the kind of day I'd never thought I would like. Being busy made the day go faster. Being busy meant I didn't have time to stress about all the other things I wasn't doing. Instead, we were playing Skyler's new demos and talking about nothing important while restocking the shelves, and I felt almost relaxed. Wonders never ceased.

"I love how it feels like the bridge swallows you up, like it completely takes over and then erupts." This wasn't our first time talking about music, and we'd developed a shorthand. "It's kind of like it's taking in the whole story of the song, all these emotions, then breaks under the weight."

I'd always listened to music, let myself get lost in it, but I'd never dissected it. I never took the time to think about the different parts and how they all came together.

"Yes! And people always credit the chorus, everyone knows the chorus, but the bridge is like the unsung hero."

"The forgotten cousin."

"The mysterious stranger who rides into town."

"I think the mysterious stranger usually ends up as the hero in the story." I finished replenishing the cups and moved on to the sugar bowls.

"Fair. Maybe more the town librarian who also tutors the kids on weekends." Skyler handed me a box of sugar packets from behind the counter. "You know, this was actually a really hard song to write."

"How so?"

He leaned against the nearest table and watched me work.

"It was inspired by this breakup. She was back and forth between me and her ex. Strung me along for like a year. Sucked."

"Sounds messy."

Was it weird that I'd never really had my heart broken? Yes, my parents dying had been devasting, but that wasn't the same thing. I'd had a boyfriend the summer after eighth grade until I'd caught him walking around the mall holding Daria Zettel's hand. It had been upsetting, and I'd had a dramatic reaction, but then Gabby and I went swimming and my heart was magically healed. The last time I'd heard, the two of them were engaged, so he'd definitely made the right choice.

"Did you always want to be a musician?"

That seemed like a safer question than asking more about his ex-girlfriend. From what I knew from his music and that brief snippet, I didn't think I wanted to know more.

"Sort of. I grew up in Brooklyn with parents who were starving artists." He looked the part of a Brooklyn artist. I'd called it the first time we met. “Well, not exactly starving anymore since Brooklyn isn’t exactly cheap, but that’s the type. All of their friends were artists. Everyone talked art. Did art. A few of them made a living from their art, but for most of them it was a vocation, not a profession, you know? So, weirdly, I think they would’ve been disappointed if I’d gone to med school. Like I’d be selling out. Crazy, but I love them. You?”

“Same-ish.” Not the community of artists part, but I understood a parent putting art at the forefront. “My mom was a dancer.”

He pushed himself off the table and walked over to the coffee machine. “Oh, so I got my ticket to your showcase. Miley mentioned it.”

I spun around to look at him. “You’re coming? That’s so . . . neat.”

Yup. I’d said *neat*. How very time-travel of me. Next I’d start talking about going to the sock hop and getting a malted.

“Is your boyfriend coming?”

“To my show? Yeah.”

“Good. I was starting to believe you made him up.”

It did seem strange that Skyler still hadn’t met Drayton. That Drayton hadn’t come by to see me at work. Even Miley hadn’t seen him since the night before his injury. My life was so compartmentalized that the different pieces didn’t connect. It had been going on for so long that I didn’t know if it was intentional or not.

“He’s real, just very busy. He’s the quarterback at USC.”

“Yes, I’ve heard that mentioned a few times.”

“That’s a big deal.”

“I’ll take your word for it.”

My cheeks warmed up. That was an unfair thing for Skyler to

say. Dismissive. Drayton didn't talk shit about Skyler. Of course, that might be because I didn't mention Skyler that often, so he had nothing to pick apart.

"You could take a lot of people's word about it. It's big."

That argument was so solid I might as well have stomped my foot after it. Hard to argue with that level of logic.

"Not running him down, Dallas. Football just isn't my thing." He walked back over and handed me a latte. The foam was decorated with a ballet slipper. "If you want to talk about why it's better to listen to Alice Coltrane at Carnegie Hall on vinyl, then I'm your man."

"I understood maybe half of that sentence."

I could hear Skyler laugh as he walked back to the counter. "Guess that means it's time for experimental free-form jazz."

"No, no! It's not."

"Afraid there's nothing we can do about it. Time to jump on the Coltrane Train."

"It's not." I waved my hands to get his attention. "No jazz, Skyler. It's a rule."

"It's out of my control."

"I'm going to report you to HR." I attempted to throw a sugar packet at him, but I was laughing too hard. "This is abuse."

"But alas, I am HR." He let out a loud movie villain cackle that only made me laugh more.

"Can I get an iced latte?"

We both jumped at the sound of the customer's voice, and I almost knocked the box of sugar off the table. Thankfully, my reflexes kicked in, and my hard work didn't slide into disaster.

"Oh my god! Nate!" I ran toward the door and hugged my big brother. "What are you doing here?"

"You didn't think I was going to miss family weekend, did you?" His hug was tight and warm. I'd forgotten how much I loved it.

"You didn't say." I pulled away then slapped his shoulder. "Why didn't you say?"

"Because this was so much more fun. Look at your face!" Nate laughed. For a second, I thought he was going to put me in a headlock and mess up my hair. "I don't think I've seen you so surprised since the infamous Christmas of the Justin Bieber box set."

"We agreed to never speak of that again." I held up a finger and gave him my most stern look. He, of course, only laughed more. "My shift is over in a few hours. But maybe you can hang out here? Unless . . ."

I spun around to look at Skyler. I didn't have to bat my eyelashes for long.

"Fine. Since you are such a dedicated and devoted worker." He shook his head, but he was smiling. "Hey, Dallas. Why don't you take off early?"

I clutched my hands to my chest. I was really committing to the rescued-damsel-in-distress bit.

"Only if you're sure." I untied my apron and walked toward the back room. "I don't want to leave you in the lurch."

"Yeah, it's dead. And you should get to be with your . . . brother?"

"And former guardian," Nathan said.

"Former *legal* guardian," I corrected him.

Skyler raised an eyebrow, curious about whatever this exchange was about. "Either way, it's nice to finally meet you. Dallas has said—"

"So many terrible things." I ran over to the counter to grab Nathan's iced latte from Skyler. "All awful." I quickly picked up two croissants from the tray too. "Okay, let's go. Thanks again, Sky!"

I grabbed Nathan's hand and we were out the door.

CHAPTER TWENTY-FOUR

DALLAS

"Econ is tough, but at least I'll never have another man explain the stock market to me."

Nathan laughed. He was playing the part of the happy and relaxed older brother, but I sensed something was up. We'd spent so many years with just the two of us, and my Nathan radar was on high alert. It might have been a low hum, but I was extra careful.

"I'm pretty sure you'd have men explaining the stock market to you even if you were CEO of Bank of America."

"But I'll be able to roll my eyes at them with more authority."

I took the last sip of my coffee and tossed the cup into a bin. We were slowly making our way around campus, occasionally stopping so I could point out a building or something of interest. It was a warm afternoon with a lot of students enjoying the sunshine, so Nathan was getting the full college catalog experience.

"Hey." He gave me a gentle shoulder nudge. "It's impressive that you're trying new things. That's so unlike you."

"What does that mean?" I kept my tone light but cautious. I didn't want to have another conversation about me being too rigid. I was dedicated and focused, not closed off. How was that not obvious? "You're saying I'm predictable?"

"Suck it up and take the compliment. Stop being so suspicious."

He nudged me again, and we both laughed. It was a familiar dynamic. Nathan had had to take on way too many responsibilities as a teenager, but he was also the fun guy, the brother who teased and prodded and kept things light. I wasn't exactly the serious one but definitely more prone to offering a skeptical side-eye. We all have our roles to play.

"How are things with Drayton?"

"Great. Good."

"Okay . . ." Nathan noticed that my voice had gone unnaturally high with that response but kindly chose to ignore it. "And other than econ, how's CalArts going?"

"Good. Great." My voice went a little less high on that one.

"It's not everything you dreamed of and more?"

Why did every conversation I had lately have to feel so weighted? Why didn't anyone want to talk about TikTok videos or Am I the Asshole threads?

"Yes. I mean, no. I don't know. It's hard to answer."

He kept his eyes forward, maybe recognizing it would be too much having him stare me down. "I'll give you a dollar if you try."

I groaned so Nathan would understand exactly how much I didn't want to have this conversation. But let's be real, I needed that dollar.

"I'm being pulled in a lot of directions." I wished I still had my coffee cup. This would be easier if I had something to do with my hands. "Like I'm everywhere and nowhere."

I wasn't the same person who'd left Archwood, but I wasn't sure if I'd become a CalArts person. I didn't fully feel a part of the dance program or dorm life. I definitely didn't belong with the USC crowd. I liked my classes but also wanted to use that time to dance or to simply *be* without having to worry about a hundred things for once.

"I guess, maybe, I'm scared I'm not making the most of college. Whatever that means."

"Yeah, that's tough." Nathan sipped his coffee, giving himself a few beats before responding. "I wish I had advice, but I dropped out."

I held in my immediate reaction, which was to hug him. Nathan didn't often talk about the sacrifices he'd had to make for me, but I felt them. He always claimed that he hadn't finished college because it wasn't for him. Maybe there was some truth to that, but there was no ignoring the fact that caring for his kid sister had played a significant part.

"Have you ever thought about going back?"

"Nah." He shook his head. He didn't look sad. In fact, he didn't look like anything other than a man trying for a neutral expression to hide his feelings. "It's expensive. And I'm too old. But I fully intend to live vicariously through you."

"Have you been listening to anything I've just said, big brother?" I stopped walking, and he turned to face me. I put my hands on his arms and gave him a small shake. "Living vicariously through me means doing your laundry in the middle of the night instead of sleeping and referring to people as skim milk latte with cinnamon or backflip dancer guy because I can't be bothered to learn anyone's name."

"But there's always the promise of a keg party around every corner." Nathan's smile felt like home. I was glad I'd come to CalArts, but I really missed the comfort of Nathan's easy nature.

"Hey, I want to show you something."

I reversed course on the pathway and headed toward the administration building. I moved quickly, but Nathan didn't complain. He followed me across the quad and up the main steps. I stopped inside the door and held an arm out, indicating the corridor in front of us.

"They call this the hall of fame. Not officially. It's just how everyone refers to it."

It was a long corridor lined with trophy cases and photographs. Nothing was in chronological order or organized by theme, which meant every viewing felt a little bit different. I always seemed to find something new.

"Weirdly, I come here a lot. It helps clear my head when things get too busy. Or I feel too messy."

"There's a lot to look at." Nathan slowly moved past one of the display cases, leaning in to read the plaques.

"There's something comforting about seeing all the people who've been here before." I put a hand on Nathan's elbow. "C'mon. I brought you here for a reason."

I led him down the corridor then nodded toward a group of photos. Nathan paused for a moment then started smiling.

"Wow. I've never seen this one." He stepped in closer. "She's so young. Must be about your age."

The camera had captured our mom mid-motion. Mid-flight. It was like the photo of the dancers on the staircase from the art show. She popped out of the photo, like she couldn't, or wouldn't, be contained within the frame.

Nathan traced a finger along our mother's silhouette, and my heart did that thing again. Maybe a little too full. Maybe a bit achy. I pulled my camera out and took a quick photo. He scowled at me.

"Warn a guy first."

"That sort of negates the point of a candid."

"At least you got my good side." His smile reached his eyes, and I felt a surprising amount of relief. "She'd be so proud of you, Dallas."

"Of you too." My words almost caught in my throat. He was holding something back. "What's going on?"

Nathan shook his head. "It's nothing."

"It sounds like something." I knew Nathan still saw me as a kid. As someone he had to look out for and protect. But keeping me safe from danger was very different than protecting me from his feelings. I could be there for him as much as he was for me. "I'll give you a dollar if you try."

"Nice callback." He took a deep breath, maybe to steel his nerves to talk. "Justin and I broke up. It was a long time coming but still hard. No avoiding the pain part, I guess."

"Nathan, why didn't you say?" Shit. I'd been so caught up in all my stress and drama that I hadn't asked questions. First Gabby, now Nathan.

"I'm okay. Really. I wasn't ready to talk about it, so I kept it to myself. Nursed my wounds for a bit."

"Sure, I get that." I looked at him closely. There was more to the story. "Is that everything?"

He sighed and smiled.

"I was so focused on taking care of you for so long. But now that you're gone . . . I don't really know what I'm doing in Archwood. I have no idea what I'm supposed to do next."

"Oh, Nate." I hugged him, though it didn't seem like enough. "And I was blabbing about my stuff when you have all this going on."

"It's not a feel-sorry-for-me thing." He squeezed me tight then stepped back so we could look at each other. "I loved being your substitute parent. Honestly. Look how great you turned out. I'll take some credit."

"All the credit."

"Some credit." He smiled. "But my point is, you have choices. Not everyone does. Don't take that for granted."

"I won't. I promise." I laid my head on his shoulder. "I want you to know that I wouldn't be here without you. But now I'm really happy you get to just be a brother."

"Are you firing me?"

"Never. I'm saying it's your turn to have choices. You deserve that."

He pulled me into another hug. "How did you get so wise so fast?"

"The expensive tuition, I guess."

CHAPTER TWENTY-FIVE

DALLAS

Miley and I were back in our usual corner of the common room. We spent so much time in this spot that they should put up a plaque. We sat side by side on the sagging but still remarkably comfortable couch with books on our laps. The room was more packed than usual. It was the end of family weekend, and there was a desperate need to hit the books. It also seemed like no one wanted to do it in solitary. Studying had become a group activity.

Miley's phone buzzed.

"Text from Mom. 'Just got home. All good. So nice to meet Dallas—finally!!' Followed by two exclamation points so I fully understand the level of her excitement. Oh, another text. 'And Nathan! What a delightful young man!!!' Sorry, friend, Nathan got three exclamation points and you only got two."

"It's hard to compete with my martyr brother." Miley's parents had been fascinated by my relationship with Nate. They'd asked a ton of questions that might have been rude otherwise but only made Nate laugh. He was enjoying the spotlight. "I fully expected them to present him with a trophy or medal. Talk to the Pope about sainthood."

Miley's parents had arrived on campus with a flourish—exactly the way I would have expected them to arrive—and treated us to dinners and replenished our dorm room fridge. Nathan was only too happy to tag along.

"I'm more concerned about how much he enjoyed it. He'll never let me live it down."

The weekend was nonstop activities for visiting families, but Nathan and I had avoided the college-sanctioned events. I'd worked a shift; we'd wandered around campus; he'd gone into Los Angeles to do the tourist thing.

"We're going to order sushi. Do you want in?" Stella wandered over to our corner of the room. She was another dancer in our program, a sophomore, and lived down the hall. She was one of those people who seemed nice and Miley was friends with, and I nodded to in hallways. "I can't face the dining hall tonight."

"Sure, count me in." Miley took Stella's phone to add her order.

"Sorry, it's my brother's last night here. We're meeting my boyfriend for dinner."

"That sounds like a better deal." Stella sat beside Miley on the couch. "Do you know Amir?" She nodded toward a guy across the room who looked vaguely familiar. "He's in the drama department, so maybe not. Anyway. He thinks your brother's kinda hot, so I thought I'd throw it out there in case he's interested."

I looked over at Amir again. I didn't actually know what Nathan's type was other than cute, so Amir would fit the bill.

"I can let him know." I had no idea how to handle this

situation. Was I setting up my brother for a hookup? "I'll text Miley if it's a yes."

"Nice." Stella took her phone back. "I'll let you know when the food gets here."

My phone rang—Drayton—and I jumped on the call.

"I'm so glad you're finally home!"

I didn't have to fake my enthusiasm about hearing from him, but I was laying it on a bit thick to make up for the away game. I'd sent him texts to check in and a voicemail to catch him up on Nathan's visit and make plans, and I'd carefully avoided headlines like *USC suffers another devastating loss to the Miami Glades*. When I didn't get much more than a thumbs-up and a heart emoji, I brought out the big guns: dogs-riding-skateboards videos.

"Me too. It's been a long week." He sounded exhausted. There was none of Drayton's ready-to-take-on-the-world energy. "We lost."

"I heard." I tried to pull out my old cheerleader instincts despite the fact that I wasn't terribly rah-rah-rah even then. "That's good, right?"

"No, it sucks." Either he didn't remember or didn't appreciate the reference to our last conversation. "If we lose again, we won't make it to the playoffs."

"Right." Okay, I was really sucking at the girlfriend test today.

Drayton shutting down, shutting me out, was a whole new thing. When he'd finally told me about Abby, it was hard to hear but also easy to make space for him and his grief. I wanted to be there for him. I was glad he understood that he could tell me anything, be as vulnerable as he needed, and I would be his rock for a change. How could I do that for him now? How could I make him understand that whatever he was feeling right now wasn't going to be too much for me? I wanted to help him.

"Does that mean things are better with Ryan?"

"No, he's still a dick." A door closed behind him. He must have just walked into his dorm room. "But look, can we not talk about football?"

"Sure. Yeah, of course." I looked up as another group of students came into the common room. They were all laughing, jostling each other as they sat down on the other side of the room. "But fair warning, Nate's probably going to ask a lot of questions during dinner."

"Shit." Drayton must have thrown down his bag or something heavy because I heard a loud thud. "That's tonight?" I could hear the exhaustion, tinged with anger, in his voice. "Do you mind if I rain check? It was a long flight, and my knee is throbbing, and I just got home."

I didn't want to say that the throbbing knee comment was a bit of a low blow. He knew I wouldn't tell him to push through the pain and come out to see me. It felt convenient that he was playing the injured knee card now. As soon as that thought formed, I felt a surge of guilt. That was unfair. Possibly true but definitely unfair. Especially when I'd spent the past few weeks encouraging him to take time to heal.

"No, I understand. It's just . . ." I didn't want to sound like a whiny girlfriend or like I couldn't survive a night without him. "It's Nathan's last night. He's at the store right now because he's making burgers. Just like old times."

See? Two of us can play at that game.

"Dallas, you know I love Nate and his burgers." Being called Dallas felt like a distancing tool. Affectionate Drayton, the one trying to convince me about something, called me Cheer. It felt like he was a step away from calling me Miss Bryant. "But I need the rest. And he used to play, he gets it."

Yes, Nathan would understand, but that didn't mean there wouldn't also be disappointment. Both things could be true at the same time. I glanced over at Miley. She was pretending to read her book.

"Look, I promise I'll make it up to him at Thanksgiving." I could picture Drayton rubbing his hands over his face. "Or maybe I can fly him out when the season's over."

Because money solved all problems and fixed the issue of not seeing each other when we'd promised to stick with our short-distance romance schedule.

"Yeah, sure. I understand." I understood being exhausted and stressed. I understood being pulled in different directions. I understood the desire to hide away and escape the rest of the world. But that was what we were supposed to do with each other. When the world got too big, or shit felt too real, we came together. It was what we did. It was our superpower. "But I better get going. We'll talk tomorrow."

I didn't give him much time to respond. I tried to keep my voice even-keeled, but I needed the call to end. I put my phone down and let out a long sigh. If I were a betting woman, my money would be on Drayton doing the same on his end.

CHAPTER TWENTY-SIX

DRAYTON

I get that a lot of people aren't fans, but I've always liked the smell of chlorine. It wasn't a childhood thing. I grew up with saltwater pools and beachfront properties. It was more about having a break from football. Putting some tunes on and gliding through the water, weightless and carefree. Since my injury, it was a great way to exercise without too much strain and one of the few extras I did that was physio approved.

My morning had been less so. I'd done the stadium stairs at full tilt, and it'd hurt like hell. Almost didn't make it a couple times and, yeah, came real close to puking. That was my new exercise normal. I was gaining muscle, though. When I got back in the game, I'd be stronger than ever. This setback wasn't going to hold me back.

I sat at the edge of the pool, feet dangling in the water, with my phone in my hand. It had taken me a hell of a long time to write the text, and now I'd been staring at it for I had no idea how long.

Can we talk?

Three words. I'd agonized over those three words, and now I couldn't hit Send. If I sent it to Dallas, then we had to talk, and what would I say? I had no fucking idea. No clue. I wanted to go back to the summer, when everything felt possible: I was on track for the NFL, Dallas was going to her dream school, and our relationship was strong. One bad game, one wrong turn, and it had all gone to hell. When we managed to get together, we couldn't shake it off. I was letting both of us down. I needed to fix me, and I wasn't giving Dallas what she needed. Fail-fail.

"Drayton, can you focus?" Charlotte stared down at me then nodded at my phone. "Girlfriend trouble?"

"How did you know?" I returned her gaze, surprised that she'd picked up on it.

"Boys gossip more than girls." She laughed and placed her hands on her hips. "I have four brothers, so you can't tell me otherwise."

I pulled myself out of the pool. My leg didn't buckle, which felt like a victory until Charlotte started poking at my knee and the pain hit me hard. I winced, hissing with a quick intake of breath.

"Drayton, what's your plan B?" She took a step back. Her look said she'd lost interest in telling cute stories about her brothers.

"What do you mean?"

"If football doesn't work out. What's the plan?"

I grabbed a towel and rubbed it over my hair. "There isn't one. I don't need a plan B."

She was overstepping. Charlotte was a physiotherapist, not a life coach, and I didn't need to hear her opinions about what I was doing outside therapy. Hell, I barely wanted to hear her opinions about therapy.

"You might want to start thinking of one. Because at the rate you're going, I'm seriously worried." She sounded more concerned than angry or judgmental, but I still wasn't interested. "You're pushing yourself too hard."

She didn't understand what it was like being an athlete at this level. Or what it had taken to get here. There was no such thing as working too hard. I didn't do steroids or rely on supplements for the extra edge. It was all me and a fuck of a lot of hard work. It was early mornings and never really taking a day off. It was sticking to a rigid diet during the season and counting grams and protein and hydration. I needed to push hard. I needed to go even harder if I wanted to get out of this rut.

"No, I'm not. I'm icing—"

"It wasn't a question. We talked about recovery time, and I know where you should be if you were following the regimen." Her voice was sharp enough to make me drop the towel and look at her again. She was still standing with her hands on her hips giving me a hard stare. "You are dangerously close to converting this sprain to a full-on tear. Grade 1 can easily turn into Grade 3, and then you're looking at surgery, and there's no coming back from that."

"That's impossible." I knew my body. Sure, my knee hurt like hell when I went that extra distance, but that was what the ice and painkillers were for. "Not gonna happen. I'm ahead of schedule. Arm is strong. Knee is getting there. I'll be geared up in a week or so."

She let her head fall back as she took a deep breath. Charlotte was objectively hot. There was no doubt that if I were single, I would have hit on her long ago. It also helped that she was smart and funny and didn't seem big on drama or playing games. There were a couple times I'd wondered if she was flirting, but it was never anything real. And I wasn't interested in anyone other than Dallas.

Dallas. I'd missed seeing her all last week. All the time the team was in Florida, I'd thought about how good it would feel to go home to Dallas. Curl up in bed with her. Sex, sure, but I really just needed her. Her warmth. Fingers running through my hair until I fell asleep. The away games were awful, shitty, and it was hard to watch the team butt heads with one another. We'd started off so strong, really working together, then crashed and burned.

It would have been different if I were still QB. I knew it. I was frustrated and angry but trying to hold it together, hoping I could push morale in the right direction. It all added up, and it was exhausting. So by the time I actually did get home, I couldn't deal with any of it. As much as I wanted to see Dallas and to hang out with Nathan, I didn't want to have to go to Valencia. I didn't want to explain myself again, or play nice like everything was okay. Because things weren't okay. Things were shit. And I didn't always do well when things turned to shit.

"Your medial collateral ligament is overstretched, and your articular cartilage is at serious risk of permanent damage unless you start taking your recovery seriously."

Bullshit. That was bullshit. She was talking shit.

"I know this isn't what you want to hear. I know you're in your jock zone, thinking exercise and dedication will solve all your problems."

My heart rate was picking up. My ears started ringing. I knew this feeling. I'd experienced it too many nights, waking up in a cold sweat, replaying the moment when I didn't follow through like planned, didn't dodge as fast as I should have, didn't get the ball into play fast enough, and the linebacker came down on me.

"But, Drayton, you need to listen. I mean really listen and take this in."

I could hear people coming in through the door behind me. There was talking, laughter, but it was all white noise echoing on the tiles.

"I doubt you're going to get to play this season."

"There is no way." My voice was low. A growl.

"This is what I've been warning you about." She turned finally, releasing me from her stare. "I told you over and over that you were doing more harm than good."

"I needed to stay in shape." I was losing the growl and getting more noticeably angry.

"You needed to recover." She picked up her bag and started collecting her supplies. "This should have been about the long game and not immediate goals. You're only thinking about next week when you should be thinking about six months, a year from now."

"I am!" What the hell did she think was happening? Everything I did was about my future and getting into the NFL. "Missing games means scouts won't see me. The longer I'm out, the more chances I have to be forgotten."

"If the goal is to go pro then . . . forget it." She zipped up her bag and threw the strap over her shoulder. "You're throwing whatever chance you had of going pro out the window every time you ignore my advice. Every time you think you know more than the therapists and your coach."

"Not going pro isn't an option."

"Sorry, Lahey. I think it's time you worked on that plan B, maybe even a plan C."

Charlotte headed toward the door.

"Where are you going? We still have thirty minutes left in the session."

She turned back but didn't stop walking.

"I can lead you to water, but I can't make you drink."

"What the hell does that mean?" My brain was spinning out of control.

"If you're not going to give a damn about your recovery, then why should I?"

Charlotte exited, and I was left standing at the side of the pool not knowing what had just happened, not wanting to believe anything she'd said about my knee, and not knowing what I was supposed to do next.

"Fuck!"

My voice rang around the pool. Some part of my brain registered that the laughing and talking stopped, but all I could hear was the sound of blood pulsing through my ears.

CHAPTER TWENTY-SEVEN

DALLAS

I didn't fully realize I'd finished my solo until I heard the applause. Weeks of rehearsing, extra time in the studio and with the choreographer, culminated in a feeling of euphoria. Arms raised, back arched, legs in perfect position. My heart was racing, breath quick, but I felt perfectly calm. I'd done exactly what I'd set out to do, and it was exhilarating.

I only had a couple of seconds to take it all in. All the dancers around me paused for the beat. The stage lights above us. The music coming through the speakers. The rows of spectators in front of me in the black box theater. Some parents (including Miley's), partners, Dean Adams, and instructors in the VIP section. No Drayton. His seat was empty.

My mind snapped back into the room, into my body, a second late, and I briefly stumbled as I caught up with the other dancers. It was only a moment, but it was enough to throw me off. Enough that I wasn't able to fully get my head back into the routine.

Drayton hadn't come. My first big showcase at CalArts, and my boyfriend wasn't there.

I fell back into rhythm for the rest of the routine. Moved in sync, hit all my marks. It was a good performance. I felt confident that we dazzled as a group and put on a brilliant show. But I was very aware of my surroundings, never completely losing sight of that empty chair in front of the stage.

Afterward, I walked around backstage in a fog. I talked to the other dancers, wished them luck before they went onstage, clapped as each routine ended, but my sense of elation was gone. Those moments of delay starting the second half of my program had messed me up. I'd let Drayton's absence get into my head. Knock me out of my zone. I was angry at myself, disappointed. This showcase was supposed to be my chance to impress Dean Adams enough that she'd invite me into her master class. Instead, I was that dancer who got caught in the headlights and missed her beat.

"Congratulations to you both." Dean Adams found Miley and me after the show. She seemed as surprised by our appearance as we were by hers. There was an awkward pause when we didn't speak, and she looked ready to bolt. "Excuse me while I make my rounds."

"Before you read too much into that . . ." Miley stepped in front of me to block my view and my path if I also decided to run. "You crushed your solo. That's all you can control."

I shook my head. "No, you're right."

It felt good when the solo finished. It felt right. But in that moment it had taken for my brain to catch up with my body, I'd let the doubts creep in. Maybe I'd put too much pressure on this performance, this one showcase. Maybe I could never live up to my own expectations. I'd spent so many years working up to CalArts and this showcase, and now I was doubting almost everything.

"Don't take my word for it." Miley threw an arm over my shoulder for a side hug. "They filmed the whole thing. You'll see it all for yourself."

I nodded my head like I was agreeing, but watching my performance didn't feel like a great idea. I wasn't sure I wanted that level of confirmation. My confidence was shattered, and I didn't know if it was because Drayton hadn't showed or that I'd let it bother me.

"Hey, that was great!" Skyler walked up carrying two bouquets of flowers. "So proud of my video background dancers. You've come a long way." He handed us each a bouquet. "No, seriously. That was really amazing."

For whatever reason, Skyler's enthusiasm felt like too much. Maybe embarrassing. I didn't think I wanted this level of attention from him. Not in that moment. But the flowers were beautiful, and receiving them made me feel a bit like a ballerina accepting honors after a performance. Okay, yeah. I was the embarrassing one.

"This is so sweet." Miley hugged Skyler. "But you do know I'm sapphic, right?"

"Yeah. The bangs gave it away."

She punched him playfully in the shoulder then ran off to talk to the other dancers. There was a lot to unpack in everyone's performance.

"Thank you, they're beautiful." I wondered if I had anything that could substitute as a vase.

“They’re from TJ’s. But I figured it’s the thought that counts.” He looked around the room. “So, where’s the famous boyfriend?”

I quickly looked at my feet and tried to catch my breath. I hated this. Feeling rattled. Not wanting to be so closely examined. It was one thing for Dray to not show but something more if others noticed too. Miley had at least pretended that my mood was all about Dean Adams’s response and my nerves about the second half of the program.

“He had something come up. He’s in season. So, it’s complicated.”

“No, it’s not. It’s pretty simple.”

I raised my eyes. Skyler held my gaze, his own eyes dark and intense.

“Whatever, Skyler.” My voice was sharp, my words clipped. “I have to go.”

I spun on my heel and raced to the door. I felt my face heating up and tears pooling in my eyes. I needed to get the hell out and far away before I started crying. I wasn’t a crier. I never made a scene. I didn’t want to give Skyler the opportunity to see my reaction or know that I agreed with him. It *was* pretty simple. Drayton could have made it to the show if he’d wanted.

~

I took the long way back to the dorm, wandering around campus and along random paths. It was dark but not deserted. The tears did come, but thankfully I was on my own so no more embarrassment. Miley had messaged to say she was going out for drinks and asked me to come along, but I wasn’t in the mood.

The cool night air was refreshing but didn't do much to clear my head. Things still felt muddled.

"Dallas! Dallas! Wait!"

I stopped, turning slowly. Drayton was running up the path toward me.

"I'm so sorry." He stopped in front of me. I noticed that for the first time in a long time, he didn't wince. "I can't believe I missed your recital."

"I feel so humiliated." Tears were brimming again. I couldn't face him. The best I could do was to look to the side, watching a couple on a nearby bench. Their heads were leaned in close as they talked. They looked cozy and in love, but who knew? Maybe their hearts were breaking too.

"I'm sorry." That was the second time he'd said it, but it still didn't sound believable. "I had to stay later for physio, and then there was traffic. Plus football . . ."

"I get it. Football comes first."

He raised his hands in frustration. "Dallas, come on. I promise I'll be at your next show."

My next show. Next date. Next weekend. Next lifetime.

"Do you know that people think you're made-up?" I turned to look at him and made no attempt to hide my fury. "I've seen your world. Your dorm and your friends. Frat parties. Stadium, practice, athletes' lounge. But you've barely spent any time in mine."

"That's not fair. You know I'm in season."

"And I'm in school! I have classes, rehearsals, shows! A *job*. Tonight was important for me. I crushed my solo, and I wanted my boyfriend there to see it."

His expression switched, suddenly became hard. "That's super ironic considering you missed my only game of the season."

"I feel terrible about that! I got there late, but I did get there. And I've tried so hard to make it up to you! Bending over backward, splitting myself in two. Do you know how much I've sacrificed?"

"You want to talk about sacrifice? I missed my first film session because I was stuck in Valencia. Coach still hasn't let me live that down."

"Stuck!?"

"That's not what I meant." He shook his head. "But I might have been able to make that play if I'd been more focused. If I'd showed up where I needed to be, on time . . ."

"Oh, so the injury's my fault?" Had he been thinking that the whole time? Was that why he was pulling back from me? He blamed me for his injury.

"No. I'm saying you're not the only one here being pulled in multiple directions."

I tried to swallow, but it felt like razors were moving down my throat.

"Football means everything, and I'm not going to let it slip away."

"Yeah, well, dance is everything to me, and I worked just as hard to get here." The tears were flowing freely now. "I'm tired of giving scraps to everyone, including myself."

"What are you saying?"

I took a deep breath then wiped away my tears. "That you're *a* dream, but you're not my only dream."

We stared at each other. It wasn't that long ago that we would have reached out. He would have held me while I cried. But this was the new Dallas and Drayton.

"Yeah . . . we haven't been the same for a while." He didn't look away. Barely paused for a breath. "Maybe we should quit while we're ahead."

"You're breaking up with me?" I phrased it like a question even though I knew it wasn't. This wasn't a surprise. It felt both too soon and long overdue.

"I'm sorry." He spoke just above a whisper. "I wanted this to work, but I don't think it is."

I wiped my cheeks and tucked my hair behind my ears, despite the fact that it was supposed to be Drayton's job. This dream was over, and I was going to have to find a way to fill that space.

"Can I walk you back to your room?" He took a step closer, but I shook my head.

"No, I'll be okay." Once again, I spun on my heel to leave, though I didn't rush off. My legs felt too rubbery and weak. "Bye, Drayton."

I didn't glance over my shoulder, so I had no idea if he was watching. If he lingered until I was out of view. He was gone. I was gone. I needed to move, and that was all I could focus on.

My dorm room was dark and empty, and I only had enough energy to crawl into bed and pull the blankets up tight. I hit the number in my contact list and felt so grateful when it didn't go to voicemail.

"I know it's late. But I could really use a friend right now."

The tears were overwhelming, threatening to cut me off, but I had no other option but to continue.

CHAPTER TWENTY-EIGHT

DRAYTON

I took the stadium stairs at full tilt. My muscles were straining, my knee aching, but I needed it. I had so much pent-up energy that I thought I might explode. Dallas and I were done. My football career was on hold. I'd always been driven, but it felt like I was now on the road to nowhere.

My watch buzzed, telling me Dad was calling. I didn't really want to answer, but my run had already been cut short, and I needed to get the conversation over with. He would keep calling until I picked up. Voicemail meant nothing to this man.

"Hey."

"Hey, Dray." It sounded like Dad was outside. I could hear traffic in the background. "How you holding up?"

I wasn't sure what I'd been thinking, but I'd left a message for my parents when I got in after seeing Dallas. I'd needed to say it out loud to someone. Like it wasn't true unless someone else had the information. I'd played it casual. Said we'd called it quits, no big deal, schedules too heavy, needed to focus on football. I could have called Josh to tell him first, but I knew I was essentially repeating the same speech he'd given me. Josh wasn't the type to say *I told you so*, but I also didn't want to risk it.

"I'm all right." That did not sound believable.

"Get any sleep?"

"Not really." That answer was a surprise. I had intended to keep up the front, but once it was out, there was no stopping. "I don't know if I called it quits too soon. Or too late." Shit. I had no idea what I was talking about or what I wanted to say. Maybe saying this out loud wasn't the right move. "Sometimes I wonder if I should have just gone to Waco."

"Dray, you chose what was right for you. I know I put a lot of pressure on you to go to Waco, but that was my baggage. My plan. I'm proud of you for choosing your own way." He held the phone away to speak to someone. It sounded like he was asking for his car, so he was probably at the valet desk at his club. "Look, it's not always going to be easy. You just have to trust your instincts. Stick with it long enough to see where it takes you."

I sat down on the steps. It was still early enough that the stadium was mostly empty. Just a few of the guys running the track. Early mornings were supposed to be a time of promise. They should have an anything-can-happen vibe.

"I just feel like I'm losing everything I came out here for."

Suddenly, I was exhausted. My limbs were heavy. My eyelids were drooping. I felt stuck in a mire.

"You've got a lot coming at you right now." Hearing his voice was comforting. So different from the hard-line coach who had a lot to say about my on-field performance. "But it won't last. Your knee will get better. And the breakup? I know it hurts." He paused, probably struggling to find the right words. "What's meant to be has a way of working itself out. One way or another. You're young."

I took a deep breath and closed my eyes. Tears felt close. I didn't see how things would work out. We'd tried. We'd made our short-distance relationship promises, and they'd crashed and burned in a couple of weeks. I thought about our night dancing. Dallas in the sexy green dress and cowboy boots. The way she moved up against me during the slow songs. That might have been our last perfect night, and I didn't even get to sleep over. It had still been cut short.

Then my injury.

Her job. Workouts and rehearsals.

Games and recitals missed.

All I had now were the Polaroids of little moments she'd sent me, and I couldn't look at them without feeling crushed. I was going to have to stuff them into a drawer or a box, and it all just made me feel like shit.

"Maybe I just need a fresh start."

"I get it." Dad sighed. His pep talk was failing miserably. "Look, if you're really unhappy, it's okay to look at other options." A door slammed as he got into his car. "But, Dray, I need you to remember to make sure you aren't running from something."

I couldn't make that promise, so I signed off with "Talk to you later" instead.

~

Things hadn't improved by the next morning. I finished my workout, did my physio exercises, schoolwork, then another workout, and once again, I barely slept. I was up against it and needed to find a way out.

I knocked on Coach Watson's door and pushed it open when I heard, "Come in."

"Hey, Coach. Have a sec?"

The look on his face told me that I looked as awful as I felt. I'd been avoiding most interactions since my fight with Dallas. Keeping to myself seemed like the wise move.

"Yeah, son. Sit down." He leaned back in his office chair, watching me closely as I sat down opposite him. "What's up?"

I had prepared a whole speech, a list of all my reasons and rationalizations, but I couldn't remember a word of it as soon as I sat down.

"Yeah, so I've been thinking . . ." When I'd told Dad that I didn't want to go to Waco, we were in the middle of a screaming match. It had been the only way I could get the words out and admit the truth I'd been feeling for a long time. But Coach and I didn't have that relationship. "I'm not sure if USC is the best fit."

"Hmm."

I was thrown off by his nonreaction. He wasn't thrown by what I'd said. He was taking it all in, listening, and for whatever reason I found it destabilizing.

"I think I should cut my losses and get a fresh start elsewhere."

There. I'd said it. Done.

"You considering a transfer?" He rocked slowly in his chair.

"I'm requesting one."

"Well, that's a damn shame." He stopped his rocking then

leaned forward. He folded his hands together and rested them on his desk. "'Cause you're a great asset to this team."

I rolled my eyes and leaned back, crossing my arms across my chest in a defensive move. I knew bullshit when I heard it.

"I'm serious, Drayton. I recruited you for a reason. You turned that Miami Glades game around."

"Turned it around? We lost. Again."

"But we went from working against each other in the first half to playing together in the second."

"Still lost."

"I don't see it that way. I've seen how it has added up since. And if that's what you can do on a bench, I'd be interested to see what you do on the field. Here or elsewhere."

The guys had pulled it together in the second half, but the Glades' lead was too large. We couldn't recover. The sports shows still ripped us apart, but they didn't see how the plays came together at halftime. Or how the postgame roundup was full of positives instead of shit talk.

"Thanks, Coach. I appreciate that."

Coach stood up and walked around the desk. He leaned against the front and looked down at me.

"I can't stop you from leaving. You're your own man, and you have to do what's best for you. But I would advise you to not make any rash decisions. Take a minute to weigh your options."

"Yeah, sure." Except how did I tell him that I didn't see any options in front of me if I wasn't playing ball? If I wasn't heading to the NFL, it was a dead end. "That sounds fair."

The conversation was over, so I stood up and shook his hand because it felt like we'd just negotiated something. I left the office feeling like nothing was solved or fixed but also like I wasn't being crushed by the uncertainty.

"And Lahey!" Coach called down the hall after me. "Mistakes happen. It's how we bounce back from them that defines us. Remember that."

I smiled and raised my hand in a quick wave because I didn't know how else to respond. I wasn't sure if there was any possibility of bouncing back from this one.

CHAPTER TWENTY-NINE

DALLAS

I pulled the blankets higher over my head, determined to pretend the knocking was far away. Not my door. Not my room. For the past few minutes—hours, days, who the hell knew anymore—the knocking had kept up a steady rhythm. *Knock-knock-knock-knock*. Then for some god-awful reason, it switched up to a jazzy beat. *Kn-knock-knock, kn-knock-knock-kn-knock*. Asshole.

I threw the blankets off and shut my eyes against the sun. The blinds were down, but it was still impossibly bright. Why did we even bother with blinds if they were going to do this bad a job? My phone said 12:24 p.m., which meant I hadn't left this bed in twenty-two and three-quarter hours.

I'd done pretty well for a couple days. Gotten to some but not all classes. Called in sick to work. Gone to the dance studio then promptly left the dance studio. Avoided the dining hall and library. I'd decided studying in my room was the best option, and

I kept that up until yesterday afternoon when a nap became my priority, and that brought us up to date.

Whoever was at the door was now experimenting with off-time knocking. I stood up, took a second to steady myself after the head rush, and moved to put an end to this madness. I opened the door, ready to curse out whoever didn't understand the meaning of *leave me the hell alone*, and was met with a smiling, far-too-friendly face.

"Hey, bestie!"

I did what any sensible person would do in response. I slammed the door shut.

I counted to five, and when the knocking didn't start up, I slowly opened it again. Gabby was still standing there, laughing.

"I had to make sure I wasn't dreaming!" I pulled her into the room with a tight hug. "Oh my God, what are you doing here?"

She was real. Gabby was in my room, and I suddenly felt a bit more like myself. I hadn't realized how much of me I'd left behind when leaving Archwood. All those pieces that only Gabby knew.

"You sounded a mess on the phone last week. And I talked to Miley—"

"How?" I stepped away from Gabby then looked around the room like maybe there would be a clue, some evidence of Miley and Gabby's connection.

"Instagram." Gabby cocked her head like that answer was the most obvious one. I had a feeling it was going to take me a bit to catch up. Sleeping for a day had done a number on my brain. That and not sleeping much for the past week. Or eating. I might have forgotten to eat a few times too. "Anyway, we were both worried about you."

I took her in. She looked good. Her dark, curly hair was

pulled back by a headband. She wore a cute T-shirt and jacket. Her cheeks were rosy. I didn't see how I could get from this stage of breakup to that level of comfort. My track pants and mismatched socks, Archwood High T-shirt, and unwashed, very scattered hair were my new normal.

"And I figured what better way to spend my fall break than in sunny California."

"You didn't have to!"

She smiled again. "Yeah, I did. I wanted to see you. It's been too long, bestie. Also, I brought you something." She held up an empty box.

"Wow. So generous, bestie." I might be sad and tired, but sarcasm would always win.

"Glad you haven't lost your sense of humor." Gabby looked around the room then grabbed the USC sweatshirt sitting on my chair. "It's cleanup time."

I watched, verging on horror but also mesmerized as Gabby threw the sweatshirt into the box. She also grabbed a framed photo of Drayton and me by the pool at his parents' place. It was a perfect picture from a perfect day and proof that we were so clearly in love. I hated looking at it now, but the thought of it disappearing also made me feel anxious. When did I have to admit that the end was the end?

I hadn't spoken to Drayton in a week. No texts. No snaps. No voice memos. It wasn't getting easier. I seemed to miss him more every day. I was forcing myself to not communicate. Feeling disappointed when he didn't reach out either.

"All Drayton items go in here. I'll take care of it tomorrow."

"Take care of it how?" I had a sudden vision of a large bonfire and Gabby setting everything Drayton-related aflame.

"You don't need to look at any of this." Gabby gave me a closer look then took pity on me. "If there's anything you don't want to lose, or think you might want later, we can find another place to hide it. Either way, we need it out of sight and out of mind."

"No, you're right. I'm officially wallowing."

Gabby handed me the box, and I placed it on my bed. This might take some time. The room was small, but it held a lot of memories and mementos. I needed to be brave because this broken heart business wasn't for cowards.

"So here's the plan. We're going to get some vitamin D, then talk about Drayton or not talk about him. And, most importantly, you're putting on something hot as hell and we're going out."

"Absolutely not." I held a hand up in defense. "That sounds awful."

I caught sight of myself in the mirror and almost did a double take. There was no way I was fit to join the outside world. There was no way I was going to be classified as hot.

"And I'm not taking no for an answer." She saw me gazing into the mirror and likely saw my look of horror. "Because you are young and hot and not wasting a Saturday night crying over a boy. That's what weekdays are for."

"You sound like Miley."

"That's because we rehearsed what I was going to say."

It was my first real laugh since the recital, when Drayton and I had last spoken. It felt so good to have Gabby here. Maybe it was possible to feel like myself again. I pulled her into another hug.

"I so needed this."

Gabby pulled back and scrunched her face. "Girl, you also need a shower."

I lifted my arm and sniffed. Yeah, Gabby might be right about that too.

~

"Great, we came." I walked into the warehouse and raised my arms. "Can we go now?"

I looked up at the tower of vintage televisions beside me. Some were playing old infomercials while others broadcast static screens. Still others contained dioramas with dolls set up in various scenes, including the couch at Central Perk.

"Woah. Dallas is here? At a party? I never thought I'd see the day."

Skyler walked up with his arms wide. He was wearing black jeans and a T-shirt. I hadn't seen him all week. He was being overly friendly, acting like the last time we'd talked I hadn't run out of the room crying.

"You don't go to parties?" Gabby turned on me. I couldn't tell if she was actually mad. "I thought we'd been through this."

"I go to parties. Mostly USC ones." I looked at Skyler because I had to get this over with. I had to say it out loud to make it true. "But Drayton and I broke up. So . . ."

"I'm sorry to hear that."

It wasn't the response I'd expected, especially after our last exchange. I got the sense he was masking something. Probably didn't want to say, *Good riddance to a crappy boyfriend* in case I burst into tears again.

"We'll take three tequila shots for our troubles." Miley held up three fingers for Skyler. "Please and thank you."

Skyler snapped his fingers. "On it."

"With lime and salt, please!" Gabby laughed at Miley and my looks. "What? I'm not an animal."

We all watched Skyler move around the bar. He held up a lime and smiled.

“Is someone going to tell me who that is? And why does he only have eyes for Dallas?”

“Skyler.” Miley smiled at me. “And why *does* he only have eyes for Dallas?”

“You’re both imagining things.” I felt my cheeks redden, which I put down to lack of sleep and overstimulation. “He’s the manager at the café. He’s a mostly nice guy and a friend. That’s all.”

This party crowd was very different from the one at the frat house. There were some people wearing designer but more in vintage. More people were standing around talking than engaging in games and competitions. There was a keg, though, so some things were universal.

“You know, the best way to get over someone is by getting under someone else.” Miley laughed when my eyes went wide. “Just saying.”

“That’s not true.” I turned to look at Gabby. “Is it?”

“I tried it, and I can attest to its merits.” She shrugged her shoulders. “I definitely had an empowering ho phase.”

“Right, you mentioned.” Her texts were usually brief updates that always felt like she was trying to prove something to herself as much as me. “There were two Dylans?”

“Three. The poli-sci frat boy, the bio engineer, and the chef.” She sat down on the couch. “But if I’m being honest, when it was all said and done, I kept thinking of Josh. I still do.”

I grabbed her hand. God, I understood. Then a thought hit me. I looked between the two of them.

“You don’t think Drayton is hooking up with someone, do you?”

“Nooo.” Gabby shook her head while Miley nodded along. “For sure.”

I didn’t have time to press them because Skyler arrived with four tequila shots. It was time I let this evening and my friends take over. We clinked our glasses together, and the drinking began.

CHAPTER THIRTY

DRAYTON

Indoor football was probably never a good idea, but that was one of the advantages to being an adult. I could make all the poor life decisions I wanted. Besides, it wasn't like we were risking any real damage. I was on the couch with my leg up and iced while I threw a Nerf football around the room with Zach and Josh. No tackling, soft throws, easy dives. It actually felt pretty good to kick back with the guys and distract myself from missing Dallas so damn much.

Zach caught the ball with one hand while holding a slice of pizza with the other. He easily tossed the ball to Josh without missing a beat.

"That's why you're our star receiver, Morgan!" I pointed at him. "Cool as a cucumber when the ball's in play."

He laughed and dropped the slice on his plate before the ball came back at him. "Maybe we need to serve food during the game if that stops the fumble."

"If we get the ball to you, you know what to do." I checked my watch to see how long the ice had been in place. Still good for another ten minutes. "It's not all on you."

Practice this week had been all over the place. I sat on the sidelines with Coach for most of the time, and there was some real improvement. There were still communication and trust issues, but I could see that the team was starting to come back together. Everyone's confidence was rattled after the string of losses, but it was finally beginning to feel like things might turn around.

"I'm mainly impressed the ball isn't covered in pizza sauce." Josh caught it with both hands. He was a good player but also knew his limits. "Multitasking was never my thing."

Josh had been a surprise addition tonight. I'd gotten back from physio and found him sitting on the front steps of my dorm. It had been such a long week, with not a lot of sleep, so my first thought had been that I was hallucinating. And yes, it was disappointing to know that my hallucinations might involve Josh.

"It is I, your handsome brother, in the flesh," he'd announced.

He stood up, and we hugged. I was confused by his sudden appearance but also relieved. I felt like I could drop my guard, even just a bit.

"Dude, what are you doing here?"

When we'd both ended up in California for school, I'd thought maybe we'd see each other more. It was a six-hour drive between USC and Stanford, or a couple hours flying, so it had seemed possible. I'd been wrong, of course. Same as I'd been wrong about maintaining a short-distance relationship with someone who was only an hour away. It was very clear that I wasn't so good with the multitasking either.

"It's my fall break, and I thought we could have some quality time." He'd placed a hand on my shoulder. He was trying for casual, but it was gentle and comforting. "The Lahey boys back at it!"

I locked eyes with him. "Mom told you about the breakup?"

"Yeah. You want to talk about it?" He looked a bit sheepish, like maybe I might take him up on the offer.

"No." I laughed when he visibly relaxed. "But I'm glad to see you."

"Me, too, bro." We hugged again, and it felt as good as the first time. Josh had only been my brother technically for a couple years, but the connection was deep and genuine. We were proof that blood didn't define family. "What do you want to do first?"

We'd walked up the steps and into the building. My knee was sore but not aching, which was an improvement.

"There's gotta be some parties we could hit up. Or a bar. Go to the Viper Room or something."

Josh was never a big partier, but I appreciated the effort. He was trying to find ways to distract and amuse, but proof that Josh was out of the loop was his suggestion of a bar that hadn't been cool within our lifetime.

"I have to take it easy this weekend. Lay low."

Charlotte's speech had been a gut punch. I was spiraling and needed to get things under control. If I wasn't going to play for USC, then I needed to get somewhere else so I could be seen. Get the attention of scouts and pro teams. Get some good stats under my belt. If that also meant trying Charlotte's recovery plan, then so be it.

"No problem. I got the perfect idea."

Josh's plan involved getting Zach over for video games and

then pizza delivery. Throw in my timed rotation of a heating pad and ice and you had the recipe for a quiet night at home. Not exactly how I'd pictured my freshman year at college but definitely what I needed.

"And just to say it one more time." Zach pointed at me. I wasn't sure when we'd become friends who aggressively pointed at each other to make a point, but here we were. "You're not transferring."

"You don't get it." I lifted the ice from my knee. Time wasn't up yet, but it was feeling a bit too cold. As ice tends to do.

"Bro! If anyone understands, it's me." He stood up to walk to the fridge. "I dislocated my shoulder last year. Took months to recover. You gotta be patient with yourself." He turned back with ball in hand. "Up top!"

Zach tossed the ball, and Josh dove to grab it. It was a bit messy, but he got it. Impressive for a science boy.

"My bad, bro." Zach grabbed more beer from the fridge.

"He's right, Dray." Josh held on to the ball, waiting for Zach to put down the bottles and me to put down the ice bag in my hand. My brother didn't have the killer sports instinct. "You were the starting quarterback as a freshman. That's huge."

He tossed the ball my way.

"Key word being *was*." And if I wasn't starting quarterback, or second-string while the knee kept me out, what was I? I wasn't big on self-reflection, but I knew enough about myself to realize that my identity was wrapped up in football. It was all I'd ever been and everything I was supposed to be. I needed to get off this topic or the downward spiral would start again. I nodded to Zach. "Go long."

"Dude, you're being too hard on your—" Zach realized a

second too late, and his sentence was cut off by the ball hitting him in the face. "Nice. Well played, QB."

Josh and I laughed while Zach reached down to retrieve the ball. It had bounced—right off Zach's face in a perfect Nerf ball bounce—and rolled under the couch. This night was exactly what I'd needed. Even if I didn't have to nurse my bum knee, I didn't think I could've handled loud music and a sea of drunk people. It would have made me think of our line dancing night and that Dallas should be by my side. I needed to snap out of it, which was why it was kind of ironic that Zach sat up holding a Polaroid instead of the ball.

"Found this under the couch."

It was a Polaroid of Dallas and me curled up in my bed. She was laughing, glowing. Damn, that was a good pic.

"Do you want me to trash it?"

"Yes." My answer was quick. Decisive. Maybe misguided. "No." Did I want to look at the photo again? Did I need reminding how gorgeous Dallas's smile was? "I don't know."

"I'll just put it back." Zach reached back down and put the photo back under the couch.

That was awkward. Maybe too revealing. I wasn't sure what my next move should be.

"Breakups are brutal." Josh cut the tension and got right to the point.

"Yeah." I took the beer Zach handed me. Took a long drink. "I think you and Gabby were smart to break up early and skip all the hurt."

Josh let out a puff of air before shaking his head. "I didn't skip past anything."

I raised an eyebrow at him. What was he talking about?

Anytime I'd checked in with him, he'd blown me off. Said he was busy, all was good. I realized in that moment, looking at my brother still looking the way I was feeling, that I hadn't checked in much after that first week. I'd taken him at his word. I hadn't made the trek to Stanford to distract him with video games and Nerf football.

"I really miss her, and I have a lot . . . I don't know." He held his beer bottle with both hands and picked at the edges of the label. "I wish I had fought harder for her."

"That sucks." Zach reached over to nudge Josh's knee. Maybe stop him from going too deep into wherever he was headed. "But if it makes you feel better, I tried so hard to make it work with my girlfriend even when we didn't make sense anymore. And I sort of wish I'd had the balls to end it sooner."

"Grass is always greener." Josh held up his beer then took a long drink.

"Have you ever thought about reaching out to your ex?"

Josh shrugged. "I've drafted the text a million times, but I can't send it."

He suddenly looked exactly how I felt, and *sad* didn't cover it. If he still felt like that after more than a month, then there was no hope for me.

"We need more beer." I carefully lifted my leg off the table and stood up. "Fire up the PlayStation. I'm done with talking for tonight."

CHAPTER THIRTY-ONE

DALLAS

In some ways, all parties are the same. At least all college parties seem cut from the same cloth. Loud music and too-drunk people, a couple fighting in one corner and someone else crying in another, and those two instances may or may not be related. There was always someone who decided they need to dance on a table or the night was a waste. At least one new friendship was born with promises of hanging out as soon as exams were done.

That last one was Miley and Gabby. They were playing beer pong, and it was hard to tell who was winning. They were both trashed and laughing hysterically at their inability to keep any of the cups upright. It was honestly delightful to watch. My oldest friend and newest friend bonding and enjoying each other's company felt perfect. My world had crumbled in the past week, so it was satisfying to see my support system was steady and connected. I was feeling both sad and lucky.

Skyler walked up with another drink for me. I remained surprisingly sober, enjoying the space and watching everyone. He stood beside me as we both stared up at the TV tower sculpture.

"Do you think it's always here or they put it up just for the party?" he asked.

"Oh, I hope this changes every week." I pointed to one of the dioramas in a hollowed-out set. "Next time I'm here, I want that one to be two figures dressed like us staring at the TV tower."

"And the TV tower in the diorama has all these dioramas in it." He nodded approvingly. "Very meta."

"Six months from now it will take over the whole room." I stepped away and started back toward Gabby and Miley. They might need an intervention soon if they kept up at that pace.

"So, having fun?"

I looked over at Skyler. Why did he sound so strange? Almost nervous. I was used to the music bully who refused to admit he actually liked the Weeknd whenever I put him on.

"Never felt better." I took too big a gulp of my drink too quickly and almost coughed it back up.

"I'm sorry for the other night. I shouldn't have said anything about . . ." He shoved one hand into his pocket. I didn't know if he was nervous about apologizing because the concept was relatively foreign to him or if the whole topic had set him off. "I hope that's not why . . ."

"Skyler, don't worry." I stopped and put a hand on his arm. "You are definitely not the reason Drayton and I ended things."

I'd thought that would put him at ease, but there was flash of something in his eyes. I might have thought it was hurt, but it was Skyler and that would make no sense. I put it down to a moment of confusion. I could just as easily have imagined it.

"Good. Good." He smiled. "I'm glad it wasn't me. Not glad? You know what I mean." He took another beat then stuck out his hand. "Friends?"

I shook his hand. "Friends."

"Thank God. Because work would have been so awkward if you'd said no. Like when you say bye to someone but then you walk in the same direction."

"Or when you go in for a hug, but the other person wants a handshake."

"Or when a girl calls you *neat*."

He remembered. This guy had the memory of an elephant. We both laughed, and it was such a relief. We'd had a fun night so far, but this was our first one-on-one. I had avoided work all week because, well, I wasn't sure why. Maybe I was embarrassed about making a scene after the showcase and running off when he'd mentioned Drayton. Though I wasn't sure if I was embarrassed because I'd run off rather than talking to him or if it stemmed from Skyler calling it. Drayton should have come. Or called. Or made an effort for a night that was so important to me. I'd made so many sacrifices for him, putting so much of my own life aside to support him, but it was never returned. When push came to shove, football was the only thing that mattered to Drayton. It would always be his first choice.

Skyler quickly stepped aside as a girl ran between us to get to the bathroom. She was moving at a fast clip and ready to bulldoze down anything or anyone who got in her way.

"Crying or puking?" I asked.

"I think we're at that stage of the night where we don't have to choose."

"See? And people say you can't have it all."

He really did have a great laugh. Skyler had an air of effortless cool about him. It probably stemmed from growing up in Brooklyn among artists. He never seemed to care what anyone else thought, which was an ethos I tried to practice, and he always seemed more curious than judgmental. I probably leaned too far into the latter, so Skyler was a good reminder of how to look at the world around us.

"I saw a cut of the music video," Skyler said.

We moved over to the side of the room. I leaned my back against the wall, and Skyler leaned on his side so he faced me.

"It's unreal. You are so great. The camera really hugs you."

"Hugs me? That sounds a bit creepy." That sounded like there were way too many close-ups.

"No, it's good." He looked out over the room, watching all the dancing and drama unfold. "Means more that it followed you around perfectly. Sort of feels like we're dancing right along with you. It has this warm, welcoming feeling."

"That's so sweet." The song and video were less about being sexy and more about love blooming, so that was good to hear. I liked knowing that we'd stayed true to the lyrics.

"Listen, my friend's this brilliant musician. They go to UCLA." He was becoming excited Skyler again. Like when he really needed me to hear a song by Jonathan Richman and then spent the next thirty minutes telling me why the Modern Lovers were the best band of the '80s. "Long story short, if you want to be in another music video, I'll recommend you. Again, no pay. But more footage for your reel?"

"I'd love that!" I turned to face him. "I'm all about my reel now. Miley has fully converted me."

"Great." Skyler broke out into a wide grin. "Because I submitted you yesterday."

It was probably the tequila shots and beer, but I felt my face warm up. It had been presumptuous of him to act without checking with me, and I probably would have told someone else to back off if they'd done the same thing. But I liked that Skyler had listened to me ramble on about getting a reel together, figuring out auditioning, and putting myself out there. I liked that he took the time to support my half-baked plan. It was what friends did for each other, and I was feeling pleased that I had officially made a new friend.

"Hey, Dallas!" Gabby shouted at me from across the room. "You in for the next round?"

"And we're not taking no for an answer, so get your ass in here!" Miley joined in.

I shrugged at Skyler. "Duty calls."

Skyler laughed as he followed me back to the beer pong match. This night was turning out to be a lot more fun than expected.

CHAPTER THIRTY-TWO

DRAYTON

It might have been a new day, but there was yet another person from Archwood sitting on my dorm building's front steps. It was Gabby this time, and she didn't look as happy to see me as Josh had.

"What are you doing here?" That sounded harsher than intended. It was more about surprise than anger. "Does Josh know?"

It was a good thing that Josh had decided to take it easy this morning and sleep in. This meeting could have jumped from awkward to intense.

"No, why would I tell Josh I'm in California? I haven't talked to him since we broke up." She held up the box she was carrying. "And I'm here to deliver a package."

I knew what was inside the box, and a voice in the back of my mind said I shouldn't take it. Accepting this box meant Dallas and I were done. Unfortunately, I'd never been great about following orders.

The box was light. I tried to remember everything I'd left behind at her place. My sweatshirt. There might have been a toothbrush. Had she sent back the gifts too? The camera? The necklace I gave her for her birthday last year? Her birthday. That was coming up soon. I'd had a whole night planned, including a fancy dinner and hotel stay.

"Dallas sent you to do this?"

"No. It was my idea."

Gabby didn't sound angry or disappointed. She wasn't overly friendly, which made sense. Friend code said you needed to be somewhat distant and overly polite with your bestie's ex-boyfriend.

"How is she?"

"How do you think?" She put her hands on her hips. Gabby still carried herself like the head of cheer squad. At any second, she could demand I do a black flip or serve as the base of a pyramid, and I wasn't sure I could say no.

"She's not the only one who's hurt here. I didn't . . ."

I wasn't sure what I was going to say. I hadn't wanted this to happen. I hadn't wanted to lose Dallas. I hadn't known how much this would hurt until that was the only thing I could feel.

"Drayton, we're not in high school anymore. I'm not going to meddle or do the 'he said, she said' thing."

"But you're so good at it." I couldn't resist giving her a half smile.

"I'm retired." She didn't quite smile in return but close enough. "If you want to talk to Dallas, you know where to find her."

Gabby walked off, and I called after her.

"I technically don't. We stopped sharing locations."

Without turning back, she raised a hand to wave me off. "Goodbye, Drayton."

I headed back inside to drop the box off. Josh was still asleep on the couch, one arm draped over his eyes to block the light. We'd stayed up late last night, goofed around, talked shit about whatever. It was good to spend time with my brother, but I had new insight into what was going on in his mind. And maybe there was something I could do about it.

~

The first thing I saw when I stepped into the coffee shop was Dallas filling up the sugar. To be fair, I was looking for her, and it was pretty easy to home in on the most beautiful woman in the room. Any room. I felt a wave a guilt that I'd never been here before. Maybe Dallas was right that I didn't have to put football first every single time. I pushed that thought aside because it didn't do me any good. All of that was in the past, and I was here on a mission.

"Hey."

Dallas jumped at the sound of my voice, dropping the sugar packets. She moved quickly to pick them up, and I bent down to help her.

"Can you talk?"

"I can't." She grabbed the packets I had already picked up. "I'm working."

I looked around the room. There was a couple in the corner, both with books open in front of them, and that was it. Dallas stood up and dropped the packets into the basket with a bit more force than necessary.

"Then I'd like to place an order."

She sighed then turned to me. She didn't look pleased. "Fine. What can I get you?"

"An iced latte with almond milk."

"That's my order."

I smiled—okay, maybe it was more of a smirk—but it didn't soften her glare. She moved quickly to the counter and rang up my order.

"That'll be seven fifty."

Wow. This place wasn't cheap. I handed her the cash, and she put my change on the counter so she didn't have to touch me. She looked more relaxed—or at least less like she wanted to have security remove me from the premises—but she still wasn't interested in talking. She kept her focus on making my latte.

"Josh came to visit me."

"What?" That got her attention. "Josh is in town? Now? So is Gabby."

"Yes, I know." The smirk came back. "Thanks for that."

Dallas dropped the espresso into the cup of ice. I could see the wheels turning in her head. I knew her so well, I could read her like a book.

"What are the odds they'd both be in LA the same weekend?" I put my elbows on the counter and leaned forward. "We should parent trap them."

"There is no 'we.' We broke up."

"I meant more the collective *we*. We as a community of concerned citizens, best friends, and brothers should parent trap them."

"And I meant that I don't think we should meddle."

Yeah, she was cute. No denying that. There wasn't anything I could do about it. I needed to push forward.

"They were always meddling with us."

"Yeah, and look how that turned out." Dallas put the cup on the counter in front of me. "Lids and straws are behind you."

I'd known this might take some convincing. I was prepared to bring out the big guns.

"Josh isn't over Gabby. Like very *not* over her. Like this could be the love of his life." I wanted to look away. There was too much to see in her gaze; it suddenly all felt too heavy. "And if there's even a chance she feels the same way, shouldn't we try?"

That last bit got to her. The wheels were turning faster.

"All we need to do is put them in the same room." I walked back to get a lid. If I kept moving, then I wouldn't feel trapped in her gaze. "If they hit it off again, great. If not, oh well."

Dallas wasn't bending. She was curious but suspicious. I was close enough that I could tip her over the edge. I sat down at the table nearest the counter and took a nice long sip of my coffee.

"So, you work here all weekend?"

She almost laughed—I knew she did. I would recognize that glint in her eye until the day I died.

"Fine." She held in her smile, but I'd take it. "What did you have in mind?"

CHAPTER THIRTY-THREE

DALLAS

Another party, another frat. I wasn't sure why or how I kept finding myself at loud parties, frat or otherwise. There was the excuse of fixing up Josh and Gabby, but I was already regretting our plan. Couldn't we have coincidentally been at the same McDonald's? Or crossed paths at a 7-Eleven? Anything that involved fewer strobe lights and an easy escape route. To make it even more memorable—or annoying, depending on your perspective—it was a Halloween party. Something I'd learned about life in California was no one else put as much effort into costumes and celebrating the theatrical. There was so much sweat and glitter at this party. A fascinating but terrifying combination.

Gabby was dressed up as a riff on a mad scientist, complete with white lab coat and safety goggles. I wore my old cheerleader outfit because that was as much effort as I was going to put into this plan. Well, that and tricking my best friend into going to a random frat party then making sure we somehow, casually, not planned at all, ran into Drayton and Josh.

"So this is Miley's cousin's boyfriend's friend's party?" Gabby was still struggling to understand the connection, and fair enough. I was also having trouble remembering the story we'd come up with.

"Yeah, she'll be here any minute."

I scanned the room. Josh and Drayton were tall, so they should be easy to spot. Of course, then I'd have to find a way to subtly signal our location. It was probably too late now to invent a secret whistle.

"Do you think my costume's too niche?" She straightened out her jacket.

"No." Absolutely. Her costume was designed for the 1 percent. "You look great."

There was a noticeable murmur through the crowd. The people around us, mainly the women, shifted positions, and my Drayton radar went off. Gabby didn't notice because she didn't know the signs. The crowd parted, and Drayton, dressed as a firefighter, and Josh, also decked out in a white lab coat, were suddenly in front of us.

"Hey, Cheer," Drayton said. "Good to see you."

"Gabby?" Josh's jaw practically hit the floor. It was like a Looney Tunes cartoon.

"Josh? Is that . . . what?" It was very rare that I saw my best friend gobsmacked and unable to form sentences. Gabby was the ever-together, always-ready-with-a-quip, never-flustered pillar. Her cheeks were suddenly bright red, and I was pretty sure I could see the pulse in her neck. "Hi."

Drayton and I looked at each other and both almost burst out laughing. I knew that Gabby missed Josh, maybe regretted her decision to call it quits so soon, but I hadn't been convinced this was the right move. Setting up friends could go horribly wrong. But the first few seconds of their reunion said otherwise. This had been the right call. I had to admit that I'd been wrong. Not out loud, of course.

"Is. What? Hi." Okay, Josh was in the same boat. Stellar in academics, perhaps lacking slightly in the face-to-face.

"Hang on. Are you also an environmental scientist . . ."

"Who has slowly gone mad because . . ."

"No one's listening!" They finished that last bit together.

Then both of them collapsed in laughter. They were so happy to see each other. The last couple of days, Gabby had mostly seemed like her usual happy, thoughtful self. I knew she missed Josh, but most of her energy had been spent keeping me distracted and occupied. She'd seemed like Gabby. Funny, reliable, kind. But watching her as she tried to process the fact that Josh was standing right in front of her and that they could still finish each other's sentences, I realized I'd only been seeing one part of her.

Josh brought out something in her that was only for Josh. I could witness it, I could be amazed by its glow, but it was all Josh.

"What are you up to?" Gabby reached out to touch his arm but pulled her hand back.

"How have you been?" Josh tried to take her hand but had second thoughts when she retreated.

"I got that internship in the lab." Gabby beamed, and I felt a sudden pang in my heart. I didn't know. I knew she had applied, but I hadn't followed up, and she hadn't said.

"Hell yeah! I knew you would."

"Really?" She bit her lip, looking shy. "I was so nervous. It was pretty competitive."

"Yeah, but you're pretty brilliant." His voice was low. Gabby blushed again. Hell, I was almost blushing.

Drayton and I really shouldn't be here. We needed to give them space. We shouldn't be watching them or feeling proud that we'd brought them together again. And I needed to get away from Drayton because it hurt to watch this reunion and know it was never going to be us because it was about more than timing and schedules.

"Can I get you a warm beer?"

Gabby giggled. Giggled! "I'd love that."

They walked off toward the keg, and Drayton and I were left on our own. I was suddenly pissed with myself for wearing this costume. I'd known I was going to see him and still I'd decided to wear the outfit that reminded us of meeting and falling in love. Hell, he called me Cheer. I didn't want him to think I'd worn it for him.

Drayton was watching me, but I couldn't read his expression, and that made me even more uncertain.

"Mission accomplished," I said.

I didn't wait for him to respond. I needed to move; I needed to be away from him. But I didn't get far before regretting my quick retreat. This whole plan had been his idea, and it had worked. Gabby and Josh were happy. I should say something more, not let him think I was mad at him. I turned back around and saw him. He was talking to a blond woman, lithe and pretty, wearing a chef's hat, a red corset, and little else. The bright red kiss mark on her inner thigh was very visible. They had their heads close together so they could hear over the loud music. Or maybe not. Maybe they had other reasons for standing so close.

None of my business. Not my concern. I turned my back and walked away.

CHAPTER THIRTY-FOUR

DRAYTON

"Want to guess?" Charlotte spun around so I could get a good look at her costume.

Chef's hat and red corset. *Ratatouille* seemed unlikely. Swedish chef? Maybe, but I wasn't sure sexy Muppet was a solid plan.

"You're a chef . . ."

She turned her leg slightly so I could see her inner thigh. A bright red lip mark.

"And kiss . . ." It took a second more, but I got it. "Chef's kiss. That's funny."

Charlotte laughed and gently punched my shoulder. "Who says jocks are dumb?"

"Every day I fight stereotypes."

I did a quick scan of the room. I'd been trailing Dallas, trying to find a second to talk after she'd bailed, but Charlotte had stopped me. While Gabby and Josh were talking, it had been so awkward. Not for them; they were happy as hell to see each other and absolute proof that we'd been right to meddle. It was us—Dallas and me—who were stuck. We were both standing there like we didn't know what to do with our hands. Like it was our first coed party and somebody had suggested spin the bottle. Then things got stranger still when Gabby and Josh went looking for a beer.

It didn't seem right to be standing so close to Dallas and not have my arm over her shoulder. That was the most natural thing to do when I saw her—touch her, claim her as my own—and I didn't care how Neanderthal that sounded. But as soon as our reunited lovebirds walked off, Dallas disappeared into the crowd, and I got distracted by Charlotte and her almost not-there costume.

I spotted Dallas across the room talking to some guy. He was dressed like a gladiator and kind of looked like that Mescal dude from that show. He was standing close to her, too damn close, and looked about ready to touch her. Not on my watch!

"So random bumping into you."

I registered Charlotte's voice but not her words. The Mescal wannabe put his hand on Dallas's arm.

"Yeah, me too." I stepped away while trying to keep my eyes on Dallas. "I'll catch you later."

There was a surge of people moving through the room as I made my way across. A group of sexy zombies who I hoped had come together, otherwise that was a very strange coincidence or the meet-cute of a rom-com, pushed me out of the way. By the time I made it across the room, Dallas was gone.

I found her in the next room, sitting alone on the couch. She had her legs crossed and held her drink with both hands resting in her lap. Her dark hair was pulled into a ponytail, finishing off the cheerleader look perfectly. It was the best and the worst feeling in the world knowing her hair was so silky smooth. And that it smelled like citrus and honey. She was watching the party with mild amusement like a biologist observing animals in the wild.

"Nice costume." When I sat down beside her, I made sure there was at least a foot between us. I didn't trust myself to get any closer.

She looked at me but didn't respond. She turned her gaze first to the cup in her lap then back to the party. Her defensive wall was up. Before we got together, we'd argued a bunch. There was a lot of back-and-forth. Dallas always spoke her mind, called me on my bullshit, never let me or anyone else get away with anything. Dallas being quiet, not telling me to back off or hit the road, was a sign, but I didn't know if it was good or bad.

"We should be friends."

"We can't be friends." She still wouldn't look my way.

"Why not?"

"You know why."

"No. I don't."

That did it. Dallas threw me her fiercest *don't be an idiot* glare. I didn't like that the only way to get a reaction was to rile her up, but desperate times and all that.

"Dallas, I know our schedules made it impossible to date." I was still getting the glare, but it was less pissed. Slightly. "But we're mature adults. We didn't cheat or try to hurt each other." On instinct, I grabbed her hand, and she quickly pulled it back. "You're the only person who makes LA feel like home."

She was about to say something but bit her bottom lip instead. I could see the light tinge of color on her cheeks, and her eyes darted over my face. She was second-guessing herself, her own instincts. Dallas was bold and brave, and I hated that she wasn't doing or saying exactly what she thought. Or that she felt she couldn't do that with me. We had always been honest with each other, which was why I didn't want to lose her friendship. Dallas was one of the only people I could be completely myself with, and I didn't want that to disappear.

We were stuck in that limbo of sitting side by side but not talking when Gabby and Josh returned holding hands. Of course. Dallas and I should go into business as matchmakers.

"We're going to get a late bite, if you want to come?" Gabby smiled at both of us. I guessed that meant she had forgiven me for breaking up with Dallas, even if it was a mutual decision.

"I'm pretty tired, and I have work tomorrow." Dallas smiled at Gabby and looked genuinely pleased with how things had worked out, but she also didn't look my way.

"Yeah, I told a couple guys I'd meet up with them here." I noticed Dallas look my way, a scowl that she quickly covered up. Did she know that was a lie? "And an early workout."

"If you're both sure?" Gabby smiled at Josh, not even pretending to care that we weren't joining. "Guess that gives us time to catch up."

Dallas laughed. "Enjoy the reunion."

"And, you know." Josh kept his eyes locked on Gabby's. "I can drive you to the airport. If Dallas is busy."

I knew Dallas was considering saying that she wasn't busy at all and was really looking forward to an airport visit. Instead, she smiled again.

"Thanks, Josh. Yeah, tomorrow is hectic. That would really help."

I ended their puppy dog stare by pulling Josh into a hug. "Braving LAX? Now, that's love."

Dallas stood up and hugged Gabby. "Guess this is goodbye. Have a good flight back East. I can leave your stuff with the porter at our dorm, if that's easier?"

"Perfect, you're the best," Gabby said.

Their hug went on longer. They whispered into each other's ears and laughed. No idea what they said, but it was good to see them together. Dallas was definitely happier when she had access to Gabby.

"Thanks for parent trapping us." Josh took his turn hugging Dallas.

"Glad it worked out." I truly meant it. This was the one good thing that had happened in my life in weeks. The win, even if it wasn't directly mine, felt good.

"Thank you for being a great best friend." Gabby went in for another hug because apparently one wasn't enough.

"A phenomenal best friend."

"The most phenomenal."

Dallas and I watched them walk away, hands clasped, then the awkward settled in again. I was about to offer to get her a drink and talk more, but she cut me off before I got started.

"Guess that's my cue to leave." She started toward the door then turned back. "Hope you and the couple of guys have fun tonight."

Then she was gone, and I didn't feel as confident in my choices as I'd thought. Maybe I was being selfish in wanting to be friends. But maybe I'd messed everything up, and now my attempt at a Hail Mary hadn't landed either.

CHAPTER THIRTY-FIVE

DALLAS

We were back in the dorm common room, our home away from home, this time so Miley could do my makeup.

"Couldn't we do this in our room?" I rolled my eyes up, focusing on the ceiling, and tilted my head back as Miley applied eyeliner. "Isn't that one of the advantages to having a dorm room?"

"The lighting is much better in here." Her hand grabbed my chin. "And hold still. This is precise work."

She finished one eye then moved to the other. I could feel her drawing soft wings at the outer edges. Miley tipped my head from side to side to admire her work.

"Green, I think." She held up a palette of eyeshadow beside my face then nodded. "Yes, green."

She was taking this very seriously. I almost laughed but didn't want to mess with her concentration. I closed my eyes as she got to work. I'd never really been a fan of the salon or spa experience, but Miley gently using a soft brush over my eyelids was remarkably soothing.

"Aren't you going to tell me where we're going?"

"Nope."

Miley loved to talk through plans, discuss all potential outcomes and who we might encounter. Secretive Miley had me worried.

"I still think a night in and a movie is a good idea." I opened my eyes when I sensed Miley stepping back. "Watching *Ever After* is a perfect birthday treat. Or *Reservoir Dogs*."

I liked the idea of watching something sweet and romantic, but sweary and violent was probably closer to my mood. I flipped my phone over—no messages—then put it back on the table.

"I just don't feel like celebrating." Or leaving the dorm. Or talking to people. Or pretending I was in a good mood.

"Too bad. I promised Gabby I wouldn't let you sit alone in your room wondering whether or not the hot jock ex is going to reach out."

"He probably won't." I cared, and I really wished I didn't.

"Or obsessing about the dean's master class."

"I'm not obsessing! I'm . . . manifesting."

I decided I should put together a vision board. Me dancing. Me with the dean. No Drayton anywhere.

"I hope you get it. But even if you don't." She took hold of my chin again and forced me to look at her. "You're still very talented, and you don't need Dean Adams or CalArts or anybody but you to define that."

I didn't know what to say. I wasn't sure I believed her, but it meant the world that Miley did. Things might feel shaky right now, but Miley believing in me was a start.

“Okay, my masterpiece is complete.”

Miley handed me the mirror for my first look. It was more makeup than I would normally wear, but it didn’t look like too much. The eyeliner swept up at the edges into soft wings. The green eyeshadow was subtle and brought out the color of my eyes.

“Wow. I love it!”

Miley looked very pleased, both with her artistry and my reaction.

“You deserve to feel special tonight. Because one day, before we know it, we’re going to be old ladies. Just bags of bones, while the earth is burning down around us, and the only thing that’s going to keep us going are the memories of our youth!”

Miley was determined to always be a little extra, and I loved her for it. More than half the time I rolled my eyes affectionately at the things she said, but sometimes they really landed. Especially on nights like this, when I was feeling a bit heartbroken and adrift, I needed to hear those things.

“Okay. You’re right.” I put the mirror down and took a deep breath. “Also, Gabby always says because society doesn’t allow women to age, celebrating your birthday is actually defying the patriarchy.”

“That’s like verbatim what I said.” She reached into her makeup bag and pulled out two tubes of lipstick. “Final touch. Do you want fire-engine red or fuck-me red?”

“Does it have to be either?”

“Think about what color you prefer to leave behind.”

“Leave behind? Where?”

“On whoever you decide to kiss tonight.”

“Miley, I am not kissing anyone tonight. Definitely no kissing.”

“Fuck-me red it is, then.”

~

Miley led me into the building blindfolded, holding my hand and giving explicit instructions.

"Walking, walking, step. Raise your foot higher. No, like a normal-size step. Another step. Step."

She'd made me put on the blindfold as soon as we got in the Uber in case I recognized any landmarks along the way. I didn't want to disappoint her, but I was pretty sure I'd recognized our destination as soon as the car came to a stop.

"Okay, just need you to step through the door and . . . voilà!"

Miley pulled off the blindfold to reveal Sally's Saloon in all its country-and-western glory.

"Surprise!"

A small group—mostly from our dance program and a few people from the dorm—stood in front of me. Skyler was standing at the back, wearing a cowboy hat and looking very rodeo ready. Seriously, these CalArts kids definitely loved a costume.

"We thought you might be homesick for them Colorado roots." Miley spoke in a truly terrible Southern accent.

"Once again, it was like a normal-size town."

All my friends came in for a hug and a *happy birthday*. Miley clapped her hands, very pleased with her party-planning skills. I didn't have the heart to tell her that her scheme to distract me from thoughts of Drayton had brought me to the bar where we'd had a truly magical evening. I decided that Miley never needed to know because this was the perfect example of *it's the thought that counts*, and I loved seeing my friend happy.

"Hey, happy birthday." Skyler gave me a nice, not-awkward-at-all hug and handed me a card. "You don't have to read it now."

I turned the envelope over in my hand. He had surprisingly nice penmanship.

"Aw, who knew you were so sentimental?"

"Literally everyone." Miley looked at me like I might be insane.

She picked up two cowboy hats from the table, putting one on my head and the other on her own. Then she took the Polaroid camera from my bag.

"Before we're sweaty." She held the camera above us for the perfect selfie angle. "Say cheese!"

The flash went off, and I was momentarily blinded while the camera spat out the photo. The room around us felt chaotic, and I was almost overwhelmed. People were doing shots, dancing, shouting over the loud music. A couple at the table next to us were furiously making out. I was on the edge, the precipice that decided if I needed to run back to isolation and nurse my wounds or if it was time to dive right in and let the night bring me whatever it chose.

"Cuuuute!" Miley held up the photo. It hadn't fully developed yet, but even under the grey haze I could see our smiling, happy faces. "All right, y'all. Line dancin's a-waitin'!"

All the dancers in our midst reacted exactly as expected: they jumped up and down and ran, not walked, to the dance floor.

"You two go ahead." Skyler waved a hand. "It's not my thing. Seriously."

"Okay, pal. Your loss." I threw him a pistol salute, pretending to shoot at him as I backed away.

"Boo! Hipster!" Miley cupped her mouth as she shouted at Skyler. He was laughing as she walked away.

We took over the dance floor, which wasn't surprising in the least, but no one minded. We actually spent time teaching others the routine, keeping it moving and having fun. I couldn't completely lose myself in it, though. My phone didn't buzz, but that didn't stop me from checking. No messages from Drayton. No calls.

"Earth to Dallas!"

Miley wrapped her arm around my waist and spun me around. She dipped me back, and I was laughing by the time I stood back up. The night had only just begun, and I needed to push all other thoughts aside. I briefly glanced over at Skyler. He was leaning against a wall watching us and laughing. And then I let myself be a college student for the next couple hours. It was exactly what I had been missing.

CHAPTER THIRTY-SIX

DRAYTON

There was nothing quite like a good old-fashioned Texas tailgate. Especially when you were celebrating a victory on the field. Yeah, you heard that one right. We won. Kicked their sorry asses up and down. I was on the sidelines, but it felt great. My man Zach caught the last throw and ran to the end zone like his life depended on it.

I clinked my beer bottle against his. "You did it, man. That last run was perfection."

"Yeah, it felt pretty great." Zach laughed. This was the most relaxed I'd seen him in weeks. "We're finally on our way."

Our team and staff had taken over a chunk of the hotel parking lot. A bunch of locals joined in and turned it into a real celebration. I was happy, but I felt a bit like an observer. I checked my phone. I still had time before the day officially ended. If I could figure out what I wanted or needed to say. Or if she wanted to hear from me at all.

"If you miss her then reach out." Zach leaned up against the truck beside me. "You're checking that phone like every ten minutes."

"It's not that simple."

"Yeah, you've said. But this is getting painful to watch."

I let my head drop back. I liked it better when jocks were all macho and didn't talk about their feelings.

"Today's her birthday."

"Bro, you've got it! That's a perfect excuse to call."

"But I'm giving her space." I put emphasis on *space*. "She said she doesn't want to be friends."

"No shit." He laughed and slapped my back. "It's literally impossible to be friends with an ex."

A couple of locals walked past, slowly so we could admire their swaying hips. Zach nodded his appreciation then turned back to me.

"How's your knee feeling?"

"Better. I'm officially cleared to play as of yesterday."

"Hell yeah!" We clinked bottles again. "That's gotta feel good."

"Not really. I'm still second-string."

I couldn't hide my disappointment when Coach gave me that news. I didn't curse or give him a hard time, but it was obvious. He gave me the speech about patience and Ryan playing a good game, and there wasn't much I could do but suck it up and listen.

"Yeah, but you're good to play." He paused for a moment. "Does this mean you're not transferring?"

I took a swig of my beer. "Still weighing my options."

"Dude, come on." Zach shook his head. "Why?"

"It doesn't look like I'm going to get any playing time with Ryan starting for the rest of the year."

"Dude, you've worked so hard to recover, keep it going." Zach called me *dude* so often I was starting to wonder if he remembered my name. "You literally have what it takes to go pro. Not everyone does. I don't. That's why I'm getting my MBA next."

I almost did a spit take with my beer. An MBA? How had that never come up in conversation? I didn't have the chance to ask anything more because Charlotte sidled up beside me.

"I heard you're thinking about transferring."

Was that all anyone was talking about? There had to be better things to discuss than what was happening with the second-string quarterback.

"Undecided."

"It's pretty stupid to quit something before you've given it a chance, but it's your prerogative."

"Wow. You never hold back."

She had changed out of her team uniform into jeans and a T-shirt that showed off her arms. I had a new appreciation for Charlotte after seeing her Halloween costume.

"Why would I? Life's too short."

Charlotte had a great laugh. Confident, assured. Just like her.

"Did you forget that you were the one ranting at me about getting an alternate plan because I was screwing up my USC one?"

"And now we're at the next stage. Let's see how well you pay attention this time."

"Oookaaay." Zach pushed himself off the truck. He smiled as he shook his head. "I'm going to get a drink. Anyone want anything? No? Good."

What was up with him? I turned back to Charlotte, and she was still smiling. It was a good smile.

"Was that your girlfriend at the Halloween party?"

"Ex-girlfriend."

"I'm sorry to hear that."

"No, you're not."

Her smile got wider, and I was surprised by how much I liked what I saw.

The moment, or whatever it was, was broken by loud cheers. Ryan had arrived. He walked into the center of the party, arms raised in triumph, soaking it all in.

"The man of the hour! Ryan Decker!" Marcus pumped his fist in the air.

"Man of the hour? I wouldn't say that." He put a hand on his chest, playing the humble card. "But ESPN did call me the comeback of the decade!"

"They said year," Charlotte mumbled beside me.

We watched as the cheers continued, and Ryan moved around the circle offering high fives and fist bumps. He stopped when he got to us. He threw an arm over Charlotte's shoulders.

"Aw, how sweet. Second-string taking my sloppy seconds."

"Screw you, Ryan."

She slammed her empty cup into Ryan's chest, shoving him back. She pushed past him and stormed off. Ryan tried to chase after her, but I got in his way.

"Back off."

He smirked at me, acting like he had something smart to say, but he didn't argue and didn't follow when I went after her.

I caught up with Charlotte at the edge of the parking lot, touching her arm so she would turn around.

"Are you okay? Can I walk you to your room?"

She shook her head. She looked more pissed than rattled. "You don't have to do that."

"I want to."

I did. It surprised me how much I did.

"Then I'll let you."

She took a few steps backward until she was certain I was following her, then we headed inside.

~

Charlotte's room was on the tenth floor. We spent the elevator ride up talking team politics and what I needed to do for physio now that I was approved to play. It felt like business as usual. We didn't touch, but we stood so close that I could feel the heat radiating from her body. When the doors opened, we moved into the hallway, keeping in close proximity.

"If you transfer, you'll end up being a big fish in a small pond. That's not going to get you to the NFL."

"Maybe, maybe not." I let my arm brush against hers. It wasn't entirely on purpose but not exactly an accident.

"Is this about your ex?"

"What? No." Where had that come from? Why would Dallas have anything to do with my decision to transfer? "I just need more playing time."

"That's bullshit. Ryan's leaving next year. You'd be up as first-string."

"You're a real hard-ass, you know."

"Did I mention I have brothers?" She laughed, and it was easy to join in. Charlotte was easy to hang out with despite her need to constantly ride my ass. "What are you really running from?"

Well, that was a loaded question. I sighed.

"I'm scared that I'll never fully get back to feeling like myself.

I'll lose football and have to figure out a plan B that doesn't involve going pro."

She put a hand on my arm, leaned in, and spoke softly. "We won't let that happen."

We were at her door. She smiled at me again, and I really wanted to believe everything she said. It would feel great to be in that space again. We stood staring at each other, not exactly sure what should come next or who should make the first move.

"Do you want to come in for a little bit?" There was that fucking beautiful smile again. A lick of her lips. "I promise to play nice."

I wasn't sure who made the first move or if we were both drawn in, like gravity taking over, at the same time. We got so close I could feel her breath, her breasts up against my chest. But that second-long pause reminded me where I was and that this was all too familiar.

"I can't." I'd been here before, done this before, and this wasn't the person I was anymore. It wasn't who I wanted to be. "I'm sorry."

I took a step back. Charlotte looked disappointed but smiled anyway.

"Don't worry. I get it." She put a hand on my chest. "It would probably get real messy real fast."

"Exactly." I laughed because it was true. I'd done messy; I'd been messy. I was trying for something else these days. "I'll see you tomorrow?"

"Yeah." She opened her door then pointed at me. "Don't make it weird."

"Wouldn't dream of it."

She stepped inside and closed the door, leaving me alone in

the hallway with my thoughts. I headed back to the elevator and pulled out my phone while I waited. Dallas's message thread was still sitting there, waiting for me to make a decision. I was still staring at it, locked in indecision, when the elevator door opened.

CHAPTER THIRTY-SEVEN

DALLAS

I'd stopped counting the shots a while back. My guess was somewhere between three and ten. It was my own fault for letting Miley take the reins on the night's activities, but I had no regrets. Well, to be fair, I might have a lot of regrets and a nasty headache tomorrow, but I was trying to live in the present, enjoy the night and not worry about whatever came next. I was trying and mostly succeeding. Miley had made a game of it and said every time I looked at my phone and got sad eyes—her words, not mine—because Drayton hadn't messaged, I had to take a shot. That was the short version of why I was many shots in.

"Thank you for tonight." I wasn't slurring my words, so that was a good sign. "You've turned this into a really good birthday."

"You're so worth celebrating! Here's to you finally figuring that out." She raised her shot glass, so I raised mine too. "Bottoms up!"

The tequila and lime made me wince—we weren't ordering top-shelf booze—which made Miley laugh and hug me. I wasn't sure why she'd decided to make me her project this year, but I was really glad she had. I didn't want to think about what my first term at CalArts would have been like without her.

"I think I met the cowboy of my dreams." Stella was suddenly beside us, arms thrown over both of our shoulders. She pulled us in to create a huddle. "Look, but, you know, don't look. Look casual."

"Which is it? Look or don't look?" I tried to glance over her shoulder, but she pulled me back in.

"Look, but casual-like." She attempted a very casual shoulder check and failed miserably. "He's the one in the cowboy hat and plaid shirt."

"You're going to have to be more specific, sweetie." Miley gave Stella a small hip bump that almost knocked her over.

"He said he wants to take me to his rodeo." Stella paused so she could think that through. "Or show me his rodeo. Or something. Do you show someone a rodeo? Is that how it works?"

"For the record, I don't think it's his rodeo the cowboy wants to show you."

"For the record, I don't think anyone here is an actual cowboy."

"Shhh. Don't spoil the fun." Stella attempted to hip bump me, and it went as well as expected.

"Okay, you're moving on to a water course." Miley propped Stella back up. "You are officially cut off from cowboys and rodeos."

"Aw, boo." Stella pouted, stamped her foot, then started laughing. She hugged Miley then me and seemed to forget all about her mysterious cowboy.

I went to get Stella her much-needed water. The bar was packed, and this time I not only recognized faces but also knew some names. So different than when Drayton and I were here together. Drayton. I resisted the urge to pull my phone out, only partly because I was done with shots for a while. I felt so torn. I wanted to hear from him but also didn't know if that was a good idea. Yet it was doing a number on me that he hadn't sent a message. Was it desperate to want even a quick, no-nonsense acknowledgment that it was my birthday? If he wanted to be friends, wasn't that what friends did? At the bare minimum?

I didn't know if it was possible to be his friend, but I wanted it. I couldn't imagine my life without Drayton in it. I respected his opinion. I cared about his welfare and his career. He listened to me whine about things. Made me laugh. Understood my ambition because he was ambitious too. All those traits we want in a friend. Those were also good boyfriend traits, but we couldn't seem to do that for each other. I needed to decide if I could be his friend and not want that extra part. If I would be okay not having that with Drayton. If we were together, I would always come second to football. And my heart hurt. And that wasn't cool.

The DJ stopped the music, followed by someone tapping the microphone to check if it was on.

"Hey, folks." The DJ stood center stage. "We've got something special for y'all." And yet another terrible Southern accent. "Give it up for . . . this guy."

The crowd clapped and threw out a few whoops as Skyler walked to the mic.

"What's going on?" I handed Stella her water.

"No idea." Miley shrugged her shoulders. "Did he bring that acoustic guitar with him?"

Skyler adjusted his guitar strap and smiled into the crowd. He looked comfortable onstage, like it was his happy place.

"So it's my friend's birthday tonight." More whoops from the crowd and a few *happy birthdays*. "She's crazy talented and so brave. Moved from a farm to the big city to pursue her dreams."

Miley cheered, and I rolled my eyes. That joke was never going to die.

"And because I'm dick broke and couldn't get her a gift, I'm going to be super cringe and sing a song she once told me she liked."

It was the song I'd heard dozens of times. The first song of his that he'd played in the café, the one from the music video. Yet it sounded different this time. It was only Skyler and his guitar, and it really felt like he was singing directly to me. For me. He'd dedicated the song to me for my birthday, but it wasn't about me. He'd told me the story of his ex-girlfriend and why he'd written it. But it resonated more. It hit differently. Every time I'd listened to it before, Drayton and I had been together. We weren't always in a good place and maybe struggling to find time, but we'd been in a relationship. I understood heartache now. I knew what it felt like to want something, someone, and the pain of not getting it.

"I think he likes you," Miley whispered into my ear. I didn't have to look at her to know she was smiling.

"You're a handful."

Skyler played the last chord, and everyone applauded. I saw him scan the room then smile when he spotted me. I suddenly felt shy, exposed, so I grabbed my camera and snapped a photo. It gave me something to do and put something—a literal camera—between us. I had no idea what to do next and might have been stuck in a state of shock if my phone hadn't started ringing.

Drayton.

Shit.

I'd been checking all night for a message, but now I wasn't sure what to do. I looked up at Skyler—he was still onstage and looking at me—then back at my phone. The DJ put on a new song, and the crowd shifted back into dance mode. I used the flurry of activity to slip away.

"Hello?" Drayton sounded confused, maybe nervous, that I'd answered then hadn't said anything. "Dallas?"

"Hey." I found a quiet corner in the bar.

"I just wanted to call and say happy birthday."

I still loved his voice. It was deep and rich. If I wasn't careful, it might still give me shivers.

"Cutting it close, QB."

"I know." He paused. Maybe cleared his throat. "But I wasn't sure if you wanted to hear from me?"

"No, I'm glad you called." I *was* glad that he'd called. I wanted to hear his voice. "It's funny. I just heard this song that made me think of you." I wondered how often that would happen. Would every song about heartache make me think about Drayton? "I don't know why I said that. Miley got me drunk."

"Are you okay?" He was being protective Drayton. He was always going to look out for me. "Do you need me to call a ride?"

"No, no. I'm with friends." I almost added, *Because I have friends now!* Things had changed since we'd last spoken. Maybe I was even a different person. "They're all taking great care of me."

"Good." He sounded so far away. I didn't know where he was because I refused to look up the USC schedule. It was strange to be so wrapped up in someone else's life and then have that door slammed shut. "So are you excited to go home?"

"Actually, I'm not going back."

"What? But you love Thanksgiving."

I could picture the furrow in his brow as he said that. Confused and worried that he had missed something important.

"Yeah, but it's so expensive and so close to Christmas. It didn't make sense."

It was going to be my first Thanksgiving without family, however small my family might be, and it would be an adjustment. I'd told myself that time alone was a good thing. I could work on assignments, maybe get some time in the studio.

He didn't say anything for a couple of seconds, and I worried that he was distracted. That his attention had been drawn away by something else. Someone else.

"Funny enough, I'm staying behind too. For practice."

"You are?" That could make sense. Football and Thanksgiving often went together.

"Yeah. I'm off Thursday, obviously. I heard the city gets pretty quiet."

No one could see me in my corner, but I bit my bottom lip anyway to hide my smile. "Yeah, probably less traffic."

"We could spend it together?" He sounded almost hopeful. Did he sound hopeful? "At my aunt's Airbnb."

That made me catch my breath. His aunt's Airbnb. The site of skinny-dipping and those little moments we'd shared while falling in love.

"Okay. I'll bring the turkey, and we'll have a Friendsgiving."

"Sure." Drayton laughed. "That's what we'll do."

I shouldn't be excited. We were spending Thanksgiving together because we were two friends without family. It was a Friendsgiving, nothing more.

I put that thought on repeat as I walked back to Miley and the others. Drayton and I were working at being friends and enjoying each other's company. It was a Friendsgiving, nothing more.

CHAPTER THIRTY-EIGHT

DALLAS

I stood outside the Airbnb, taking a few extra deep breaths for good measure. The week before the holiday had been busy with assignments and prep for the end-of-term showcase. I felt like I was running around like a madwoman trying to get everything done, including shopping for this meal. Then, suddenly, it was over. It was Thursday, everything was crossed off my list, and I was standing on the front steps and thinking about what might, or might not, happen in the next few hours.

He answered the door quickly, like maybe he'd been waiting on the other side, with a big smile. Unsurprisingly, Drayton Lahey remained a very handsome man.

"I come bearing gifts." I held up the bag of groceries, which was no easy feat considering it contained a small turkey.

"Just in time, Cheer." He stepped back so I could enter. "I finished watching the 'how to cook a turkey' YouTube videos, so we're all set."

"Should we follow up with a 'how to prevent salmonella' video?"

"Have some faith, Cheer." He took the bags and headed toward the kitchen.

The place looked just as I remembered it: cozy and comfortable but with a touch of elegance. Clean lines on the furniture and art on the walls. Drayton moved around the place with ease. He wore sweatpants and a USC football T-shirt, no socks. Everything hugged him perfectly, showing off his biceps and slender hips. I needed to keep my distance today. Maybe make sure we always had a table or counter between us.

"How long did it take to get here?"

He was back in the kitchen, groceries on the counter. He slipped an apron over his head and tied the strings behind him. That shouldn't have looked as sexy as it did.

"Twenty minutes." I sat on one of the stools at the breakfast bar. "You were right about there being no traffic."

"LA's easy to get around when no one else is on the road."

"Guess now we know our relationship would have survived the zombie apocalypse."

His eyes shot up, but it wasn't a *too soon* look. He was surprised, but he laughed, shook his head, and started prepping the bird.

"Pass the garlic."

"Yes, chef." I jumped to attention and pulled the garlic from the shopping bag.

"Thank you, chef."

We had clearly both decided to cast aside any tension. It was so easy to fall back into our banter and return to friendship basics. It was so natural. There was a lot of back-and-forth as we went through the recipes, including an animated discussion of what a "bias cut" meant for the carrots. After one call to Drayton's mom and two to Nathan, we got the bird into the oven with stuffing and vegetables cooking on the stovetop. Somehow, we accomplished all of that with no injuries and no arguments, only one broken plate and a lesson about putting hot dinnerware in cold water. I had been so worked up about not having anything to say to each other, but the conversation was as relaxed and free-flowing as always.

"I can't believe I'm in this house again. The location of my greatest embarrassment. I thought I would never look your aunt in the eye again!"

I held my hands over my cheeks, worried that I might be blushing. My face felt a bit flushed, but that might have been the wine.

"She was supposed to be in London!"

"Drayton, I was naked in her pool. She came home and found a complete stranger naked in her pool."

"Well, you left an impression?"

I threw a carrot stick at him. He, of course, easily caught it and popped it into his mouth.

Drayton could make anything fun. Getting caught here naked was a top-five embarrassing moment for me, but he'd somehow turned it into a funny, charming story about meeting his aunt. Admittedly, she had been lovely about the whole thing and welcomed me into her home, albeit after I was toweled off and dressed. That incident had also let me see another side to Drayton. He played the bad boy at school or on the field, but he was kind and sweet with his aunt. Played with her kid. It's entirely possible I was already falling in love with him before that night, but there was no denying it was happening after it.

That night had held a lot of firsts for me. I'd let my boundaries down. Trusted Drayton to keep me safe. I'd lived such a careful existence before him. He really made me see all the possibilities.

A phone rang, and we both looked around.

"Yours or mine?" Drayton reached into his pocket.

"Mine." I held it up to show him the screen: Unknown Caller.

"You gonna risk it?

"Sure, why not?" I shrugged my shoulders. "I'm all about the brave these days." I hit the green button. "Hi, this is Dallas."

"Hi, Dallas. This is Edgar de la Luna."

Breathe. Breathe. Remember to breathe.

I must have made a face—possibly one of horror—because Drayton mouthed, *Are you okay?*

I might have nodded. Or maybe not. Maybe this was all a fever dream, and I was still back in Archwood with malaria. Because, yes, Colorado was a hotbed of malaria.

"You came to an open call a few weeks ago."

"Oh. Hi. How are you?" Did that sound suitably casual? Totally believable?

I put my phone on the counter and clicked on the speaker. I looked at Drayton with wide oh-my-god eyes so he would understand my excitement.

"Doing great." Edgar sounded very enthusiastic. "Sorry to call on a holiday, but I have some good news. I'd love for you to come in for a callback. It's for the next movie I'm choreographing. It's a theatrical release. Filming starts in January in New York. It's for a very famous director. I signed an NDA, but let's just say . . . *E.T.*"

"*Oh my god!*" I was done trying to act cool. I was completely out of chill. "I'd absolutely love to. Yes. That sounds great."

Drayton's smile was impossibly wide. He leaned on the counter and stared at me with genuine awe.

"Perfect. I'll send over the details. We're moving fast and want to have our dancers selected ASAP."

"Of course. I'm here. I'm ready. I can't wait."

"Great." He laughed. I'd made Edgar de la Luna laugh. "Talk soon."

"Yup. Talk soon."

I ended the call then jumped from my stool. I ran around the counter and threw my arms around Drayton. He lifted me off the ground and spun me around.

"Congratulations!" He put me down, then his hands cupped my face. "That's amazing. Wow. January? That's soon."

I stepped back, and he dropped his hands as soon as we both realized that might be too familiar. Reality seeped in.

"Yeah, except . . . wait. This is insane. I can't do this."

"What are you talking about? There's no harm in auditioning."

"But if I get it, then what? I'm just going to quit school and move to New York?"

Moving to New York had never been part of my plan. To be fair, my plan had never extended beyond "get into CalArts," but it was still a big leap. Going to New York meant so many unknowns. So many more chances to fail, for things to go completely off the rails.

"Why not? I love college football, but if the NFL wanted to scout me, I wouldn't say no." He took a step forward, closing the gap between us. "It's your choice. But for what it's worth, that's the most excited I've heard you in a long time."

"That's not true." I crossed my arms over my chest. "I've been excited about the dean's master class."

“No.” He wrapped a hand around my wrist and pulled my arm down. “You’ve been anxious about the dean’s class. There’s a difference.”

“I just don’t know.”

“Look, if you don’t do the callback, you’ll never know.” He gave my wrist a small squeeze. “If you do the callback and get picked, you can still say no. You’re not locked in.”

The oven timer went off.

“Dinner’s ready.”

He held on to my wrist and didn’t drop his gaze. Why did looking into Drayton’s eyes make me feel so seen? Like anything was possible.

CHAPTER THIRTY-NINE

DRAYTON

Dinner went off without a hitch. Mostly. At least no hitches that caused any real problems. We ate way too much food and had way too many leftovers, but it was all good. Really, really good.

Everything about this felt right, and I was constantly fighting with myself to not hold her hand. Run my fingers through her hair. Ask her to sit on my lap. Would it be crazy to ask her for another chance? Or maybe we could keep this going until she took off for New York. I had no doubt she'd get the job.

We stacked the dishes to the side to clear space for our game of Sequence. I had to explain the rules because Dallas had never played it before, but she took to it right away. All that competitive spirit that I loved about her. The game was a lot closer than I liked.

Dallas picked away at the brownie I'd served for dessert by slowly licking her fork clean. She was lost in thought, enjoying the chocolate, and I was about to lose my mind.

"Is this your strategy? Distract me with this fork display?"

She looked up, obviously surprised that she was doing anything suggestive or that I'd noticed, then she laughed.

"What can I say? I'm a fan of your work." She put her fork down on the plate. "You were definitely a chef in another life."

"The only thing I was responsible for was picking them up at the bakery. But maybe I should've got some whipped cream too."

She watched me move a marker on the board. "Do you ever wonder what would have happened if you'd gone to Waco instead?"

"Sometimes. I try not to go there." I liked when she watched me. I always felt better knowing her eyes were on me. "When I was first injured, it was really easy to think about the what-ifs."

I didn't like thinking too much about that time because it was all such a mess. I'd been so angry. Mostly at myself for letting it happen at all, but at everyone really. The linebacker who took me out. Coach for calling the play. Dallas for getting there late. That was the one that really did me in. There was some part of my brain, deep down and way back, that thought I would have handled that play differently if she'd been in the stands cheering me on. It wasn't like Dallas brought me luck, but I'd felt sorry for myself and needed to spread that pain around.

"But I'm learning a lot. About myself and football. And if I had gone to Waco, I would have missed out on some pretty great memories with you."

"Like almost getting arrested for having sex in a car?"

"Amongst other things." I didn't want to turn away or lose her gaze. What if I never got it back? "Not only the big ones. And yeah, I'm going to tell everyone that story."

"Don't you dare!" She playfully slapped my arm. "I do *not* want that story getting back to . . . well, anyone."

"Sorry, Cheer. It's already all over TikTok."

"Please. If you had TikTok, all your content would be you throwing a football and commenting on your perfect arc. Or you talking about your motorbike."

"Ouch. So shallow?"

She laughed as she picked up a card for her turn. "Shoe fits."

"It's the smaller memories that get me, though." I knew she was thinking about her camera and all the shots she'd taken since I'd given it to her. "Mornings with you. How confused and cute you are before coffee. Watching a show. Sitting around and doing literally anything. Or nothing."

She watched as I spoke. A smile slowly formed, her eyes bright and beautiful. She reached out to, I thought, place her hand on mine, but it went to the game board instead.

"I win."

I looked down to see her put her final piece down.

"What else is new?"

Our faces were close, only inches apart. She glanced from my mouth to my eyes.

"Do you think about us often?" she whispered.

"Every day."

Damn, her lips were soft. Perfect. It took about a second for the kiss to turn hot and passionate. I moved around the table without breaking contact and pulled her to me. We were making up for lost time, running fingers through hair, pushing shirts up and out of the way. I lifted her up, and her legs wrapped around my waist. It felt so good, so right. I walked as quickly as I could across the room and up the stairs.

~

We were both on our sides, lying face-to-face in bed. Her hair was spread in a mess across the pillow, the comforter pulled up high. We'd left the lights off, but I'd opened up the blinds after our first round, and the moon cast a perfect glow over her face.

"Dancing in a movie would be pretty cool." She readjusted her head on the pillow. "I think I like the idea of being a small part of the bigger puzzle. You know?"

"I do. That's how football feels when it's at its best."

It was one more thing that was so easy with Dallas. We moved seamlessly from sex to conversation then back again. There was never the awkward moment of wondering if you should leave or if a topic was too serious. It all felt like the same thing. It was all connection and learning and being in the present with each other.

"Is that what you love about it?"

"That's part of it for sure." I ran a finger along her jawline, still amazed that I was allowed to touch her. "But also, it's like no matter what's happening in my life, when I get on that field, everything else fades away. I feel . . ."

"Like yourself?" She smiled.

"Exactly."

"Yup. That sounds familiar."

She took my hand and laced our fingers together. Her hand was so much smaller than mine, but I always loved how strong she was.

"I'm scared that if I leave CalArts, I'm abandoning my mom." She focused her gaze on our hands, rubbing her thumb along mine. "We both wanted this for so long. It was our dream, you know?"

Dallas was so careful with her grief. She'd helped me with mine, supported me in bringing my feelings about Abby to the surface, but she was careful how she spoke about her parents.

"Yeah. But at some point, you have to live for you and not the ones you've lost."

"Easier said than done." Her voice was laced with hurt. She didn't sound sad, though. It was more like resignation. The understanding that memories sometimes weighed a lot.

"True. But as someone who's finally doing it, it feels amazing." I smiled as her eyes met mine. "I'm not saying I'm done grieving. You helped me understand that grief comes in waves. I mean, I sometimes wonder what Abby would think about a certain thing. Or person. But I worry less that I've disappointed her, let her down, if things don't work out exactly as planned. Abby and I talked about a lot of things, but I can't be that version of me anymore. If that person ever existed, it's not who I am now."

"Okay then." She let go of my hand and tucked hers under the pillow. "So what is your big plan? For the new and improved Drayton."

"Oh, easy. NFL. Eight Super Bowl championships. Dunkin' commercial."

"Going for Brady."

"Hell yeah, Cheer." I smiled at her laughter. "I'm dreaming big."

If that was true, though, then I'd tell her that she'd be at my side. We'd say fuck it and do whatever it took to stay together. Except I knew that nothing had changed. I still loved her, but we had wildly different paths we needed to take.

“I’d love to start a nonprofit to help missing children. Either finding them or offering services to the families. I’d call it Abby’s Angels. Or something like that.”

“That’s beautiful.”

“I hope it happens.” I felt a lump in my throat. I didn’t care about crying in front of Dallas, but that wasn’t where I wanted tonight to go.

“It’ll happen.” She sounded so serious. Maybe she heard the hitch in my voice. “Where would you want to get drafted?”

She tucked her other hand under her pillow and pulled her legs up. We were lying close, and her bent knees now acted like a small barrier between us. She didn’t look angry, but I got the idea that she was pulling into herself. Protecting herself.

“Ah, thought you’d never ask!” I wanted to lighten the mood. “I’d be happy to stay in LA. But also Kansas City or Baltimore could be cool. Buffalo’s not too far from New York City. Anywhere but Florida.”

“And then it’s the life of an NFL star.”

“No complaints there.”

“That’s a lot of time on the road. You said even during off-season your dad was often away.”

“Yeah, training camps, promotional tours, sponsorship deals. If you want to make the money, it’s a year-round gig.”

My dad had been away most of the year. Mom took us out to visit as much as she could, and we did all our holidays on the road with him, but it was constant.

“You’re going to go so far.” Now it sounded like she might have a lump in her throat.

“You too.” Suddenly exhausted, I threw my arm over her waist and pulled her in close. “I really hope you get this movie.”

She licked then bit her bottom lip. Lightly touched her fingertips to my jaw then pulled away.

"I think I hope so too."

I wondered if I should tell her that I loved her. That she was the best thing that had ever happened to me. That her believing in me was one of the things that had gotten me though my recovery.

Dallas leaned in and kissed me. One soft, gentle, perfect kiss.

"Good night, Drayton."

"You too, Cheer."

~

Drayton,

I know it's a cliché to leave a letter on a pillow, but I hope you'll forgive me. Last night was wonderful. I'm so sorry to leave like this, but I couldn't see any other way. It would have been too hard to say goodbye. I'm not sure I could have done it. You probably would have said something charming and sweet (and you know how much I hate it when you do that). You would have swept me off my feet again. You would have forced me to defy all rational thought, and I need to be strong.

Despite what I'm going to say, I love hearing about your dreams and plans. I believe without a doubt that they will come true. I realized last night that football will always be the biggest part of your life. It will be your life. I don't know where I'll be in six months or six years. I hope I'll be dancing, but I also know that's not something I have complete control over. Which is to say, it isn't likely that our paths will cross. I don't want to force us to fit in each other's lives. I want us to remember all the reasons we loved each other. Because the truth is, loving you was everything I never knew I needed. You made the mundane seem extraordinary. You made the extraordinary seem possible. I hope all your dreams come true. I'm just sorry that I couldn't be one of them.

Dallas, xo

CHAPTER FORTY

DALLAS

I found myself back in the hall of fame in the administration building. I had a legitimate reason to be there—to check my exam schedule—but it was also a good excuse to stop by my mom's photo. I hadn't been there since Nathan had visited, and there was a good chance I'd been avoiding it. I had some big decisions to make, and I felt almost guilty that I hadn't visited her.

The photograph was exactly the same, but I felt different staring at it. I wasn't looking for my mother around every corner anymore. I didn't miss her any less, but campus was starting to feel like someplace I could claim as my own, not just something I'd inherited. I had the photo of Nathan staring at Mom's picture on my corkboard, and it held almost as much significance for me. It was impossible at this point to separate Mom and Nathan in my mind.

"It's good to see you, Ms. Bryant."

Dean Adams smiled as she walked up beside me. She almost always exhibited such a serious, don't-mess-with-me front that the smile threw me off guard.

"I, too, often revisit these photos. We've had some marvelous artists come through our doors during my time at CalArts."

She scanned the wall of photos, letting out a soft sigh.

"It's a nice place to come and think. Reflect. The halls are always much quieter at this time of year. Far less hustle and bustle between Thanksgiving and the new year."

All of campus was quieter these days as everyone prepared for finals and their showcases. I was in more of an in-between state. Working my shifts, rehearsing, but also pushing myself to get out of my room and off campus. Miley had helped me put together my reel, and we'd been to a few open calls and auditions. Nothing major, but it felt great to be trying new things, putting myself out there. Stella and a few others from our program came along too, and it was nice to have a small pack of friends. I'd been a bit worried that things might be weird with Skyler after my birthday, but we were good. We still spent most of my shifts talking about music or his plans postgraduation. It was fun to have a no-pressure friendship.

I hadn't heard from Drayton since Thanksgiving. Thanks to the Josh-to-Gabby pipeline, I knew he'd been upset, maybe a bit pissed off at first after reading my letter, but he was back to football, and life was moving on. I hadn't asked for any specific details, but it was what I'd needed to hear. It confirmed that I'd made the right choice for both of us even if it felt terrible in the moment. And for many moments after. It possibly still felt terrible at times, but those moments came less and less frequently, and I considered that a small victory. I had to think about it like that because I needed to move on too.

"Do you remember her?" I pointed to the photograph of my mother.

"Of course." Dean Adams furrowed her brow at me like she needed a moment to process the alien words I'd spoken. "I remember your mother very well."

My mother. She knew the connection. A part of me felt angry that she'd never mentioned it before, but mostly I needed to know more.

"What was she like when she was my age?" I had no one to ask that question. No one else who carried that memory.

"She was talented. Kind." Dean Adams stared at the photo and seemed lost in thought. "She was also young and away from home for the first time, so she was a hot mess, as the kids say."

"People don't say that anymore."

Dean Adams gave me a solid *watch it* side-eye then smiled.

"It was my first year teaching, and your mother made it memorable." She turned to look at me. "She's actually the one who lobbied for a showcase after the master class."

"Really? I didn't know that."

She chuckled. An actual chuckle. There was no other way to describe it.

"She was very passionate about dance. Ambitious." Dean Adams cleared her throat. Readjusted her posture. "I thought she might have become a teacher. She was so good about sharing her knowledge. Liked directing others."

"You didn't think she would be the one to become a professional? Stay with the artist's journey?"

She examined me, letting her eyes scan my face, before

speaking again. "I have lots of stories that I'm happy to share any day." Dean Adams reached into her bag and pulled out an envelope. "I was just about to put this in the campus mail."

I felt momentarily confused as she handed it to me. My name and dorm room were on the front. Dean Adams's insignia was on the back. It looked official and permanent.

"Sometimes history repeats itself. Sometimes it doesn't. But it's always good to glance back."

She touched my shoulder, a gentle tap of acknowledgment, then walked off.

I carefully opened the envelope and got as far as the opening paragraph: *Congratulations, you have been accepted into Dean Adams's master class.*

I looked back up at my mom's photograph, half-expecting her to be smiling back, maybe giving me a thumbs-up. I felt frozen in place. It can be a terrifying thing when your dreams come true.

~

Early-morning shifts at Emmy's helped to distract me. I was getting better at running on autopilot until the caffeine hit. I stood at the coffee machine making myself a latte while Skyler counted the money in the register.

It was nearly a week later, and I was still reeling from the dean's letter. Miley wanted to go out and celebrate, but I wasn't ready to share it with the world. It was exciting, and I was proud about being accepted, but it also didn't feel quite real. Gabby and Nathan had both pointed out that it would feel very real if I shared the news, but I needed to give myself time to let it sink in. I had Drayton's words running through my head, and I needed to work out if this class was still as much my dream as my mom's.

"What was going on last night?" Skyler dumped a pile of change on the counter. "Why are there so many quarters?"

"At least you're set for your next laundry day."

"My laundromat uses an app." He looked over his shoulder at me. "You need to upgrade."

"Talk to CalArts's residence program. Arts schools love retro."

Skyler was about to reply, probably something about keeping up with the times, when my phone rang. It was 6:00 a.m., so not likely anyone in this time zone. Gabby was the most likely bet. I looked down at the screen.

Oh crap. Oh no. Oh boy. I hit the green button.

"Hi, Edgar de la Luna." I wasn't sure why I'd addressed him by his full name, but there was no turning back now. I glanced at Skyler. Yup, he was staring at me with very wide eyes. "How are you?"

"Dallas! I'm glad I caught you." He had a lot of enthusiasm. The callback had been so much fun. "I'm calling with some great news . . . I would *love* to offer you a spot as a dancer on my upcoming project."

"Wow. I mean, wow!" Apparently, I'd lost the power of speaking in a complete sentence.

"An assistant will be sending over all the details. But as I said earlier, we're moving fast." He was also speaking quickly. I needed to take a few deep breaths to concentrate on his words.

"This is great. So great. Wow. I'm really honored for the opportunity."

Thank god I'd impressed this man with my dancing because I wasn't doing a great job talking.

"Of course. Oh, one more thing. You can call me Ed."

"Thanks . . . Ed." I made an *OMG* face, biting my lip, at Skyler.

"We'll talk soon. Watch out for the email. You'll need to reply ASAP."

I put down my phone and tried to regain my composure. Calm down. Think about the consequences, the ramifications, the reality of that phone call. Unfortunately, the only thing I wanted to do right now was run around in circles screaming.

"What happened?" Skyler stepped closer.

"I can't believe it!" Screw composure. I was literally bouncing with excitement. "I got the part!"

"Hell yeah, Dallas!" He held both hands up, and I hit them in a double high five. "Never doubted you. So are you going to take it?"

"I don't know. It's a big move." Reality was setting in. Stupid reality. "And I got into the dean's class."

"When? Why didn't you say anything?"

"I—I don't know." I let out a long, slow breath, getting my heart rate back in check. "These are real princess problems, right?"

"You earned both these gigs, Dallas. This isn't some fluke or about who you know." Skyler leaned back against the counter. "Want my ten cents?"

"The saying is two."

"I adjust for inflation."

I took a sip of my latte then leaned on the counter beside him. "It's like I have two really great options in front of me. One that I wanted for so long and another that's unexpected?"

I held my cup in both hands and looked up at him. It was easy talking to Skyler about these things. He understood the artist's perspective. Hard work did not mean a sure thing. Success didn't always mean a solid income. I valued his opinion. A lot.

"You'd be stupid not to take it."

"Excuse me?" I'd expected a story or some nuanced evaluation based on my circumstances. Something about his mother and living in New York City in the '90s. The straightforward response was a surprise.

"This could be your big break to actually make a career out of your art. So many people would kill for this chance." He took the cup from my hand and sipped from it. It was a bold step, but I didn't really mind. "I'm not saying you'll never have this kind of chance again, but you've got momentum now, so go for it."

"But it's just so fast. I've never been to New York before. I'd have to find a place to live . . ."

"You can crash at my parents' place until you figure it out. There've got plenty of room. Done."

"And what about CalArts?"

"You defer for a year. Or you just start your life and don't look back." He put the cup on the counter and turned fully toward me. "Look, it's your choice. But you have to chase the thing that scares you, because that's art!"

Excited, worked-up Skyler was new to me. He waved his arms to emphasize his point and looked like he might jump up and down. I liked it. It was a good look.

"I just feel like . . ." My chest felt tight. The back of my neck and cheeks were getting warm. "Like something's holding me back."

"Something or someone?"

I didn't have an answer. At least not one I could say out loud.

CHAPTER FORTY-ONE

DRAYTON

I took the last tier of stadium steps two at a time. It was a good finisher for my workout, pushing me just past the brink for a high-intensity rush. I walked back and forth along the top tier to cool down. Shook out my limbs. Stretched and enjoyed the feeling of coming down from the high. I was sweaty and hot, my muscles ached from the stress, but I felt great. My knee was healed, no pain, and I felt stronger every day. If they ever let me back in as QB, I'd be set.

Instead of music, I used a sports podcast as the day's motivation. All I needed to get me moving was to hear, "USC's Bowl game is this Friday, against De Leon University, a rivalry as old as sin." That was an understatement. It felt appropriate that our last game would be against De Leon. We'd pulled ourselves out of the basement and hit our stride and our winning streak just in time. It was a nice bookend to a messed-up season.

I sat down and looked out over the stadium, letting the podcaster's voice drone on in my ears until it was no longer words, only a soft white noise to lock me in my personal bubble.

I'd arrived at USC with the promise of getting us to a Bowl game, and we'd done it. Not because of me, though. I'd played a small role behind the scenes and working with the guys during practice, but I wasn't going to get all-star accolades for my performance. I wasn't the season's superstar, and that was a hard truth to accept. I'd started off strong, top of the world, and then hit a low I could still barely comprehend.

It had taken some distance, and some long talks with Coach and Josh, to realize it was more than the injury that had gotten me down. I'd never seen myself as someone who might get depressed, so I didn't know how to pick up on any of the signs. Losing Dallas might have been the last straw. It wasn't all about physical recovery.

When I'd read Dallas's letter, I'd been furious. I'd let myself believe we could be friends and lovers. I'd let her see how much I loved her, loved spending time with her. The letter made me feel like she blamed me for everything. It was all about me putting football first when she was just as devoted to dance. Hell, she had a callback for a job in New York. Did she think I should drop everything and follow her?

I pulled my earbuds out and stared across the field. I loved the stadium when it was full of cheering fans, but there was something extra special about these quiet hours. It was the dawn of a new day, a road trip just about to happen, a first kiss with a pretty cheerleader. Anything was possible.

It was messy for a while after Dallas. I was distracted and mopey. *Mopey* was Zach's word, but he was right. We'd already been through a breakup, but I'd had it in my head that we could be friends. We could be in each other's lives. Thanksgiving had had me convinced we could be more than friends, though I hadn't worked out what kind of situationship we could have. I only knew that I wanted her in my life, and when her letter made it clear that wasn't going to happen, I kind of lost my mind.

I didn't know what had turned that around. One day I was checking my phone constantly and thinking about asking Josh to check her Instagram, and the next I was taking an extra lap on the track and talking plays with Coach. Once I put my mind to it, it was exactly where I wanted to be. I put in extra time with Coach and the physio team. Got myself up to speed on all counts.

Closing my eyes, I focused on my breathing. Deep breath in, count to five. Release, count to six. It had been Charlotte's idea to try some mindfulness practice. She'd tried to get the whole team in on it, but only Zach, Marcus, and I had put in the time. It was a way to push back all the noise. Enjoy this moment before the chaos started up again. It helped me be more present, in the now. Pay attention to the sounds and smells, the movement around me. Like the sense that someone was nearby, moving closer, sitting down beside me.

I opened my eyes.

"Nervous for tomorrow?" My dad leaned forward to rest his elbows on his knees. It looked like he'd considered hugging me before noting the level of sweat.

"Not for me. I'm just watching from the bench."

"Still in the game. Still part of the team."

"Not nervous for the team either. They've got this."

It was true. We weren't perfect, but the team had found a real groove. They had the plays down. Their reaction times were stellar.

"You're good?"

"Yeah, great."

The grounds team was walking across the field, checking the turf, getting ready for today's practice and tomorrow's game. They were dwarfed by the giant field, the empty stadium around them.

"Dad, I should've seen the safety drop."

I felt like a little kid admitting I'd broken a lamp. Or like when Abby and I had taken one of Dad's game-winning footballs to play catch and lost it in a lake. We were so scared to tell him what had happened. As much as Dad and I fought after I'd defied his plan for Waco, I still never wanted to disappoint him.

"Or I should've stepped up in the pocket." I continued to stare out over the field. "I should've felt the pressure from the weak side."

"That's a lot of should'ves."

"Yeah, well, I can't help it. I keep replaying everything over and over."

"Dray, beating yourself up won't change the play." He put a hand on my shoulder. "Sure, we spend a hell of a lot of time watching game tapes, reviewing the minutiae of every move and throw. But sometimes we have to take the lesson and move on. You circling the drain won't make you a better player or teammate."

"Why did I force that throw?" I shook my head. "I could've told any other player what to do. I know better. But I did it anyway."

"You were trying to make something happen." He rubbed his hands along his thighs. He was struggling to find the right words. It occurred to me for the first time that maybe Dad was worried about disappointing me too. "I've been there. That exact spot. I went from being a high school superstar who could do no wrong. Then first time I stepped on a college field, everything felt different. Everyone was bigger, faster, smarter."

"Yeah." That was the feeling exactly. It was why it was so tempting to throw in the towel at USC and find a smaller school where it didn't feel so all-important. "And the coaches are expecting way more from you."

"Everyone's expecting more from you. The fans. The reporters. People back home who followed your career and think all the hometown pride is hinging on your success. Suddenly, there are way too many people watching. Even people who don't care about football suddenly care if you win or lose." Dad paused to look out over the field. I knew he got the same sense of peace looking at that view. "I had a great run at Waco, but not right away. I thought I had to live up to something. Be perfect."

I'd never heard Dad talk about this before. He'd always hyped Waco up as the perfect place to be. He never wanted to let me see his cracks. His vulnerabilities. I wanted to hug him, tell him he was exactly the person I needed in that moment.

"You're gonna mess up, Drayton. We all do. I've made mistakes I regret every day. But you can't waste time wishing things were different."

My mind jumped to Dallas in the Airbnb, asking me about my plans postcollege, and me listing them off one by one. I hadn't included her in any of them. I hadn't made room for her or her dreams or a way that we could be together. I'd shut her out without even realizing it. I'd created this perfect story without any cracks or places for someone else to hold on.

"That's easier said than done."

"I know. But you have to try to look at what's actually in front of you." He put a hand on my shoulder. "You're not the starter right now, but your knee's better. All you can do is keep showing up, keep working, and let go of the should'ves."

I shook my head and smiled at him. "You know, you're pretty good at this."

"Coaching?"

"Parenting."

Dad laughed and pulled me into a hug.

CHAPTER FORTY-TWO

DALLAS

It made no sense that we had more boxes packing up than when we'd arrived. Our already small dorm room seemed even smaller now with stacks of boxes and piles of clothes and books to donate or sell taking over. I had done a fair job of staying on task and working my way through my possessions. Miley, on the other hand, was deep into Google investigating our new neighborhood.

"So Queens is actually much closer to Manhattan."

"Geographically?" I had only a rudimentary knowledge of New York City and its boroughs, but that sounded wrong.

"No. In style. Tone."

"Queens is closer tonally to Manhattan?" That made even less sense. "Maybe you need to reevaluate your search terms."

Miley looked up from her phone. She was sitting on her bed, legs tucked beneath her, surrounded by a pile of half-folded, definitely-not-packed clothes.

"What I'm saying is, I hear Queens is the new Brooklyn."

"Then what's Brooklyn now?" I tossed my economics textbook on the donate pile. As much as I'd enjoyed the class, it was very unlikely I would look at it again.

"A bunch of yoga moms shopping at Whole Foods."

Miley had called me about ten minutes after I'd spoken with Edgar—sorry, Ed—screaming so loudly I thought I might go deaf. It took a few seconds before she could form coherent words, but her level of enthusiasm told me she'd also gotten a part. She replied yes to the email as soon as it appeared in her inbox. I gave myself a day to talk to Nathan and Gabby, take some time to let it sink in, then said yes. It was all forward motion after that. I finished my exams, danced in the showcase, organized for the move, talked to Dean Adams, and dealt with admin and financial aid to defer the rest of my year. Almost everything was crossed off my list. Almost.

"What do you think?" I held up two books. "Modern set design?"

"Oh, hells no." Miley barely looked up from her phone. "Don't carry anything that will weigh you down."

Miley made a good point, but I wasn't ready to part with them yet. I didn't know what life in New York might bring. Maybe these would come in handy.

"Knock-knock."

Nathan stepped into the room carrying a tray with three coffees. I was always happy to see my brother, but especially now. It was late morning, but my coffee intake was still low. My life as a barista had impacted my caffeine tolerance, and now I could almost always have more.

"Skyler said these were on the house. They're a going-away

present." He handed me my coffee with a very serious look. "Perhaps he's a little in love with you?"

Nathan winked at Miley as he dodged the pillow I threw at him.

"You two are trouble."

"Thank you." Miley looked genuinely pleased with herself.

Nathan sat on my bed. He lifted up a stack of papers then dropped them again.

"Anything you want me to do?"

"No. I have to sort through everything first. We'll take advantage of your generosity when we need to get this all in a van."

"Oh, did I tell you?" He held his shoulder and moved his arm in a slow circle. "My old football injury has been acting up."

"Nice, brother." I was tempted to throw another pillow his way. "Well played."

Miley jumped when her phone rang.

"Why does that always scare the shit out of me?" She swung her legs over the side of the bed. "It's my mom, again. She's freaking out about this gap year, but I'm like, Mom, getting a sweet film job *is* a reason to drop out of school and move to New York! Anyway . . ."

She answered the phone as she walked out of the room.

"Guess you're on your own with packing." Nathan sipped from his cup.

"In Miley's head, we're already in New York. I don't think she cares what she leaves behind."

I put the box of discarded books on the floor and moved to my closet. I planned to bring everything with me, as long as it fit in my two suitcases.

"Nervous?"

"A little." I glanced at Nathan and smiled. "But the fact I won't be drowning in debt helps."

My financial aid officer was still pushing the loans even as I left her office. She wanted to believe that tuition was the reason I was deferring and not that my plans had changed. Or that I could work for a year then come back without any debt. Okay, that one seemed a bit far-fetched.

I pulled a sweater from the back of my closet. It was rust color with a turtleneck and short sleeves. It was a soft wool, well-loved and comfortable. I used to sniff it, thinking it still smelled like her. I'd wanted so desperately for her perfume to linger. I'd never worn it, but I always wanted it with me.

"I wish I knew what Mom would say right now." I held the sweater close to my chest.

"She'd say she's happy for you. And maybe a little jealous because she always wanted to live in New York."

"She did?" I thought I knew all Mom's stories. I thought I'd already asked all the questions.

"Yeah. I was cleaning out the attic, and I found some old journals." Nathan moved the papers so I could sit. "I skimmed a little because there are some things a son doesn't want to know, you know?" We both laughed, trying not to picture anything. "But I saved them for you."

"Thank you." That felt overwhelming. I wanted to know more, but taking it in stages would be good. "Wait, so why didn't she go to New York?"

"Oh, she and Dad were saving up, but then . . . they got me instead." He held out his arms and smiled. "Which I think is the better deal."

"Definitely." I nodded solemnly, and Nathan laughed.

“Anyway. They used that money as a down payment for our house.” He fidgeted with his coffee cup while we both thought about that turn of events. “It was nice to realize that even they had to accept their dreams changing.”

It was strange to think that I’d come to CalArts because Mom had and now I was altering my plans too. Not for the same reasons, but we’d both reacted to what life threw at us. She’d wanted to go to New York, but I was the one to get there. I looked over at the corkboard. It was covered in the Polaroids from this past semester, all those little moments. There was still one of me with Drayton, taken in a moment of pure happiness, and it felt like a different lifetime.

“Guess you need to sort through those too.” Nathan gave me a knowing look.

“I thought I should keep one.” I felt almost guilty saying it.

“Smart.” He put a hand on my shoulder. “Sorry it didn’t work out.”

I mouthed a quick thank-you then sat up straight. I needed to work on my posture, and I needed to change the topic.

“Why were you cleaning out the attic?” I blinked a few times to make sure I didn’t cry.

“Funny you ask. It’s because I might have to rent out the house soon . . .” He paused for dramatic effect. “I decided I’m going back to college.”

“Wait, what? Nate, that’s amazing!” I hugged him.

“Is it? I feel sort of old to be in school.”

“Dude, you’re twenty-seven. That’s hardly ancient.” I folded the sweater and held it in my lap. “Also, there are plenty of mature students in college. Even here.”

“Even here. Nice.” He rearranged my pillows and leaned

against the headboard. "Anyway, I think it'll be good for me to finish."

"I need a lot more information. What do you want to study? Where are you applying? Any schools in New York?"

"I applied to Rutgers early decision for their social work program. So New Jersey."

"*Get out!* Way to bury the lede!" I shoved his leg. "Why do men keep doing this to me!?"

"That question is definitely outside my pay grade." He nudged my leg in response. "I didn't tell you earlier because I didn't want to influence your decision. It needed to be yours."

"That's so selfless. You were the best legal guardian ever, and now you're going to be the best social worker ever."

He held a hand up. "Calm down. I still have to get in." His smile lit up his face. "But it feels good to have choices."

"My brother and my best friend on the East Coast." I got back up to resume packing. We were on a deadline. Nathan was picking up the rental van first thing tomorrow morning, and then we were gone. "Does Gabby know?"

"Yeah, she helped me with the application process over Thanksgiving." It was obvious that he had more information to impart. My brother was a font of revelations tonight. "It was her and Josh. He mentioned his family really missed Drayton."

Nathan knew a bit about my dinner with Drayton. I hadn't given him all the details except to say that had been the last time we'd spoken. "Yeah, it sucks he had practice."

"Except he didn't." A sip of coffee for a pause. "I heard he chose to stay behind."

I froze. "Why would he do that?"

Nathan's look said, *Isn't it obvious?*

"He told me he had practice. He didn't stay here for me."

"Maybe he didn't want you to be alone on Thanksgiving. Or he didn't want to spend the holiday without you."

"I—I don't know."

"He loves you, Dallas. That's probably the only *why* you need."

"He stayed here for me? That's so sweet." I could feel my heart rate rising. My head was spinning. I felt almost giddy. "And generous. And so . . . Drayton."

I was leaving Los Angeles in a few hours, and I hadn't told him. He didn't know I'd gotten the job in New York.

"I have to go say goodbye."

"Doesn't he have a game tonight?"

I grabbed my coat and bag, pulling up Uber on my phone. "At least I know where he is then."

CHAPTER FORTY-THREE

DRAYTON

I couldn't say how many locker rooms I'd sat in waiting for a game to start. Hundreds. More than a thousand? More than I could count was the most obvious answer. I'd also been lucky enough to be in locker rooms before a championship game. I understood the mix of nerves and excitement, satisfaction and terror. Our season had started in the dumps—especially for me—but we'd pulled ourselves up, and now we were about to cross the finish line. The guys were pumped. We were primed. We could taste victory.

Ryan walked in with an actual swagger. He liked making an entrance, wanted all eyes on him. He stood in the middle of the room, raised his hands above his head, and announced, "I have arrived!"

He walked to his locker, giving high fives and the occasional shoulder slap. Ryan was an arrogant son of a bitch, but I couldn't fault his energy. He'd had a solid season, and I had to give him his due. The trouble was, in Ryan's mind, he was the one who'd gotten the team this far. He acted like his throws downfield were the only reason we scored. He didn't acknowledge the wide receivers who caught the ball and ran it into the end zone. The linebackers who took out the other team's defense. The kicker who put the ball through the uprights. The quarterback was the linchpin of a team, but the operative word was *team*.

"Just talking to an NFL scout." Ryan spoke loudly so everyone in the room heard him. "Wanted to know how I was feeling before the big game. Since so much was riding on me."

I'd noticed a few scouts sniffing around lately, talking to a few players. No doubt, Ryan was at the top of their list. But they weren't only interested in the high scorers or the showboats like Ryan. They needed players to fill in gaps, players who could bolster the team they had. They looked for potential and chemistry as much as superstars. It sounded like a great idea to have a team made up of Bradys, but that didn't cover all the skill sets. You needed the pawns as much as the kings.

"Told him I actually thrive under pressure." Ryan pulled off his shirt and tossed it on the bench. "Unlike someone."

Gee, whoever could he mean? He was still trying to get under my skin. Still thought I was his main opponent. I didn't understand his endgame. We could go at each other, but that wouldn't solve anything. Might even mean a game suspension. It was like Ryan on the field when the play didn't go as expected. His reaction was scattershot. Throw as much as you can at the target and hope something lands.

"Ryan, why don't you give it a rest?" Zach sounded exhausted more than anything else. "Let's focus on the game."

"Oh no, Zachy. Did I offend your delicate sensibilities?" Ryan was taking his role as schoolyard bully to the next level. "You're gonna have to toughen up when we get out there. De Leon is gonna eat you alive."

"Don't worry about me. I'm ready to go." Zach was dressed and prepped and looked ready to take on all of De Leon at once. "Just saying we don't need you throwing shit at anyone who isn't De Leon."

"Ah, I get it!" Ryan winked at the linebacker standing next to him like they were in on some clever joke. "Sorry, Zachy, did I offend your girlfriend?"

That was my breaking point. Take all the swipes you want at me, but leave Zach out of it. Especially if you're going to throw in some vaguely homophobic slurs. I jumped up and got to Ryan in seconds. It was fast enough that I could've taken him down no problem, but I stopped inches away.

"This ends today." I knew he wanted to clock me. I could see his fists balling at his sides. His jaw twitching. "We all know what you think of me. We all know you think you're king shit around here."

He almost smiled. He thought he was ready for his victory lap and for me to finally concede his superior football prowess.

"But here's the thing. I've been through shit. Real shit. Football, life, everything." I could feel everyone's eyes on us. The room had gone completely silent. "And I'm betting you have too."

Ryan hadn't expected that one. His eyes narrowed. He was suspicious that I had some dirt I was about to reveal. I almost wished I'd asked Charlotte for some compromising information to throw in his face.

"None of that matters right now. Whatever you've got against me or I've got to carry around with me doesn't matter. There's only this game. Us against De Leon. So tonight, I do hope you win. I hope you go out there and play the best game of your life. I hope everyone does. Because this isn't about you or me. We don't matter, man. It's about the game and our team."

Ryan blinked a few times, which was as close to a reaction as I got other than his hands relaxing as he stepped back.

"We win this together or we go down together. That's all that matters." I took a step back, feeling a bit dazed.

"Couldn't have said it better myself." Coach Watson clapped his hands. He was standing just inside the locker room. I had no idea when he'd arrived. "Let's go out there and kick some ass!"

~

We were down, and we really needed a jolt to get our heads back in the game. The cheer squad was doing their part, trying to keep everyone's spirits up. The fans weren't losing faith—or at least not letting on that they were—and kept the shouts and applause going. The stadium blared music designed to energize and motivate. But the clock was running out, and we had only so many chances left.

"Ryan, I want you to tuck and run." Coach pointed his clipboard and shouted.

We could still gain those final yards. De Leon's defense was stellar, but if we kept the ball long enough, we could force them out of their comfort zone. We could beat them at their own game.

I stood beside Coach, both of us coiled and energized, watching as Ryan took the team into a huddle. He got the ball at the snap then took a few quick steps back.

He wasn't going for the tuck and run. Instead, he lined up and fired deep as the De Leon players rushed him.

I didn't know if he couldn't see them run into position or if he panicked when he realized he'd waited too long and there was no opportunity to run around them anymore. The ball went high, a good arc that seemed to hang in the air like a bird, a prayer, and my stomach fell with the ball because I could see exactly what was going to happen. Anyone watching the game could see how it was going to play out.

Zach leaped into the air, got a good five feet off the ground, and caught the ball, but he didn't make it down before the De Leon player leveled him. If we'd been watching a cartoon, the word *BAM* would've appeared above him.

"I told you to tuck and run!" Coach Watson threw his headset down. He pointed his clipboard at Ryan. "You wanna be the hero? Try a solo sport. Sit the hell down!"

Ryan looked shell-shocked. He couldn't believe he'd messed up so badly and lost those valuable yards.

"Lahey—you're up!"

"Yes, Coach." I threw my helmet on, strapped up, and ran onto the field.

As I passed Ryan, I slapped his shoulder. "You got us here. We've got the rest."

I didn't wait for his reaction. I got the team into position and got to work.

There was more back-and-forth with the ball for a few plays, but we gained ground. It felt like we were moving one yard at a time, but we tied it up with only minutes to spare. The crowd was going wild, with both teams' colors flashing across the stands. It was electric, and both teams were feeding off the energy. This game could go either way.

I called everyone in for our huddle.

"I want you all to know, whichever way this game goes, every one of you rocked it. I'm proud to be on a team with every damn one of you."

"Yeah, yeah." Marcus threw me a wicked grin. "Save the speech for the victory party."

I laid out the play for them—go long and around their defensive line. Once Zach was clear, he could make the final dash.

"You got this, Drayton!"

I looked up into the stands to see Dallas. She was beside my dad, screaming her head off.

"You can do it!"

I counted us out, and it was game on.

As soon as I had the ball, I spotted Zach. He was in position but completely covered. I scanned the field, did quick calculations of all possible scenarios, then ran. Tucked the ball under my arm and ran faster than ever before. It was every run I'd taken to the top of the stadium steps. Every extra lap on the track. The hours in the weight room. I was running on pure instinct, years of pushing my personal best, vaguely aware of De Leon players dropping as my team cleared my path of obstacles. I could hear the shouting. Coach yelling, "Come on, Lahey!" Dad calling, "Bring it home!" Dallas was in the mix too, shouting my name.

Zach was in the clear, and I threw the ball just as the De Leon linebacker took me down. I watched those last few seconds—Zach passing the posts for the final touchdown—from the ground. I lay there, staring at the blue California sky, listening to the chants of "USC!" and "Lahey!" while I caught my breath.

We'd done it. We'd won the damn thing. After everything that had happened, and the mess of a season and semester, we'd won.

Some of the guys helped me up and threw me onto their shoulders. It felt fantastic and also a bit ridiculous to be carried off the field, but I'd take it. I looked back up at Dallas. She held her hands in front of her chest forming a heart.

CHAPTER FORTY-FOUR

DALLAS

I leaned against the wall in the stadium archway, halfway between the field and the real world. There were the usual groups of fans, mainly women, waiting for players, and a few more lingering toward the parking lot. I guessed a postgame tailgate was in the works. The stadium had gone wild when USC scored that final touchdown, and it was going to be a while before the excitement ran out.

I'd picked this spot because it was relatively quiet. Most of the team and staff had already passed me. I'd said hello to the few I recognized then went back to standing and waiting. I didn't bother with my phone or any other busywork. Instead, I enjoyed the peace. Listened to the faraway voices and laughter. It would probably be a while before I was in a football stadium again, so I took the opportunity to absorb as much as I could.

Zach and Marcus made their way down the passageway, stopping to give me a hug.

"Maybe I should get the star player's autograph?" I smiled up at Zach. "That was an amazing rush, Zach. A spectacular way to end the year."

"Yeah, it felt pretty good." He was back to golden retriever mode, looking almost shy about the compliment. "That's definitely the story I'm telling for the rest of my life."

Marcus pulled him away, declaring there would be plenty interested in hearing all about it when they got to the party.

"Gotta make the most of it while the highlight reel is still playing."

I'd gotten to the stadium right after halftime. They weren't going to let me into the VIP section until Drayton's dad saw me. I was a bit surprised when he called me over, but he gave me a big hug. Said Dray would be glad I was there.

When Drayton took the field, I thought I was going to lose my mind. I felt proud even though I had no right. He belonged out there. Watching him run down the field, dodge players, then know exactly when and where to throw to Zach was mind-blowing. Dance could look like that, like minor miracles when everything came together, but it was precise. Cheerleading too. You always knew exactly where the other person was because they were following the same rules, the same choreography as you. That was how trust worked.

I spotted him as soon as he stepped into the stadium corridor. He was striding toward me with the calm Drayton energy that I loved so much. He caught my gaze and didn't let go. My heart swelled, seemed to float in my chest, as I watched him. I wanted Drayton to always be walking toward me. Always moving in my direction.

"Hey."

"Hey, Cheer." He looked and sounded like my Drayton, and I

wondered if that would always be the case. Would there ever be a time when I didn't feel like a piece of him belonged to me? "So I'm back to being first-string."

"Hold on." I lifted my camera. He tilted his head and smiled as I snapped a photo.

"After that game, I'd be surprised if the NFL doesn't call you tonight." I pulled the photo from the camera. Color was already starting to push through the flat grey square.

"Funny enough, there were a few scouts at the game." He continued his walk toward me. "Not sure they were there for me, but I'll take it."

"Does that mean you talked to them?"

"Means I *might* be talking to them."

Whatever was I going to do without cryptic Drayton messages? The truth was, as much as they could annoy me, I was going to miss them.

"That final run . . . wow." I flicked my fingers against the side of my head in an exploding mind gesture.

He didn't laugh, but he looked amused. Maybe curious. He stood a few feet from me and shoved his hands into his pockets. "I was surprised you came."

"What can I say, QB? I'll always be your number one cheerleader."

It was true. I would always be in Drayton's corner. Always want the best for him. Never doubt that he was going to get it all, Dunkin' Donuts commercial included. I handed him the Polaroid. He grinned as he watched it slowly come into focus. I knew the photo was perfect without having to look at it.

"I got the part."

He looked up and smiled that heart-crushing smile. I would

always count myself lucky to have been on its receiving end even if only for a short period of time.

"Never doubted you could do it." His eyes still did a number on me. Weak knees and soft center. "When do you leave?"

"Tomorrow. It all happened really fast." It still felt like a blur. I didn't think I would truly believe it was happening until I was in our apartment in Queens. "Phone call done, contract signed, school deferred. But I wanted you to hear it from me."

How much more was there to say? Was this door actually closing? I thought about that moment at the start of senior year when Drayton threw a wild football and I caught it. Maybe that was our first little moment. Something that had seemed small, inconsequential, but it had set us on a new path. One that would change us forever.

I'd thought we were going to be in each other's lives forever. We'd chosen each other, and I'd thought that would be enough.

"I'm happy you're living for you."

"Me too." My voice was breaking up a bit. "I'm glad that you didn't need to activate plan B."

"I should probably get working on one. You never know when it might come in handy."

"I've been thinking more about that one too." I pushed myself off the wall and stepped closer to him. "I don't think we need multiple backup plans. It's all one plan. It might shift. It might divert. Sometimes it's a tuck and run. Other times you throw it into the pocket. And sometimes you end up in New York City because an unexpected door opened and you took the chance."

"And who knows where that door will take you."

"Exactly. But it's all one plan."

A couple of women, likely cheerleaders, walked past, but

Drayton didn't acknowledge them. We remained silent, eyes locked, until they were out of hearing range.

"I need you to understand something," I said. "Just because we broke up, it doesn't mean the relationship failed. I see it as a win, actually."

"Really?" He raised an eyebrow. "How so?"

"Because my life is so much better having spent this time with you."

It was true. I might not be heading to New York if it wasn't for Drayton supporting me, keeping me sane when things got too hectic. He'd helped me see that I couldn't live my life for my mom in the same way he couldn't live his for Abby.

"So, I guess this is goodbye."

He flinched slightly. We were already broken up, but having a country between us felt far more permanent.

"Well, in that case, come here."

He pulled me in and wrapped his arms around me. In typical Drayton fashion, he was sturdy, and the kiss was soft. In a weird way, it felt like a first kiss instead of our last. There was promise and hope in it, even though it signaled an end.

"Do you believe in right person wrong time?" I whispered.

"I'm not sure . . . but I think what's meant to be has a way of working itself out." He kissed my forehead.

"Me too."

We let go of each other, and I took the first brave steps away. I gave him the briefest of waves then headed outside. The day was bright, and it could lead me anywhere.

ABOUT THE AUTHOR

Rachel Espy is a Toronto-based author who loves pop culture and walking her dogs.